A KELLY CHERRY READER

Selected stories, novel excerpts, essays, memoir, and poetry

A KELLY CHERRY READER

Selected stories, novel excerpts, essays, memoir, and poetry

For more information:
Stephen F. Austin State University Press
P.O. Box 13007 SFA Station
Nacogdoches, Texas 75962
sfapress@sfasu.edu
www.sfasu.edu/sfapress

Distributed by Texas A&M Consortium
www.tamupress.com

LIBRARY OF CONGRESS CATALOGING-IN-PUBLICATION DATA

Cherry, Kelly.
A Kelly Cherry Reader / Kelly Cherry

p.cm.

ISBN: 978-1-62288-070-6

Acknowledgments

I acknowledge with pleasure and many thanks the publishers who generously gave permission to reprint work in this re-collected volume: the Boson Imprint at Bitingduck Press for "Her, in His Story" and "Art and Aberration" from *The Woman Who: Stories* (2010); University of Missouri Press for "How It Goes," "Chores," "Not the Phil Donahue Show" and "Love in the Middle Ages" from *The Society of Friends: Stories* (1999); University of Tampa Press for "On the Isle of Bards" and "Postmodern Poetry in Ancient Rome: On Translating the *Octavia* of Seneca" from *History, Passion, Freedom, Death and Hope: Prose about Poetry* (2005); Louisiana State University Press for "An Underground Hotel in Leningrad" from *The Exiled Heart* (1991); and BkMk Press for "I Was a Teenage Beatnik" and "Why I Write Now" from *Girl in a Library: On Women Writers and the Writing Life* (2009). "Where There Is Writing" and "Letter from the Philippines: Crossing a Street in Manila" are reprinted from *Writing the World* by Kelly Cherry, by permission of the University of Missouri Press. Copyright ©1995 by the Curators of the University of Missouri.

Rights to the novels from which excerpts are drawn have been returned to me. The novels are *Augusta Played, In the Wink of an Eye,* and *We Can Still Be Friends*; the last of these, if I'd had my way, would have been called either "American Minuet" or "Dancing with Ava Martel." Rights to *My Life and Dr. Joyce Brothers: A Novel in Stories*, from which "The Hungarian Countess" is taken, have also reverted to me. (If, as I hope, my trilogy of short story collections set in Madison, Wisconsin, is reprinted, I plan to change that title to "What I Don't Tell People.") With the benefit of hindsight, I have left my first novel, *Sick and Full of Burning*, and a later, titled *The Lost Traveller's Dream*, on the shelf.

My choice of poems is limited by the rights available, but most of my poetry collections are relatively easy to find, which is not always true of the fiction. Hence, short seemed to be the way to go when it came to making a selection of poetry. Seven of the poems are used by permission of Louisiana State University Press. The rights to "Questions and Answers" were previously returned to me.

I have a number of other books in mind and should like to complete them. My hope is that this book serves meanwhile as both introduction and guide.

In memory of my sister, Ann, and my brother-in-law, Paul

Contents

INTRODUCTION

POINT OF NO RETURN
by Fred Chappell

In collecting the materials for this amazing Reader, Kelly Cherry has dropped two of her published books from consideration for excerpt, following "the benefit of hindsight." In a way, that decision is disappointing; it would be enlightening to see passages from what she considers her lesser work. If we set out to follow the forward progress of her artistry, we would need to know the paths she did not pursue, as well as those that lie open before us in these pages.

One reason I would like to glimpse those roads not taken is that I have a theory. Cherry is a flambeau example of the extremely conscious artist, a writer who mediates ceaselessly upon the problems and possibilities of the poem, the novel, the short story and the essay. She ponders what she has done and how she has done it; she thinks about the approaches and techniques she has employed and she labors to extend and expand them. This kind of effort is not common to all writers, many of whom will write this year pretty much the same novel they wrote year before last, the same poem they wrote twenty years ago.

But for those who strive to push against their own boundaries, the accustomed methods and aspirations will not suffice. Something new has to happen so that something new can be made. There comes an hour when the will must come to the aid of the psyche, when the writer asks herself, Is this the way it has to be? Then she scrawls furiously at the head of the page, *Es muss sein!* And afterward there is no turning back. *Les demoiselles d'Avignon* is one of the ugliest paintings ever to grace a canvas, but Picasso had to paint it, then own up to it, to display it in public, and to bow to the inevitable. It was his new starting point. There was no going back.

I have been trying to locate such a crossroads moment in Cherry's fiction and will propose that the first piece she places in this gathering, "Her, in His Story," may be it. It is in this brilliant story that she demonstrates her concept that no personal narration is singular; a story takes place in the past and the future as well as in the present. It is taking place in the lives of all other characters as well as in the life of the central character; the narrator is perceived in different terms by all the characters and by author and reader as well; the incidents of the narrative include within their actions interpretations of those actions. The conclusion of the action does not curtail its possibilities. In truth, the action never concludes—but that is a different story.

"Her, in His Story," is a thorough anatomization of the desire of a woman for a man. The focus is close and intense. But the ninth paragraph begins with this sentence: "Although he had not imagined her, he had imagined a character imagining a hill like a teardrop, the long grass weeping, blue as water." Gadzooks, thinketh the reader, the point of view has changed. —But it has not. It has voiced the other part of itself which was present from the beginning. He was a writer; his language is literary. Yet he could not possess those words if *she* had not imagined his way of imagining things.

Please spare me the carping adjectives: *convoluted, baroque, precious, exhibitionist*. None of those terms apply. The story does indeed require concentration, but the rewards are immense. In fact, the rigor of concentration—savoring the sentence the sentences and the swift insights and the perceptive glances—is its own reward. Any aspiring writer (that adjective includes all of us) must ask how Cherry got from the sentence, about a woman who loves a man she has not met, to the last sentence: "If he wrote that story, he thought, he would put those flowers in it."

I propose the fanciful notion that "Her, in His Story" represents a dramatic turning point because I feel a need to account for "The Hungarian Countess," one of the very finest masterpieces of the contemporary short story. I tell myself that it could not have appeared in the world above; it must have had an ancestry. It bears a family resemblance to the other story, but it is of a different order. The styles of both of them are set in closely related keys, but the closure of "Countess" is in a seemingly distant key. A mysterious, veiled figure bearing the Rose as a traditional symbol of beauty enters, like a being from the world of fairy tale, into the analytical discourse about love. The story concludes with this extraordinary key-change that is both inevitable and utterly surprising. My neck hair prickles every time I read it.

But why should I devise silly fantasies to account for "The Hungarian Countess"? It speaks for itself; it does not require a pedigree. One may proclaim, "The reason it is so marvelous is because Kelly Cherry wrote it. 'Nuff said." That rejoinder is unsatisfactory because Cherry herself has written at length about the processes of composition and the demands of art. To dismiss in offhand fashion the reflective toil that has gone into her work would be to engage in distasteful false ingenuousness, unworthy of the achievements that have been so hard-won.

Cherry has written searching autobiographical accounts also. *The Exiled Heart,* in large part a memoir of star-crossed love at the mercy of Soviet politics, records some episodes of her struggles with illness, depression, and crushing loneliness. That book, along with several of her essays, furnishes a glimpse of how personal misfortune is made into art by the fully engaged passions of the intellect. Cherry's almost Pascalian methods are dangerous ones for a writer to choose, for they demand escalating efforts for each new piece, each new page. Baudelaire said that a writer "entering into the abyss of himself" shows as much courage as a warrior on the battlefield. His pronouncement may more accurate in the case of Kelly Cherry than in his own case.

She addresses the subject directly in her essay, "The Place Where There is Writing":

> In the beginning was the Word, but we learned to say "I," and that prideful self-assertion was the original sin. It was also the beginning of language. It is not consciousness but self-consciousness, which allows us to see ourselves as subjects, and to see ourselves as objects of our subjective seeing, and so on as in an endless series of mirrors, that separates us from God. That separates us, period. The ability to refer to ourselves grants us history and hope, the foreknowledge of our death and legacy, the knowledge, to put it in other words, of good and evil. For with the reflexive recognition of ourselves as subjects that are in their own objects comes the inescapable awareness of cause and consequence.

> With discovery, or the first articulation, of "I," we brought irony into the world. The children of irony—Socrates, Lao Tze, Montaigne, Bacon, Locke, Newton, Einstein, and all the others—fashioned us into was we are becoming. Their children and grandchildren, along whom we must prominently number Cherry, are still at work on the project.

I have engaged in pointless, enjoyable fantasies in trying to find a single turning point in the evolution of Cherry's fiction. I have done so partly in order to increase my own appreciation of her work. Why, then, do I feel no urge to find a corresponding crucial point in her poetry? It could not have arrived full blown upon the currents of a Botticellian breeze.

Yet it seems to me to have arrived in just that way. From her earliest work, the Benjamin John sequence, to the late collection, *The Life and Death of Poetry,* her voice has been consistent. It varies to some degree as the subject matter varies, but the essentials are always there: lyric tautness, economy of means, intensity of expression, rigorous musicality, and the ambition to form every experience, even every intimation of experience, into art. The most fleeting apprehension of that same ambition may be captured and expressed, as in her longish poem, "Questions and Answers":

> Things are not simple, it seems, as certain ones
> who have gone before us have suggested:

there are implications everywhere,
whispering in the tops of trees, urgent,
restless, waiting, darting across the ground
just a second before you turn your head,
so you never quite see them, just their shadows,
the light stabilizing itself after the sudden disturbance.

This wary awareness, this sensitivity that is as restless and vulnerable as a candle flame, is our helpless mainstay, necessary because we are "surrounded by unseen eyes in the dark." The way forward is into the dark and we have no choice, once we have become ourselves but to enter.

We will go into the unknown together,
drawing the long sentence of ourselves after us,
until only the tip end of it is visible,
a scant bit of blackness, a point, like a period.

I

HER, IN HIS STORY

"Eternity is passion."

—W. B. Yeats

She saw his films, read his books, was ravished by the way he could write about the suburban gardens humming in late afternoon, how when he walked out in them he realized the sound was lawn sprinklers. She carried on secret conversations with him, conversations replete with references to singing gardens and other things that were out of his work. Nobody knew this. Nobody knew what she was doing. She lived alone and there was no reason nor any need for anybody to know what went on in her mind. If she wanted to have an imaginary conversation while she washed the dishes or made the bed it was nobody's business but her own.

She imagined him in her bed. She knew she was older than he was, but perhaps not by too much. Anyway, for months, before she had ever read his stories or even knew about them, she had been half-wild with desire, for what she didn't know. For love, yes, but not just that. Whatever it was, it was something she must still be hoping could be found—she realized this, surprised—since, it seemed to her, we don't desire what we cannot imagine receiving. Wind blew in through the screens and hit her in the face.

 She was a woman who had been hit by a man, but long ago. She was not a woman who had stayed around to let it happen again and again. There is a strength to be located in despair, and it gets you out the door. She knew perfectly well that when a man glared at you with contempt like that and with one vicious smack imprinted his palm on the side of your face there was nothing to do but leave. Leaving might be something you were ready to do or it might not; if it wasn't, you would spend months, maybe years, weeping over what had been lost, but you wept silently, secretly, and nobody knew it.

They might think they knew it but they didn't, not really.

They couldn't know it because they had not seen how his distaste for you yanked one side of his mouth down, a scowl/sneer/scornful scoffing. *That mouth you had kissed. That mouth that had kissed you.* It was a palsy of disparagement.

You left because when a man despises you all is lost.

Hate can be turned to love, but despisement and contempt cannot. Not any way she knew, at least.

A season of desire, she thought of it as: these months leading up to now, in which she had felt absence sleeping beside her at night, grief and longing walking beside her by day, the wind like a hand lifting her skirt. When she discovered his stories, she fled into them, away from absence, grief, longing, the wind and anything else that would assault, strangle, suffocate.

Although he had not imagined her, he had imagined a character imagining a hill like a teardrop, the long grass weeping, blue as water. Everything liquid and flowing and dripping. She imagined him imagining. She knew you could write shoreline hills and suburban gardens into the middle of a city. She imagined the stiffness in his shoulders from working all morning at his desk, the muscles tight in the back of his neck, the abstractedness he carried into bed at night. She was old enough to imagine other scenarios. He might be, instead of her lover, her son. She wasn't old enough for him to be her son, but she was old enough to imagine this alternative configuration of elements. Whereas, once upon a time, she would have seen him only in the one role: her lover, her hoped-for lover, a man with a talent for tenderness, capable of forgetting himself long enough to forget his fear.

Desire drove men into women but as soon as it was fulfilled they grew wary and wanted to leave. But she felt—she made believe—that he would want to stay and stay and stay. She remembered that moment when a man retreats from a woman's body as an abandonment, a rejection. She remembered it as a moment in which she felt stunned, as if hit, maybe murdered. Yes, it was as a dead person that she had sat up, the jism leaking from her and making the sheet clammy, and she felt as if she should apologize for that, as if it were her fault, this wanton exchange of bodily fluids, this overflow of passion, and she hooked her bare heels down on the inside of the bedframe and hugged herself, willing herself not to say anything, not to utter endearments or formulate claims or make demands. But also not to apologize.

In those days she smoked, and she lit a cigarette but her throat was dehydrated, and her mouth felt stretched and pulled, like some faded garment blocked to dry, from what he'd wanted done to him. Which was merely what they all wanted done to them—there were not *that* many scenarios. She could imagine being his sister, his daughter.

New York at night—in those days when she had smoked, she lived in New York—had been a place without parties, restaurants, theater, concerts. No salons, no gallery openings, no first-run films. It was simply a place where you worked a day job, a night job, a most-of-the-weekend job, trying to earn enough to get by on. The subway to work, to the second job, the bus home, buying Cheerios and cat food on upper Broadway at nine at night, the garish light in the store leaching the third dimension from everything, so that everything was depthless and transparent. Working at her typewriter on into the night, perhaps planting on the page, extravagant in the only way available to her, a garden in the grid of shadowy streets. She thought now of all the people she had never met there, because she had always been working except for the Saturday nights with men, all of whom were periodontally impaired or repressed or puddingy, or maybe only uninteresting-looking, and all of whom required perfection in a woman. The irony of it was, at the time she had overlooked their bad teeth or latent (as long as it remained latent) hostility or their love handles, or their being emotionally lethargic, but she could not overlook their requirement for perfection and her inability to meet it. She had smoked and hung her bare feet on the bed rail and her long, straight hair swept forward at the sides of her face, and sirens and horns had tuned up for the evening performance, an orchestra of traffic, but the man she'd just been with barely turned in his sleep, oblivious. Red lights on radio towers blinked against the black sky. She wondered where he was now, that man, although she wasn't even sure which man she was remembering. It had all been so long ago it was like a story, something she might read about someone else, another woman.

He wrote about women. He paid attention to their perfume, their hair and eyes, the different ways in which they asked for love. Some asked outright, laughing at themselves, maybe even at the men they slept with. Some blushed. Some hated their own neediness.

She never asked, she had given up asking. She pretended to a certain gruffness, making fun of anything she might feel. She was afraid her feelings might be a nuisance to others.

And yet she felt.

She felt, in his stories, a tremulous awareness of beauty that made her think he would know why he had written the particular stories he had written. When she set the soap back in its dish and peeled off the latex gloves she sat down on the kitchen floor, eye level with the sink pipes, which were still sweating, and rested her forehead in her hands, thinking she could be in a story by him, if he knew her. But he didn't. He didn't know her, and therefore he did not know that she was, already, in his story and would be until the end.

After a while she got up from the floor and went upstairs to work, which she did in a small room the house's previous occupants had used as a nursery. When she was a little girl she had imagined that when she was grown up she would have twins. Twin girls. She was going to dress them in red and white polkadot raincoats. She had seen such a raincoat on another child and thought it was beautiful, the shine and slick and cheerfulness of it. It was *such* a beautiful raincoat she thought there should be two of them. Beauty was meant to be magnified, made more of. Her twins would be dark-haired. They would be talkative, at least with each other. They would have secrets but none from each other. They would have umbrellas. Rain would roll off the umbrellas and the twins would stay dry. When they got home from school she would see that they left their umbrellas open in the hallway and she would hang up their raincoats and serve them tomato juice, and crackers with peanut butter on them. When they took off the raincoats, the twins would smell, faintly and enjoyably, a little like rooms whose windows have been briefly shut against a summer storm.

She pulled the door shut and turned on the air conditioning unit. It was the only unit in the house, a small unit for this small room.

The room got colder. It got colder and colder. She put on a sweater. She wondered if he, too, could be in a small room somewhere with an air conditioner making it colder and colder. She thought not. She thought he was probably somewhere swank—a premiere, a book publication party. Or no—she decided he would be somewhere not swank at all. He would be visiting his parents, she was sure, in a rundown part of town, soot on the windowsills, furniture arranged to hide the spots in the carpet. The lace curtains snagged on a nail where a picture had been taken down and not replaced, the tea cozy in the shape of a camel. He'd be good to his parents, going to see them often, taking them out on the town now and then. They would look old but still be relatively young, perhaps not all that much older than she was.

An air conditioner was like a sea, drowning out other sounds. You couldn't hear a garden when the air conditioner was on. You heard the air conditioner humming, not the garden.

It was possible, she supposed, that she had gone a little bit crazy, but she knew that mostly she was just lonely. She didn't like to think about that now. What she felt now was simply this pain and longing, the pain of knowing life could have been different—was different for him, for everyone who knew him—and never would be any different for her, though it was probably going to get harder, because it got harder, and colder, for everyone, as time went on.

She tried to think of ways she might meet him. If she found out where he worked, where he lived. If she knew someone who knew someone who knew him, at least a little bit. If she did something that attracted his attention—but what would that be? What would cause him to turn his gaze from wherever he was in her direction and, seeing her in this faraway place, this place that was inland and like a coffin, notice that she was here?

She could think of nothing. She was completely dependent on him to notice her, to think of her, and he didn't even know this. He didn't know that she was out here, waiting in the margins of his life. She wanted him to read her. She wanted him to find in her a meaning like the meaning she had found in him. Then he would begin to love her the way she loved him.

Of course, she reminded herself, he might already be in love with someone. He probably was—men usually were. And having reminded herself of this, she put on a pair of gloves.

From the window of the small room, high above the street, she could see kids in shorts; drivers of convertibles with the top down and their left elbow where the window would be if the top were up and the windows rolled; small birds with dark crowns in a tree. The more she thought about it the more she realized he had to be in love already. His girlfriend or wife would be blond, or perhaps a redhead. She would be intelligent. She would be smart enough to understand him and keep him interested in her but not so smart that she distracted him from his own work. She would be kind, too, this girlfriend or wife, because if she weren't he would not have been attracted to her. In fact, it was her kindness that first attracted him to her.

So that was that. She herself was not, she knew, kind. She was mean, driven, and envious. She had tried to change these things about herself but failed, which left her feeling meaner, more driven, more envious. And perhaps she was not very smart, either. Perhaps she could think a thing through, all the way to the bottom, she gave herself that, but that was not the same as smart. To be smart you had to be willing to forget, for a little while, how other people felt. You couldn't be constantly worrying about them or gauging their reactions.

So maybe his wife or girlfriend was kind but not all the time, because sometimes she forgot about others; she tucked her blond or red hair behind her ear and smiled and said something bright and funny, and even if it wasn't kind it was so clever and entertaining that everyone forgave her, even the person she had hurt. When he and his wife or girlfriend got into their bed at the end of a long day—work, conferences, a meeting at the bank to refinance their mortgage, dinner with his agent—maybe even dancing at a private club later— he pulled her to him, fitting her small bright head into the place between his shoulder and neck, because a man in love needs to touch, a man in love doesn't want to let go.

A man in love had thoughts he wouldn't tell his buddies. Florid, floral thoughts. He thought about how embankments of flowers were like choirs, the deeper tones tall at the back, soprano peonies up front. He walked home instead of taking the subway or a bus or cab, because, even though he lived in a city where *urban renewal* was a synonym for *decaying infrastructure*, he thought the late-afternoon light edging the buildings was like a soft answer turning away wrath. A man in love was like that. A man in love noticed the white butterfly that strayed out into the streets, that it danced around the hood ornament of the passing car before it flew off again, weaving invisible currents of air into a single invisible braid. He noticed the way shoulders brushed his in passing, male and female shoulders, shoulders in sports jackets or Liz Claibourne dresses or bare beneath tank tops. He became conscious of his own body in a new way, and he fell a little in love with it, too, his own body, fondly grateful for the pleasure it could both provide and receive.

But a woman in love might never tell the man she loved. She might love in secret. She might love a man who didn't even know her.

And so he would go on walking home, and he wouldn't even know about her, anything about her. When he reached the entrance to the apartment building where he and his wife or girlfriend had taken a flat, he smiled at the doorman, and he stood to one side to let his neighbors in 5A onto the elevator first. When the lift's doors closed he felt suddenly fearful, as if something had seized him and was ferrying him to some unnamed destination, and his heart began to pound, as if on a door and demanding to be let out, but then the lift stopped at his floor and he got out and he walked down the hall and turned the key in his lock and went in.

She was already there, his wife or girlfriend, waiting for him. Even before she said hello, even before she moved over to him and lightly touched her lips to his, he admired the translucence of her skin, like a butterfly's wings, the answering softness of her hands. He was a man who had the good fortune to recognize and be pleased by his good fortune. He never wanted to run from the happiness in his life. Sometimes, though, he felt overcome by it. There were times when all he wanted was to cry, and he *would* cry, he would wait until he was alone and then step into a closet and feel buried among the hanging shirts and dresses and he would cry, tears splashing onto his hands as he covered his face. His hands on his face felt smooth, the palms like shell-less sea creatures attaching themselves to his clean-shaven cheeks, and deep inside the closet there was an odor like the sea in a cottage, the way the salt smell gets into the wood and revives whenever there's rain. It frightened him, sometimes, to realize how long and hard he could cry.

The gloves made it impossible for her to touch herself. And they were warm. But especially, they made it impossible for her to touch herself.

His wife or girlfriend—it was hard to see her, at first, beyond the bright hair, the smooth skin. Nice hands, probably—manicured, with the skin still fitting closely to the bone, even the knuckles. And her teeth would have benefitted from modern orthodontics, been straightened, whitened. No lines in the face yet, except for a few around the eyes when she smiled, and those were lovely, more like grace notes than like lines.

Her own face was vanishing. It was disappearing behind another face, one that belonged to an older woman. Sooner or later, the day would come when no one would stop to look at her face anymore, because it would no longer be there to be seen. And it had been rather beautiful.

His wife or girlfriend's face would fade too, but not for another twenty years. By then, she imagined, doctors would have devised or discovered a way to keep people from ever looking their age. Or if his wife or girlfriend did age, he wouldn't mind, because he loved this wife or girlfriend so much that he loved not only who she was but who she was becoming. If his wife or girlfriend cut or curled her hair it was a small change but one that added to his sense of her. Every change deepened her image for him, this portrait in time. He loved how she had been and how she would be, and this, to him, was what devotion was, staying with the same person as she changed.

He could tell that his wife or girlfriend had something on her mind, but he didn't want to press her. He wanted her not to feel that she had to tell him what it was until she was ready. He took off his jacket and threw it over the back of a chair and went into the kitchen. Little roach traps and ant traps were placed at intervals along the counters and floors. Pasta was packed in tightly sealed cylindrical containers with green lids. Light from a ceiling fixture streamed evenly down. All day, he thought, this room had been exactly like this, silent and still, though with the light off, which she had turned on.

In his work there was always the smell of water, a beach or strand, dune grass, often a ferris wheel or roadhouse dance hall. This was what he had known growing up—a sense of loneliness, people wanting a bit of fun, a band in the background, and later, after everyone had gone home, wind blowing lights in the dark water, a cruel moon, clouds shifting like moods.

But she was inland. She was so far inland that he would never find her, even though she was in his story. He didn't know, yet, how much had gotten into his story. He still thought that when he wrote something, that was it, but stories changed too, they began as narrative and then took on the multiple dimensions of poetry, becoming their own possibilities of being, ever new re-visionings of loss and gain. He thought he had written what he had written, but because what he had written had changed her, he had written her as well. The problem was that now she was lost. She didn't know what was expected of her, because he didn't yet know about her or that he expected anything of her.

On a hook on the back of the door was a coat. She put it on. There was also a wool scarf, and she put that on, too. In her scarf and coat and gloves she sat down at the computer, turned it on. It was still summertime outside. Her neighbors were still mowing their lawns. They were still having cookouts, grilling chicken with pesto. The twin Korean toddlers rode their tricycles under their father's watchful eye. Now and then the father mopped his brow. This was not a scene that would be in a story by him. It was too inland, and too ordinary.

He was not an experimentalist. While he did intriguing things stylistically and structurally, style and structure were not the essence of his work, were not what made it extraordinary. What made it what it was, was its openness, a quality of attentiveness that amounted to receptivity. He was a person who could believe anything. He was willing to give up all his preconceptions and accept anything. This was how she knew he would accept her, had accepted her, even if he didn't know that he had. He had left room in his work even for her, the likes of her.

She had to be careful, she knew, not to upset the wife or girlfriend. She wouldn't want to take up too much space. After all, he had never intended for her to appear in his story, and he wouldn't want her to get in the way of the narrative. He had just left room for her, or someone like her. That's all.

So she wouldn't presume.

The thing was, to leave room like that was kindness itself, and no one should presume on kindness. No one should ever try to take advantage of someone's kindness.

She began to type on the keyboard. The gloves hampered her typing but didn't make it impossible. She felt the keys, through leather and cashmere, as padded, like cat's paws.

She was inland, even if the air conditioner sounded sealike.

She turned the unit up, as high as it would go. She was shivering, even in her coat and scarf, but her heart was on fire, it was a thing that had smouldered but not gone out and now flared up. There was a burning inside her that was a kind of localized hell, self-hatred an eternal penance, the flames of it eating at her forever. She had tried to be cold. Cold to herself.

Not to him, of course, but then that was an academic point, inasmuch as he was not someone she had or ever would meet.

If she did—just for hypothesis' sake—what would she say to him?

Whatever her words might be, they could not be the words his wife or girlfriend said to him. He rested two fingers on that lovely left wrist when he came back out from the kitchen. She was sitting in the black leather chair. He had a glass of milk in his other hand. "What's on your mind?" he asked.

She put her gloved hands over her ears. She didn't want to know what was on his wife or girlfriend's mind. It would be something important, probably something that signified how much his wife or girlfriend cared for him. Or she was pregnant, and he would respond with delight and love. Or—but it didn't matter. Whatever it was, it would take him farther and farther away into that world where he lived, the world of premieres and publication parties, of women who were still young or youngish with bright hair and smooth skin and nice nails. It would take him farther into his own life, during which he would become famous—receiving awards and other honors—and then retreat a little, wanting to recover the excitement he'd had when he first began to write; and then, still later, when most of his work was done and his children were grown, he'd stand in front of the hall mirror, on his way out, and notice how his form had thickened, his jaw was a little jowly now, his eyes were tired-looking though he certainly didn't feel tired. He'd pick up his umbrella from the stand but wait just until he'd stepped outside to open it—some superstitions a person just couldn't shake—and as he walked swiftly to the tube stop, rain falling lightly with a hollow sound like flutes or fossilized bones, he remembered a story he meant to write, once, started, in fact, and then had set aside. It was around somewhere, in a drawer or filing cabinet. He thought he would dig it out and see if there wasn't something he could do with it. He thought he remembered that there had been something in the story worth working with, if he could figure out how to use it, though for the life of him he couldn't recall why he had ventured into that particular story in the first place.

He had never got used to the way ideas simply appeared. They were just there, like weather.

The underground stop was at the corner—a short walk, hardly long enough to follow his train of thought, beyond making a mental note to look up that beginning. *Lord!* he thought, dashing down the steps past a flower stall. *How beautiful to find flowers here, on the street, in the rain!* He had caught a glimpse of color—Van Gogh yellow; pink so pale it was peach; and scarlet, crimson, and cerise. And the leaves! The leaves all washed a dark, deep green. It was a medley.

Then he was stepping onto the train, going wherever his life was taking him.

She waited to see where that would be. She had given herself over to his story and waited to see how it would turn out. (She wasn't worried. She trusted him.)

He was still seeing the colors of the banked flowers, their dampened leaves and petals, as the train entered the tunnel. If he wrote that story, he thought, he would put those flowers in it.

HOW IT GOES

At five-thirty I pick up my wife and she says Let's take home Thai. She parks her briefcase on the floor under the glove compartment, her toes on it like a footrest. She's wearing alligator shoes and her legs in stockings look both substantial and definite enough to squeeze and somehow hazy, cloud-hazy, kind of close and far off at the same time, like late afternoon through a screen door, like childhood, it makes me want to cry, but I know I'm just strung out it's been a bitch of a day. I'm just back from Chicago nine inches of rain in twelve hours the streets were like canals like irrigation ditches who am I kidding? like open sewers would be more accurate, the taxicabs like sickly yellow turds, the city suddenly less a city than an insane jumble of rocks at the base of a (what I need now is a long hot shower) waterfall and no sleep for three days while we wooed the boys from Kansas. Oatmeal. I say to her Well we made love to the oatmeal boys and now they're ours how about that and she says Fine that's good I'm glad the trip went well and I don't say a word about the rain but of course she saw it on the news and she says I was worried and I say You were?

She turns to look at me. Her face is like a cookie, cute and sweet, I guess I've got oatmeal on my mind but a child would go crazy with yearning looking up at that face, reach for her like a cookie jar but we don't have kids her career comes first. She's a lawyer. Everyone I know is married to a lawyer. Sometimes it's the husband sometimes the wife.

Of course I was worried she says I saw it on TV and it looked awful. There were people swept away. Whirlpools at intersections.

Tell me about it, I say.

And she closes up the jar of her face and turns to look out the window. This is how it goes.

At Bahn Thai we settle on one pork one chicken, there's beer in the refrigerator. She's still not talking. Neither am I.

The housekeeper has been here today and the place smells of Pine Sol. I keep saying we should get rid of cat that pees on the couch but she won't hear of it she says the cat is like her child and I say The hell it is and she says I have no heart and I say she might be lacking an organ or two herself the way she carries on about that cat and I have her brain in mind but she thinks I mean she's not a complete woman because she'd rather raise a cat than a child and maybe there's something to that and she starts to cry and this is how it goes.

But tonight I don't say anything. I know we are walking a fine line here. I don't want to be the one to make us take an end-of-the-world, it feels like it would be that, misstep. I carry the food into the kitchen and serve it up on plates and bring the plates back out to the porch. It's still light outside and we can eat on the porch and watch the neighborhood. The cat follows us and takes up a position on the floor and sits there on her haunches gazing up at us like a reproof in person. She is old, that's her problem and I don't blame her for it I just don't like the smell of cat urine who does?

How did your day go? I ask, all ears but they're taking in the lawnmower across the street, the Medflight helicopter overhead, the boom-box making its way down the sidewalk next to the tufted tie-dyed gelatinous hair of what I would guess is a ninth-grader, the dog barking and the cars in their homebound rush.

How did my day go she says. She seems to be turning the question over, asking herself how her day went. Finally she says, Larry, I want a divorce.

My mouth is hot, Oriental. Snowpeas on my fork and what she says is she wants a divorce.

I ask you.

Look, I say, I know we've been having problems we got some big things we disagree on but a divorce? Do we need to zip right into a divorce? People aren't doing that so much anymore you know I say, they're taking time to work things out, AIDS, etcetera.

A divorce, Larry, she says.

I am so tired I'm just back from a twelve-hour flood in Chicago and kissing Kansan ass and countless hearty jokes about sowing wild ones and then driving the car home from the airport and picking her up and what she has to say is—well, you know what she said.

I look at her unhappily for a minute and wonder where we go from here when Sam comes around the side of the house and says You're back why don't you come over to our house we're planning to watch *My Brilliant Career* on the VCR tonight and I think great, that's just what my wife needs to see, frustrated ambition in the Australian outback, but we go anyway and Sam and Mary pop corn and we drink strawberry daiquiris and my wife is so fucking brilliant herself, so witty, You'd never know, she seems to be saying, how my heart is breaking I'm a great actress myself. Not until the movie's over do I start crying, and then the tears come, like rain in Chicago they fall and fall I'm out-Chicagoing Chicago and everyone's solicitous and embarrassed but no one really knows what to do about it least of all me.

They negotiate. They try to figure out do Sam and Mary leave the room so Lisa can comfort me, or since Lisa may be the cause of this do she and Mary go and leave Sam with me? This is a quandary. Meanwhile I am still crying and part of me is saying to myself Look, if the roles are reversed one of the things I get to do is cry so I just keep crying but the roles aren't reversed, not really, and this I know because Lisa throws me a look of deep disgust, which I catch before she changes it to one of concern and helplessness. There is such calculation here. She *is* a great actress.

Then it's just Sam and me and he says Hey, fellow, you go ahead, cry for all of us it's our turn. He's cheering me on. That makes me smile at least after a fashion and I say Lisa wants a divorce and he says Mary and I sort of thought that was coming sooner or later and I say I was hoping it would be later and he says Well if it's going to happen sooner is probably better don't you think and I say All things considered I'd prefer later if you don't mind and he says Maybe she'll agree to hold off and I say Maybe and he says Life's a bitch and I say Right and he says Hey and I say Hey and this is how it goes.

Look, I say to her in bed, we've made it this long, why don't we hold off a bit. We can divorce anytime, you know. We don't have to do it this minute.

She's asleep. You'd think she'd stay up and suffer some but she's sound asleep. I turn on the light just to make sure she's not faking but she's not I guess it's not like an orgasm, I think meanly and hate myself for it. But let's face facts, she's a lawyer not an actress.

When she sleeps her face softens, it kind of melts, the bones under her skin sink and blur and she looks about seven years old. Night is like a hole we drop into, a hole in time. You go to sleep and you fall down this hole and all night long you're seven years old. But I don't sleep.

In the morning she sits up and says she's thought it over though when she's done this beats me because all she's done all night is sleep. Larry, she says, I don't want to wait. I want to get divorced now. This is how she announced she wanted to get married. Larry, she said, I don't want to wait. I want to get married now. But I don't think this is a good time to remind her of that.

So I say Okay and we get dressed, moving around each other in little circles but never touching, little circles in the bedroom, the bathroom, the kitchen. When I'm in town I drive her to work. In the car we're stuck side by side. For the first time ever she props the briefcase on the left side of her seat so it's like a partition between us. When I shift gears my hand grazes the briefcase and I say Excuse me realizing as soon as I do that it's stupid nobody apologizes to a briefcase.

The sun is shining in my eyes and I turn the visor down. Unless a god-damned bird landed on the car hood an olive branch in its freaking beak you'd never know how it had been raining in Chicago. God, I think, impressed by this, it takes only a minute or two for the past to become past. It's like time is a kind of fast-drying glue that the present keeps getting stuck to and no matter how hard you tug at it you can't pry it loose again.

Listen I say I know I've been putting too much pressure on you. I guess we could wait where a child's concerned.

Children are not the issue here, Larry, she says. Children are a screen.

Then what's the issue?

Disappointment.

I could pursue this but I don't. Traffic is snarled on West Doty.

I drop her off and park under my building and go to my office. Billie is there ahead of me, flipping through files on her desk while the receiver's perched on her shoulder. She has one of those phone rests that lets her keep her hands free. Her red hair is pulled straight back in what ought to be a schoolmarm effect but what happens when she does this is that her flawless complexion, her high forehead look so brave, so touchingly exposed, so unself-conscious, that it breaks my heart and makes me want to weep I'm afraid I'll start crying again for some reason it seems lately I've got waterworks on the basis of which I should probably declare myself a public utility or should I say futility. Looking at Billie's forehead makes me feel hopelessly old so when she signals for me to get on my phone I just nod at her and throw myself in the chair and say Yo, of course I say Yo, who doesn't, I say Yo, Larry here, and it's Oatmeal on the line.

We've reconsidered, he says.

You're reconsidered, I repeat, parroting him.

And he says, it's just like racquetball the way this keeping coming back, they've reconsidered. They think maybe they don't want to sell after all.

This is my cue to dance but I'm so tired my verbal feet don't want to move. Well I'm sorry to hear it I say I think you're making a mistake, which is the worst thing I could say because what else can Oatmeal do but take offense nobody wants to be told he's making a mistake this is basic sales psychology don't you think I know that?

Billie is looking at me hard.

What's wrong? she asks when I get off.

Nothing's wrong I say, what makes you think something's wrong?

Jesus Larry she says, what kind of dunce do you think I am I can tell when something's wrong. Tell me.

Oatmeal just canceled.

What else.

Lisa wants a divorce.

Oh.

Oh is right I say.

It was inevitable.

I know it's inevitable it still feels like I've been kicked in the balls.

I don't know what that feels like, she says. Please use terms I can understand.

I am maybe ten years older than she is but she looks so young to me it's like she's light-years away on the edge of the universe, that clear face shining bright as a star a quasar, too far to even think about reaching. Billie, I say, I'm going home.

You just got here she says.

I need sleep.

You learn things in business that's for sure, I'm thinking as I head home. Take oatmeal. They store it in these silos like the Quaker Oats silos in Akron, Ohio, and every so often some poor sucker falls in it's like drowning. The guy tries to climb out but it's like quicksand he just keeps sinking deeper and deeper. Oat dust up the nose down the throat. Now here is the goddamn paradox the fucking oats are so dry they suck up all the moisture in the vicinity. When the crew finally vacuums out the oats and find the body it's drowned and dehydrated both. Looks to me like they oughta be able to mix it with a little water and reconstitute the poor bastard. What would it feel like, I'm thinking, to be condensed. What would it feel like to be yourself but take up less room. You wouldn't have all that empty space that your molecules float around in now. You wouldn't be all watery and wavering. You couldn't cry.

It feels strange entering the house at ten in the morning. All along the street, houses are shut up, as if they sleep during the day while the people are awake and working. I sit down and take off my shoes but I'm too keyed up to get into bed right away so I wander from room to room, not exactly thinking about things but not not thinking about them either. When I get to the screen porch I stand there for a while looking out through the screen. The mesh makes the day look muzzy, gauzy, something with a z in it. It makes me think of childhood, those summer days of riding my bike back and forth on the sidewalk in front of my house there were elms then and riding through the patterns of sun and shadow, well it was a kind of lace-light, something like a curtain and billowing, and there was this feeling of having so much energy and power in you that if you could pedal hard enough you'd propel yourself into the future and I decide to call my father. I go back into the living room to do this and as I dial, the cat comes over to me and starts curling around my feet, purring. She must like the smell of my socks. I think about sticking a knife in her belly or chopping her head off and sneaking it into Lisa's briefcase something really vicious like that and then I hear my dad's voice on the phone god he sounds old, creaky. Hi, Dad, I say, like it's normal for me to call him at ten in the morning on a weekday but it's not normal and he is instantly alerted I can tell, there's this energy of expectancy shooting over the wires all the way from Florida.

Howzitgoin? he says.

It goes, I say. You know how.

So what's up?

Nothing much, I say, I just felt like calling.

Something's up, he says.

How's your blood pressure? I say, speaking of what I hope is not up. He had this heart attack a couple of years ago after Mom died, and retired and moved to Florida but he has to watch his blood pressure no red meats lots of fish oil. I can't help it I see him rattling around in his dinky little apartment which even though it's only two rooms and a kitchenette is too big for him, because ever since Mom died, his whole life has been too big for him, there are empty spaces all around him.

Blood pressure's fine, he says.

How'd you like me to come for a visit, I say, knowing a visit would do nothing but make us both hurt more, but what are you going to say. You could say Yo. You could say What's up or Hey. You could take a flying leap into a silo of oats and turn your brain into food for a horse.

Lisa's left you.

Well, I say, not yet but she's planning to.

I'm sorry, son, he says.

One second I feel too old the next too young, because I think I'm going to cry when he says son, when he says son I feel so young I feel much too young for him to die which I know he'll probably do in the next year or two and I want to cry again but I can't not over the phone with this old man who would just feel bad not being able to do anything about it so instead I kick the cat.

It's such a shame he says, but fifty percent of marriages fail these days I read it in *Newsweek* so don't feel bad it's not your fault it's the times. Everyone is a victim of his times. For your mother and me, it was the war. For you it's divorce.

I know, I say.

Your mother and I he says, your mother and I, we had our rough spots too everyone does.

I know, I say, although actually I don't and I don't want to think about my parents having rough spots I want to think their marriage was as smooth as anything. As smooth as Billie's forehead. As smooth as time, which just goes on being what it is, the same thing always, behind you, ahead of you, smooth as anything, smooth as a lawyer, a smooth cookie.

Everything works out for the best in the long run, he says.

In the long run, I think, *you'll be dead.* In the long run everything just falls apart the house the lawn work love marriage whole impossible cities, even empires. Empires launch wars that are death rattles in their own throats. They think they are making history but history is just something they become. Life's such a swindle. You keep hoping if you play the angles right you can come out ahead but all the time you're losing more ground than you're gaining. There's this torrent of events that makes you feel like you're being swept along somewhere a tremendous force carrying you in its current like it matters but then it's all over and where you are is exactly nowhere, nowhere, time goes by and leaves you high and dry. Look at this cat I think, she's falling apart too her kidneys are going, her eyesight. She's whimpering in a corner, under a chair, gray-and-white fuzzball she looks like one of those furry slippers with whiskers on them that little girls wear. I'm such a shit. No wonder Lisa wants out.

I tell Dad I'm glad he's doing okay and I'll be okay and I'll be in touch and I hang up and crouch down on the floor trying to get the cat to come to me but she's having none of it smart cat. So I pick her up by the scruff of her neck and carry her into the bedroom with me. The blinds are down and the room is dark. I unmake the bed that Lisa and I made a couple of hours ago trying not to look at each other from our respective sides, tucking the sheets in as if a sheet is a sheet is a sheet and not just about everything else you can think of too. I put the cat on the bed and peel off my clothes down to my underpants and crawl in and pull the maroon top sheet up over me and from the bedroom, street sounds are muffled you could hear yourself think but I don't want to hear myself think, so I lean over to the cat and whisper in her ear her pearly pink ear, Hey, where are your pajamas, the cat's pajamas? and she just looks at me and blinks, and I say, Listen, I'm sorry, I'm not going to hurt you I don't want to hurt anyone if you want to pee on the bed you go right ahead it's a free country and I'm saying this to her in a low voice and I stroke her back and she pushes her nose into my face like she wants to kiss me I miss being kissed, Lisa, once upon a time we were students then, stepping into the circle of my arms and lifting up to me her beautiful complicated face pale and freely given as a communion wafer that sweetest sweetness and I wrap my arms around her and say I'm sorry I'm sorry I'm sorry I'm sorry this is how it's going going gone.

CHORES

Conrad hired a Czech to shovel his snow. She is a graduate student in mathematics, still in her twenties, with dark, revolutionary eyes that shine bright against her absolutely clear, un-made-up skin. She enlisted her mother, and now he has two Czech women, one in her fifties, scraping and shoveling his sidewalk. He watches them from his bedroom window, peering between the slats of the blind. When Milena answered the ad, he realized she needed the money. He wanted to help. Now he feels like a shit. This is not how he wants to see himself: as landed gentry, an overseer. He wants to be kind. He wants to make broad, humanitarian gestures. He wants to be Václav Havel.

There is a lot of snow. He has a lot of sidewalk, a driveway. Next year, he thinks, he will shovel the snow himself (but how will Milena pay her tuition? he wonders). It is good to have things to do, chores to occupy your time.

Fortunately, there is no end of things to do in a house you have only recently moved to. There are floors and walls to clean, shelves to build. He buys books—it is his one indulgence—and he needs to put them somewhere. He has designed cabinets for the study. The cabinets are to have glass doors and will take a long time to construct. Many of the books are first editions—not old, but someday they will be *you can say that about an object not always about a person*, and so they deserve a certain respect. And anyway, it is good to have something to do with your time.

In the evenings, he sits in his study and tries to read. First editions, alas, are not necessarily more riveting than subsequent ones, but there is always the possibility that a new book will jolt him out of his despair—if he can just concentrate on it long enough. He has taken to reading Czech writers—Kundera, Kafka, Čapek, Havel.

Eventually he puts the book down, marking the page with a small copper clip someone had given him He is not an old man, not even middle-aged—he's only thirty-five—but at this point in the evening he sometimes forgets, for a moment, where he is, what he means to do—go to bed—even who he is. He will discover, a few minutes hence, that he has been staring at the wall as if he were watching a slide show *their faces like works of art not life their marvelous postmodern, oh, god, post-everything faces.* Then he will be annoyed with himself, and a little frightened as well, and he will say to himself, harshly, Snap out of it, and sometimes he will actually snap his fingers, too, as if he were accompanying himself in a rendition of some well-known refrain, backup to his own band.

Lying in bed, upstairs, the blinds turned against the night and snow—he knows it is snowing again because traffic sounds are muffled, reaching him only as strangled cries, as if automobiles were coughing and dying all up and down his street, as perhaps they are—he draws up a mental list of everything he must do the next day. There is dry cleaning to drop off and pick up. He needs to put salt in the water softener. The list is endless. There are always things to be done.

In the wintertime, there is snow to be shoveled—next year he will do that himself (unless, of course, Milena is still as much in need of the money as she seemed to be when she answered the ad, her eyes bright with opportunity, her skin flushing with shame). In April and May, there'll be chores to do in the lawn—the hedge to be trimmed, a crabapple tree to be planted, shrubs and flowers to be mulched. In the summer he will mow the grass every Friday afternoon after work, unless it is raining or promising to, in which case he will stay inside, fix himself a drink, and pick up around the house. (The pizza boxes from Domino's will have to go into the trash, he can wash the week's dishes while listening to MacNeil-Lehrer.) The rain will hurl itself against the house, angry at being shut out. Wisconsin seldom has the kind of rain he grew up with, steady all-day downpours. In Wisconsin, the rain lurches across the sky, a stumbling drunken rain-god. It'll be raining but it'll be hot in the house and he'll run a fan even though the windows are closed and he'll work on his drink and read and send out for ribs instead of pizza and there will be the continuous low whoosh of the fan and the rattle of rain on the roof.

By then, the house will no longer seem so strange to him. A little strange maybe, the way any place he could think of would now be strange to him *because without them he is a stranger to himself he no longer knows who he is he is certainly not Václav Havel,* but not so strange. He'll have grown used to it, the way you grew used to being yourself even if you couldn't say, and who could, who that was. In early September, while the house is still dreaming of summer (winter will wake it soon enough), he'll mow the lawn. Quite likely, he will buy a headset and listen to music, undisturbed by the roar of the mower. He will listen to Smetana.

When she answered the ad, she said, "My name is Milena. The accent is placed at the beginning. It is on the first, the first— Do you see?" Her cheeks were red with a kind of revolutionary fervor, her lashes dark even without mascara, glistening from melted snow like animal fur.

It was a soft "i," almost an "e"; a soft "l." "What an unusual name," he said, smiling, though he knew it might not be unusual at all in Czechoslovakia. "You must be very bohemian."

Before he knows it, it will be the time of year when mice find their way into suburban basements—he'll have to call an exterminator. He'll worry about chemicals, the environment, himself. He'll worry about the mice, their eating poison and crawling off like tiny furry French legionnaires in search of water, dying horrible, lingering deaths in the laundry sink. He is such a shit, he knows it. Would Havel call an exterminator? Would *Kafka*?

As winter approaches, he'll have to put up the storm windows. This is a major job, requiring several hours. He'll have to take the screens down, then bring the storms up from the basement. He'll have to hose the storms down and wipe them with Windex, and then fit them into the frames—which can be tricky, especially on the second floor. Then he'll have to rope-caulk all the windows—more hours. Some chores are major, some are minor, but there are always plenty of things that need doing in a house.

After it happened, people said Why don't you get an apartment it's not as if you need, and then they stopped while he finished the sentence for them, but silently, to himself, so much space, and he said to them, I thought I'd look for a house.

At about the same time, there will be leaves to rake—the leaves fallen from the black walnut tree, the maple seedlings, the locust tree, the newly plant-ed crabapple. He'll like the heft of the handle in his gloved palms, the deep draughts of bright air, the feeling of being alert that you get when you attend to the changing of the seasons. He'll stand in his lawn, leaning against his rake as if were a staff, and the November sun will slide across his shoulders without really warming him, and he'll be surprised at how fast time goes when you have things to do. The gutters will need cleaning, the outside faucet must be turned off. He may have to call a chimney sweep, a cement contractor. He could plant bulbs and in the spring there would be tulips and hyacinths. He will definitely buy a tape of *The Moldau* and listen to it via earphones as he mows the lawn, and the tulips and hyacinths, if he has gotten them in, will stand tall and straight, as if they were listening also, just waiting for the proper moment to applaud.

In the evenings he'll read, opening glass doors and taking from the cabinet some book or other and settling into the chair in the study. Sometimes he'll for-get, for a moment, who and where he is, and when he remembers these things—that he is head of a medical library, that he is in the house he bought because it is within easy walking distance of work *if they'd been walking not driving; the freezing rain turned the Subaru into a bobsled*, that he is still a young man—when he remembers, he is stunned to realize how easy it is to lose track of everything, to let go. Suppose you could forget to live in the world. Suppose you could forget to eat, to sleep, to wake up, ever. You could wander through your dreams forever, an echoing hallway lined with candles in sconces, the flames blurring into the jittery darkness, shadows of varying depth, some as deep as time.

In his bedroom, he'll empty his pockets, dropping the loose change into a small brass tray on the bureau. He'll turn the blinds against the snow and the night. By now, he'll know the couple next door—the Wallaces—because she is a nurse at the hospital, and he has met her, walking to and from her shift, and they have acquaintances in common. He will know the woman with the dog who lives across the street. He will be a fixture in the neighborhood.

If he runs out of things to do around the house, he can offer to help out. There is a widow who could surely use some help. He can mow her lawn, he can shovel her snow if the boy she hires fails to show up. The kids in this city—they turn sixteen, they get a driving license, they can make much better money at McDonald's. Only third-year graduate students in mathematics are desperate enough to hire themselves out as snow shovelers. Only women from Czechoslovakia are willing to get out of bed at six in the morning and walk several blocks to shovel snow. When he wakes, he hears them scraping and shoveling, Milena and her mother, it is what calls him back from the mysterious place he has been, the hallway lighted by candles in sconces, their shape-shifting flames. When he wakes. . .

He tries to think of everything he knows about Czechoslovakia—anything. King Wenceslaus. Or Alexander Dubček. Though he was only twelve, he remembers television images of Dubček on a balcony, he remembers the words *Prague Spring* like the title of a song. The tanks lumbered through downtown Prague, stiff with arthritis. The soldiers, boys who would be middle-aged now, but he remembers them as younger than he is, remembers their confusion, their haircuts that made them look overexposed, as if they were not flesh at all but just pure film. . . .

He lies there, listening to Milena and her mother, and he feels like a totalitarian government, but all he wanted to do was help. He expected a teenage boy to answer his ad, but it was Milena who called, Milena who came by to look at the sidewalk and driveway, and say yes, she could handle it. Her eyes were dark, shining with an inner light, and her skin, bare of makeup, was like a part of the world he had never visited, full of points of interest (her cheeks as red as *The Communist Manifesto*, her mouth as mobile as America).

He hired her. He didn't want to be sexist. She straightened her shoulders and raised her arms as if she were flexing her biceps but of course she had on her coat and so it was only a gesture, not for real, and said, "I am *very* strong."

He had never meant for her to put her mother to work too. "It is good for her health," she said, speaking for her mother, even though, he knew, her mother spoke English. At least some. Milena and her mother worked in concert, a New World symphony.

Downstairs, in the kitchen, he confronts the pizza box that he left out last night and that now smirks at him from the vinyl-cloth'd table, gaping like a mouth, dried tomato paste clinging to the sides. He stuffs it into a Hefty bag and ties off the bag with a blue twist. He has dry cleaning to drop off on his way to work, to pick up on his way home. He must go to the grocery store. He needs milk, cereal, salt for the front stoop.

There is so much he has to do. He never understood just how much there is to do *she had done so much of it, cheerfully, efficiently, never complaining, she had been on the way to the store when it happened Caleb not yet five.* He realizes now that there are baseboards to be scrubbed, floors to be waxed, moldings to be dusted, radiators to be vacuumed. There are toilets that want scouring, waste-baskets that want emptying, sheets that want changing, walls to contemplate painting. He is building bookshelves, cabinets with glass doors, doors that will open and shut with a polite, satisfying click, the sound that things make when they acknowledge their gratitude, knowing they have their own place and are safely in it.

As he has and is, here, in this house that is within walking distance of where he works. But how dark it is when he arrives home, in the evening! How terribly, dreadfully dark! He turns the key in the lock and enters the hallway, his shoes leaving a Hansel-and-Gretel trail of salt and melting snow. He hangs the dry cleaning in the hall closet. He hangs his anorak in the closet, slipping the loop inside the collar over a hook on the wall. He finds his way in the dark to the lamp in the living room, and when he turns it on, the light is as sudden as accidental death.

For a moment, he forgets where he is, who he is. He stands there blinking, his shoes as heavy as chains, a worker's chains—the chains of a man whose life is a chore—the room dancing in and out of the lamplight. Then he remembers, and he goes to the study, picks up a book, and settles down to read. This book could be by Hašek, Siefert, or Škvorecký. From time to time he looks up from the book and stares out the window. It has begun to snow again—he can see it tumbling around the streetlight, a busy snow, a well-traveled snow blown this way and that (up from Iowa, down from Minnesota) by a no-nonsense midwestern wind. Now the whiteness is everywhere. It has filled up the rectangle of window like milk poured into a glass. Upstairs, undressing, he turns the blinds against the snow and the night, but then he pulls two slats apart and peers out between them. Milena must come in the morning, with her mother; the shovels are waiting for them, on the front stoop.

"Mathematics?" he'd asked, startled, impressed. Her eyes shone like candles in sconces, her lashes were as dark as shadows. Color bloomed in her face, a kind of warmth, like springtime, though it was snowing and she had on her coat, a fur hat. "I can't even balance my checkbook," he said, becoming aware of what he had said only as he said it, and then he was blushing too, while she looked at him with a mild pity, perhaps the ways she regarded all Americans, as a weak people with money and bad puns. She is strong and beautiful and smart, a worthy compatriot of Václav Havel.

Sometimes he forgets—himself, everything, almost everything—and then he is annoyed with himself, and a little frightened as well, but he is also a little proud of himself, amazed by his own great weakness, his enormous weakness, for he is capable of far more weakness than he ever suspected might be in him. He never knew how easily he could be defeated. The snow dashes across the street in drifts; the sky seems to have dropped, and clouds lie over the street, the sidewalk, the driveway. Who is he? What did he mean to do? Wasn't there a dream, a dream he woke from? These are questions he asks himself when he has time on his hands, when he has nothing to do, nothing to keep him from thinking about a future as oppressive as the history of a small Eastern European country.

THE HUNGARIAN COUNTESS

Blessed are they that have not seen, and yet have believed.

—John 20:29

While I was in the mental hospital, my brother ran off with a Hungarian countess. I found this out when I called Connecticut. Maureen, the woman he had been living with before he came back from the countess and moved in with Alma, answered the telephone. "He's in Spain," she said, "with a Hungarian countess." You hear far stranger things than that when you are a patient on a psych ward, so I just said, "When's he coming back?" He was the only stateside relative I had, bad blood though some might call him. "How should I know," Maureen said. "He's in *Spain* with a fucking Hungarian *countess.*"

I hung up the telephone and crawled back to bed. I stayed there for three weeks. It was a semiprivate room. Then I went home because there had been a blizzard and I had to shovel my sidewalk. Living in Wisconsin, I devote much of my energy to worrying about snow. Will it? Should I stay up late to see whether it stops before midnight so if it does I can get up early to clear it off before I leave for work, since there's a noon deadline, or will it go on after midnight, in which case the city will give me until noon of the following day and I can get to sleep early, except that I will have stayed awake until midnight to determine this? Excessive worrying was one reason I wound up in the hospital, and it was the reason I left.

Wisconsin is a state made for worriers. Our hyperbolic legalism is both a symptom and a cause of the extreme worry that goes on in this state. We march against U.S. imperialism and big brotherism and send Joe McCarthy to the Senate. We tax people out of sight to support social agencies and then pass a Grandparent Liability Act to make private citizens ineligible for state aid. What do all those inaccessible agencies do? Whom do they serve? Wisconsin is working on these questions right now. It plans to draft a report to the American people as soon as it discovers the answers.

Meanwhile, my brother had come back from Spain. Without the Hungarian countess. A true member of the jet set, she had moved on to Costa Rica. My brother was now with Alma, who had up to this point been best friends with Maureen but who was now Maureen's archenemy. "How was Ibiza?" I asked him on the phone.

"Fine," he said, "but the countess was a teetotaler."

My brother, once arbiter of my life and still at that point bound to me in ways so subtle I had yet to understand them, was dying—to use a short word for a long process. I had consulted with his doctor, also by telephone, who said my brother was about seventy years old internally. I imagined an old man inside a not-so-old man. I imagined a decrepit liver, a withered heart. His insides would have a sheen of green, like time-tarnished bronze. The cause was alcohol, which was what my brother thought flowed in a real man's veins instead of blood. It certainly flowed in his veins, and had been so flowing since his first year in college, at a Baptist institution in Virginia from which each of us was in turn expelled, one for cutting classes, one for taking more credits than was considered healthful for a clean-minded young woman.

"How was the mental hospital?" he asked in return.

It was the first of December, I hadn't yet unpacked my bag. I had shoveled the sidewalk first thing. The red shovel lifted the snow like a giant mitten. The pale sun gleamed in the sky behind the blue spruce like a fragile Christmas tree ornament.

"Ninotchka," he said, "inasmuch as I'm dying, will you do me a favor?"

He was forty-seven. He had refused the liver scan. If he continued drinking but what he had was only cirrhosis, he could last six months to a year. If it was liver cancer, three months. This was from the doctor, so I accepted it—if it had come from my brother, I wouldn't have known to what extent he was dramatizing the facts: My brother had never allowed himself to feel restricted by the truth.

"Of course," I said, "but if you'd just quit drinking, you could perhaps live for a long, long time and I could do you many more favors."

"But if I gave up drinking and died of liver cancer anyway I'd resent being a sober corpse. Besides, this is all academic. You know I can't quit."

"You could if you wanted to," I argued. I was not yet knowledgeable about the biochemical basis of alcoholism. "I wish you would have the liver scan done."

"I can't afford the liver scan."

"I'll pay for it."

"Honey, I'm losing weight every day. I have jaundice. My liver's so big it feels like a football, pure pigskin. It's too late." I wanted to cry when I heard this, but I was also rather bored, because I had heard it many times. We always talked about him and his problems. He would ask a pro forma How are you? but the conversation quickly reverted to him. He was the center of the universe. "Besides," he said, "I don't care about living anymore."

"Does Alma know that? Does Babette know that?"

"That's what I called about," he said. "My daughter."

I wished he would just call her Babette. I knew she was his daughter. Whenever he said "my daughter," I was reminded that I had no children.

"What about her?"

"She's here."

She was supposed to be in Athens, Georgia, with her mother. Who was Wife Number Two (Alma, Maureen, and the countess were girlfriends. Andrea, Janice, and Carlotta were the wives, in that order. These were the main players in a cast of thousands.)

"How did she get there?"

"She hitchhiked." He said this with pride, as if to say: How much she loves me!

But what I thought was, Thirteen years old, hitchhiking from Georgia to Connecticut! Jesus!— though I sensed his need to view this feat as confirmation of his superior parenting. See, he was saying to himself, she prefers me to her mother. He seemed not to understand that because of his drinking he had been an erratic, improvident, sometimes self-pitying and often sarcastic father.

"I wish I could keep her here," he said, "but Alma can't run the risk of having a teenager in the house. You know how tenuous her health is."

I didn't like Alma. She had black penciled-on eyebrows that charged at each other over her eyes like two mad bulls, pulled together by a permanent frown. She was stingy. She had turned on Maureen like a vicious dog—according to Maureen, at least. I kept track of all these developments from long distance. It was better than "As the World Turns."

"Send her back to Janice."

"That bitch," he said. "She put out an all-points bulletin, but now that her daughter turns out to be safely here, she doesn't want her back."

"You want me to take her." Light dawned, as I remembered now that he had asked for a favor.

"Do you mind?"

Did I mind? Never! On the contrary, his request made me feel as if I had a purpose in life—and not having a biological purpose in life was another reason I'd wound up in the mental hospital. So I said yes. He didn't tell me that the reason she'd run away from home was that she'd gotten knocked up.

She stood in the middle of the bus station, shivering in a brown coat that had lost its buttons. She was clutching both sides of the coat collar to keep it from falling open. It fell open anyway, over her little hillocky stomach. On the floor next to her was a blue-speckled Samsonite suitcase.

She had long brown hair, freckles on her nose, the bone structure of a

Vogue cover girl, and a hearing aid. She wore her hair long to hide the hearing aid. When you could glimpse it, it looked like a small mushroom growing in the cave of her ear.

"We'll have to get you a parka," I said.

"Did my father tell you I was pregnant?"

I nodded, lying, and picked up the suitcase.

"I'm too far gone to have an abortion," she said defiantly. I think she expected me to take her straight from the bus station to the abortionist.

"Okay," I said. "You still have to have a parka. It gets a lot colder here than it does in Georgia."

"It's pretty damn cold in Georgia."

I could see she had not been going to her geography class.

After supper, we sat in front of the fire and she attempted to cure me of my lack of sophistication. "My boyfriend's name is Roy," she began. "He's quite mature."

"How mature?"

In her honor, I had lit candles. I had put chrysanthemums in the center of the table in the dining room. Soon I would buy a Christmas tree that would stand shyly in a corner of the sunroom. My little dog sat next to me in the reading chair, but from time to time he darted over to the couch to let Babette pet him.

"Twenty-two," she said.

I thought that was entirely too mature for a thirteen-year-old, but I held my tongue. She was my niece, not "my daughter"—though considering a black night some years ago, she might have been.

"He deals," she said, determined to strike terror in my heart.

"He what?"

"Deals. You know, drugs and stuff. Naturally he's always got lots of money."

"That's nice," I said.

"Yeah," she said. "So I decided to go to bed with him."

"Because he's got lots of money?"

"Because he's mature."

"What does your mother think of all this?"

"She likes him."

"She does?" I found this hard to believe.

"She says she wishes *her* boyfriend was as nice as Roy is."

"I thought they were married."

"Mom just likes people to think they are. She's afraid he'll lose interest in her and leave. She's afraid he'll get interested in me. She said so. She said she thought it was a good idea for me to go out with Roy because then Eugene would know better than to try anything. She says Roy is protection for both of us."

"I see."

"Do you want to know how I got pregnant?" she asked.

I had naively assumed I already knew how she got pregnant.

"We were watching television. Me and Roy. There was this neato movie on where everybody got killed. Like there was this one scene where this girl had her head cut off and she still ran around in a circle like a chicken. Gross." Babette got up and walked around in a circle, holding her neck with both hands, then fell back on the couch. "It was July and awfully hot so we started taking off our clothes. And then we just did it. I turned my hearing aid off since I couldn't see the movie with Roy blocking my view anyway."

"That was sensible," I said.

"And afterward," she went on, after I thought the story had ended, "because it was so hot, Roy went into the kitchen to get a beer and he bought me one, and I had turned my hearing aid back on and was watching television the way I like to, like this." She swiveled around so that she was backward on the couch with her head over the floor and her legs against the wall behind the couch. My dog sprang from the chair and went over to sniff her hair. He began to lick her face.

"You still didn't have any clothes on?" I asked. I wanted to be sure I got the picture right.

"It was *hot*, Aunt Nina. Anyway," she continued, from the floor, "I was watching the end of the movie like this and Roy brought me a beer and I started trying to balance the can on my forehead, just for the hell of it. I don't know if you've ever tried to balance a beer can on your forehead. It requires concentration."

"I'm sure," I murmured.

"Anyway, that's what did it."

"You got pregnant from drinking beer?"

"You're so funny, Aunt Nina," Babette said. "My father always said you have a really good sense of humor."

"Your father exaggerates."

"Well, don't you see? It was because I had my legs up against the wall like this." She righted herself on the couch. There was a baby in that stomach—probably a very dizzy baby. "All that stuff—you know that stuff?"—I nodded to indicate a tentative acquaintance with semen—"all that stuff was running up inside me, because I was upside down. It couldn't leak out the way it always did before. That's how I got pregnant." Her smile disappeared and she looked glum. "If only I hadn't been balancing the beer can on my forehead, I wouldn't have gotten pregnant."

I got up and went into the kitchen for scissors, snipped a burnt-sienna blossom off the chrysanthemum plant, and tucked it behind her ear, the "good" one. Much depended on how hard she was trying to listen. "You better go to bed," I said. "It was a long trip."

I banked the fading fire, blew out the candles, and led her to the bedroom I'd prepared for her. She asked for a glass of water to put her chrysanthemum in, and I brought her a shallow glass bowl. The blossom floated like a little boat. From her blue-speckled suitcase she extracted a pair of pajamas and put them on. They were white with tiny dogs and cats all over them, and black teardrops representing rain. There was a drawstring around the waist instead of elastic. Her stomach had a soft bloom to it, like the chrysanthemum. "Aunt Nina," she said, "there's something I have to tell you."

"What's that," I asked, savoring the maternal pleasure that went with having her in my care, though only temporarily. I pulled the covers up around her shoulders.

"Roy said he might come out here," she said. "You know, to visit?"

I enrolled Babette in school. She didn't want to go because, she said, everyone would make fun of her condition, but in a few days, she had girlfriends who dropped in after school to talk about boyfriends. I gathered that they wanted Babette to tell them what it was like to "do it." She would tell them about the beer can but she never really said what it was like to do it. They giggled incessantly, a sound like crystal beads spilling on a floor. If you said, "How are your parents?", they giggled. If you said, "How's school?", they giggled. They spent a lot of time picking out names for the baby.

I took Babette to my gynecologist. He told me she was malnourished. "Make her eat three good meals a day," he advised. "Plenty of milk, protein, vegetables. Where is her mother?"

"Georgia."

"I don't like this," he said, beating a tattoo on his desk blotter with his pencil. Babette was waiting for me in the waiting room. This doctor had helped me try to get pregnant. He considered that he had an almost uxorious interest in me. "Why isn't she with her mother? Are you sure you can handle this? Are you sure you want to?"

"I don't know," I said. "It's certainly painful to watch someone else being pregnant, but on the other hand, I like having her around the house. I think her mother feels threatened by her because she's so gorgeous."

"I see," he said, wrinkling his forehead. He was a sexy, vigorous man still in his thirties. And open-minded: He'd had a permanent. His dark blond hair rippled in waves like wheat. "Well, make her eat three meals a day. Lots of milk, protein—"

"Vegetables," I said.

Babette's mother called. "Hello, Janice," I said. "I guess you want to know how Babette is doing. She's fine." I didn't say anything about malnutrition. This was a tightrope I was walking—I could wind up with everyone angry at me.

"Listen," Janice said, "it's not my fault she got pregnant. It happens to girls all the time. I did my best."

"I know you did."

"I can't be watching her every minute of the goddamned day."

"I know," I said.

"You just don't know what it's like," she said, "living with a teenager."

"I guess I'm about to find out."

"Well," she said, "call me if there are any problems or anything. Good luck."

"Don't you want to talk to her?"

"Not now." She whispered into the phone: "I'm not alone."

"Would Eugene really mind if you talked to your daughter?" I was beginning to think of Eugene as the Monster of the Hemisphere.

"Mind?" She laughed. "He'd kill me. That man," she said, "is a tiger. I have to hold him by the tail."

She hung up. Babette was standing next to me.

"She didn't want to talk to me, did she," Babette said.

"She said she couldn't. Eugene was there."

"That's just an excuse. She didn't want to talk to me."

She ran upstairs and slammed the door to her room.

I was afraid to get too close to Babette—and not only because she was subject to the higher authority of her mother and father and would be leaving at some as yet unspecified point. Her presence in my house seemed to me to be a kind of victory for my brother. A thousand miles away, I was his fourth wife, mothering his child. I had been haunted by an image of the two of us growing old together, a parody of a marriage. I had looked for a husband, hoping to escape that destiny—but for twenty years I never told a man why I was so eager, or why I felt so unfit. My one actual husband, who for sure didn't stick around for long, accused me of caring about my brother more than about him—and that was true if "caring about" meant "being in the Svengalian thrall of." My brother had always been determined to keep me in his control. For many years I misunderstood this as love. That's what he called it, and I wanted to believe that's what it was. I *had* to believe that's what it was, or else, I thought, I would hate him and myself and possibly everybody else. After twenty years I learned to defy my brother and stand up for myself and I no longer felt I needed a husband to separate me from him, but destiny is destiny, and here was his daughter, full of phrases she had adopted from him and with his propensity for self-dramatization, as well as the deep sea-green of his eyes.

When I was in the mental hospital I learned that life is a comedy of errors. Previously I had recognized it as sometimes a comedy, sometimes a tragedy, but I hadn't realized the extensive role error plays. I began to think of my own mistakes less as a message that I had no right to live and more as a series of necessary stitches in the hem of existence, which one way or another we have to fit to ourselves.

My roommate was a farmer's wife named Wanda. She had two small children. When her husband told her he was leaving her for another woman, she tried to kill herself. She still had the suicide note she'd written, and showed it to me with satisfaction. It was the longest thing she'd ever written—to her, a novel. *"I have took poison,"* the note said, *"and now I am going to lay down and go to sleep and when I wake up Ill be with Jesus in heaven and you can marrie Tessie Jo. Please take good care of my babies Billy thats all I ask."* She had been sure her husband would come back when he read that note. Every time *she* read it, she felt sorry for herself, so she was sure Billy would feel sorry for her too, and tell Tessie Jo to go fuck herself, and then he'd come back and be a good husband and father again. When it didn't work out this way, she lost all faith in fiction.

"You should show this note to your doctor," I urged.

"What goes on between a man and his wife," Wanda said, "is a sacred secret."

"Tell that to Tessie Jo," I said.

"Tessie Jo gave my Billy a sinful disease," Wanda said. "And now I have it."

"What kind of disease?" I asked.

"I itch all the time. Down there."

"You have to tell your doctor about *that*," I said. "Unless you want to itch forever."

The next night she said to me, "I told the doctor. About my itch."

"And?"

"He gave me something."

"That's good," I said. "Now the itch will go away."

At the end of the week, Wanda said to me, "Nina, you know my itch?"

I said yes, I knew her itch.

"It still itches. It's driving me crazy."

"Well, you came to the right place, Wanda. Are you using that cream the doctor gave you?"

"Every morning and every night, just like he told me," she said. "I rub it all over my chest. But I still itch."

Realizing this called for a professional, I fetched one of the nurses and told her what the problem was and hung around the lounge playing pool until the nurse came back out of Wanda's room.

Wanda was standing in front of the mirror, brushing her hair. "Now the itch will go away," I said.

A few days later, I asked her how she felt. "I don't itch anymore," she said, "but when the nurse looked at me, she put a radio up there."

I tried to suggest this was unlikely, but she insisted it was the case. "You can't tell me I don't hear what I hear," she said. "I get 'A Prairie Home Companion.' I even pick up St. Louis."

Wanda was transferred to Mendota State. I heard later that Billy was adamant about a divorce. He told his lawyer he didn't want his kids being raised by a woman with a radio in her vagina.

Babette never wanted to do homework, but I made her. I said, "I'll do the monthly bills and you do your homework, and when we're both done, I'll make us each a cup of cocoa with a marshmallow in it."

She said she'd prefer grass.

Once I had to send her to her room. I turned off the Christmas tree lights. She came back down in an hour, sneaked up behind me, and put her arms around me and said, "Does Aunt Nina forgive me?"

"I don't like being manipulated, Babette," I said.

She glared at me as if I'd betrayed her by calling her bluff. She held my little dog under her chin and talked baby talk to him. She said she was "practicing."

Maureen called. "Have you talked with your brother lately?" she asked.

"Not lately."

"That son of a bitch."

"He's dying," I said to Maureen. "Doesn't that cancel out some of the hard feelings?"

She thought for a while, as if trying to decide whether it did or not. I could hear the ice cubes clinking in her drink at the other end of the line. Alcohol had been her and my brother's strongest mutual interest. "Has he made a will?" she asked.

"I don't know. Why?"

"Because if he thinks he's going to get any of this furniture back, he's crazy."

"Maureen, he'll be dead. What would he want with a bentwood rocker after he's dead?"

"You never know," she said, darkly.

"Possession is nine-tenths of the law," I said, to comfort her.

"There's Janice. She might try to get her hands on the stuff. And Carlotta." Carlotta was Wife Number Three, a broker by day and playwright by night. "Not to mention Andrea. Or the Hungarian countess."

"The countess is in Costa Rica. What does she want with a bentwood rocker? She's rich."

"And not to mention that completely reprehensible woman he is living with now."

"She's your best friend. Her name is Alma."

"I hope you don't blame me for the breakup," she said. "I had to kick your brother out because he was living with her."

"Absolutely," I said, not questioning her sequential logic.

"She's old enough to be his mother."

I had indeed pointed that out to my brother myself. I'd told him he was too old to be acting out incestuous fantasies. He'd said that inasmuch as he was dying, he'd better act out all his fantasies fast. He'd asked me if he could come live with me (he didn't know this was one of my nightmares). I'd pointed out that that was an incestuous fantasy he's already acted out. In repartee, our lives move past each other like people on a sidewalk, barely grazing sides but going places. The real conversation takes place intramurally: with ourselves. It goes nowhere. Meanwhile, we are full of facts that nose their way out of our pores no matter how thick-skinned we say we are, germs that crawl to the surface of our bodies and say I am the true you.

"So are you," I reminded her. "Old enough."

"He must have an obsession."

"Several," I agreed.

"Did you know," she said, thoughtfully, "that the countess has had two face-lifts?"

"No," I said. "I didn't know that."

"Not one. Two."

"That's interesting," I said.

Maureen had descended into another moody silence.

"How does she look?" I said.

"Who?"

"The countess."

"How should I know? She's in Costa Rica."

How I liked having Babette in the house, the rooms like cardboard boxes for her self, which she was constantly unwrapping! Even her scowls and tears were welcome, the ribbons and bows on the packages. Oh but the presence of Madonna I could have done without, for like a virgin, like a material girl, Babette went to school wearing lace gloves and a black leather jacket studded with rhinestones over a short skirt skewed by her condition, and when she returned, music, of a sort, billowed in the rooms like veils. One day I put my keys in the lock getting ready to yell hello and opened the door to find Babette on the couch with a young man who could only be Roy. I switched off the record player.

We shook hands. He had a kind of fluid good looks, his head flowed into his neck, which flowed into his shoulders, on down to the long, rivery tributaries of his legs and the crepe-soled puddles of his shoes. He had that gently flowing grace some young men have that can be diverted or channeled but not easily dammed, though life may do that to them later.

While we were eating dinner, he told me how he was going to make a quick million in Hollywood. He had a surefire idea for a screenplay. It was perfect for Don Johnson of "Miami Vice" or maybe Mel Gibson. It took place in Afghanistan. It opened with a close-up of the hole in the front end of a rifle, a Kalashnikov rifle. At first the whole screen would be black and as the camera pulled back the blackness would take on this round shape and then you'd see you were looking right into the wrong end of a rifle and the camera would just keep pulling back, slowly and steadily—I looked at Babette and saw that she was entranced with the sexual poise of his measured description—and you'd see the rifleman, the mountains like skulls with caves for eye sockets, and the tall gumless teeth of the trees, the David Lean blue sky.

From the bedroom, where I slept with my dog in a double bed, I could hear the two of them—the narrow cot sang, the narrow cot shrieked. From time to time loud bursts of laughter floated across the hall like balloons.

Their youth dragged me down like a net, I felt tangled in it, and I could feel myself beginning to drown in memories. We start life on dry land but memories, which are like tears, discrete as they occur but cumulatively one element, rise until we are standing in the middle of an ocean, washed by time. Currents we have unwittingly created ourselves now tug us in unanticipated directions, all of them pointing to the past. In the hospital, I had been amazed to discover that I had never advanced beyond my brother's image (the shadow of which I have since cast off)—my past with him surrounded me so that even when I'd thought I was moving into the future, it was only the past in new guises. My first reaction was to blame myself for having been so dense, so stupid. I told the doctors—I had quite a few, a brigade of doctors—that I felt ashamed, I was so stupid.

"How can a woman of your accomplishments feel stupid?" they said.

"I don't know," I said. "I know it's stupid."

They didn't even laugh. They just shook their heads. I saw their head-shaking out of the corner of my eye because I couldn't look straight at anyone. I kept hiding my eyes from everyone. I kept my head down and if I had to walk down the corridor I felt my way by sliding against the wall. When I came to a blank space, I knew it was time to make a turn. There was method in my madness.

"What's stupid," they tried to explain, "is going from *it's* stupid to *I'm* stupid."

"That's what I said," I said.

"What is?"

"That I'm stupid. I know it's stupid to do that, to go from *it is* to *I am*."

"Then why do you do it?"

"Because I am."

"But you aren't."

"Then why do I do it?"

"You have to answer that yourself."

"I can't answer it. I don't know the answer. I *told* you I was stupid." I glared at them—they were so stupid!

I made a visor out of my hand to hide my eyes from them. The truth was, my neuroticism on the subject of stupidity—while delightfully, from a psychiatrist's point of view, traceable to sibling rivalry, or perhaps even to a female fear of outdoing the parental figure who set the standard, in this instance my seven-years-older-than-me, father- and mother-substitute brother—was a red herring, designed to throw doctors off the track of my precipitating anxiety, which was a fear of feeling my lifelong condition of not being loved. It was easier to blame myself for this condition, since that allowed me to imagine I might someday find the means to revise it, than to ascribe it to causes outside my control—such as unhappy parents, a psychopathic brother. I was definitely in hiding: from myself too, as at that point not even I suspected my apparent candor was an illusion, if not a delusion.

They had my medication increased. For three days, none of the doctors came to see me. I began to look where I was going.

At home, lying in bed, I reviewed my life to the musical accompaniment of bedsprings. I remembered how Babette's father had claimed my bed like a birthright. A great many years later, he told me that I made too much of this. It was as inconsequential an event as a one-night stand, no different from any of the hundreds of nights he'd picked up a woman in a bar and taken her home with him. (But that night he had sworn me to secrecy, saying: If you tell anyone, I'll deny it, I'll say you lied. This is monstrous, he had said the next morning. Yes, I am a terrible person and you have ruined my life by letting me do what I did! he said—and so of course I hated myself and felt sorry for him. And he laughed at my confusion.) For twenty years I had felt like a piece of shit—Darwinian shit, unfit for evolution, selected by nature for genetic extinction. This was not a consequence?

Now "his daughter," who in my opinion should have been playing with dolls, was getting laid, exuberantly at that, across the hall. I couldn't decide whether she was paying for the sins of her father's generation, or reaping the benefits.

In the morning, Roy was gone. Babette was in the kitchen, communing with the toaster so far as I could tell. She had her back to me.

"Babette," I said, "where's Roy? Did he leave already?"

She didn't answer me. I thought she was sulking.

"Answer me, Babette," I said.

Then a thought struck me, and I shouted her name. Still no answer. She had her hearing aid turned off.

I put my hands on her shoulders and gently turned her around to face me, so she could read my lips. She was crying—silent, adult tears trickling down her stunningly sculpted, dedicated face.

I told her to turn the hearing aid on.

"He's not coming back," she wailed. "Ever."

"Oh," I said, "he might. He might even make a movie and earn a million bucks. You can't say for sure he won't."

She shook her head. Behind her back, the toast popped up.

"He doesn't want to come back. He says he's too young to be a father. He says it wouldn't be fair to the baby."

"Maybe he's right," I said.

"He doesn't need a million bucks. He's already got money."

"Drug money," I said, as if I knew, "can't be banked on. Connections go cold or get killed."

"I want to go home," she said, starting to cry louder. "I want my mother."

But first she developed a fever and chills. I felt her forehead, the tight skin hot under my hand. "I'm going to call the doctor," I said.

She was pissed because vacation had started so she wasn't missing a school day. She turned over on her side, away from me. She had kicked off the covers. She was wearing the it's-raining-cats-and-dogs pajamas, and the pants legs had ridden up to her knees and the top had gotten twisted, exposing her midriff like an undeveloped film.

I called the OB/GYN. "Two aspirin and some rest," he said. "No problem."

I wanted a problem. I wanted to feel needed—too soon she would be gone from me, the amphitheater of her mind filled exclusively with visions of Roy in Hollywood. "That's all?" I asked. "For a pregnant teenager?"

"Even pregnant teenagers," he said, "get uncomplicated colds. Especially when they're from Georgia. Are you feeding her well?"

"Milk," I said. "Protein, vegetables."

I got in the car and drove to the mall to buy presents for her: a pretty maternity dress, a tiny pot of lip gloss, stationery, some items for the baby's layette. The enclosed lobby that sidled along the full length of a dozen stores was carpeted with the thick, spongy smells of perspiration and wool, the tangerine sharpness of manufactured pine-needle aroma (sprayed onto artificial Christmas trees). Dazed shoppers trudged by lugging bulging bags with ropy handles that banged against their sides, like oxen balancing milk pails. And then all at once, there was the man I had loved more than any other, my most Significant Other, coming toward me with the woman he had prioritized over me. I ducked into Gimbels, grabbing a Chaus blouse and skirt to give legitimacy to my desire for a fitting room where I could sit on a stool until my hands stopped shaking. I slipped on the skirt and blouse. The skirt was a cotton tan trumpet-cut, rather long, and the taupe blouse had a V-neck and loose sleeves that stopped at the elbow. I liked the way I looked in them so I bought tnem, a Christmas present to myself, thinking Cliff would be sorry if he could see me in this outfit. However, he would never see me in it, because even now I was afraid of how I would behave if I ever ran into him. I might weep, or plead, or stutter some nonsense, or even reflexively flirt, or worst of all, act like everything was fine, thereby colluding with all the women who had preceded *me*, including his mother, in their decision to shield him from the effects of his actions. We are such good little girls, all of us, reluctant to wreck our hopes for the future, no matter how unrealistic they may be, on the shoals of calling men to account for themselves. What they get away with, just because there are so few of them! Think of it: Women are waiting in line for the privilege of taking care of broken-down drunks like my brother. Anyone who doesn't think men get away with murder should remember that on "Leave It to Beaver," Beaver's last name was Cleaver. That made him Beaver Cleaver. What does this say about America?

I dumped my packages in the trunk of my car and drove home. It was my birthday—the longest night of the year. I put on my headlights. The snow, plowed and heaped along the sides of the road, glowed like glass at the bus stops where people had walked a smooth path over it, grinding the crystals like a lens. In a beautiful short story by Fred Chappell, the mathematician Feuerbach asks his students, "If a man construct an equilateral triangle on a sheet of paper, what is in the triangle?" No one raises his hand. "The correct answer," Feuerbach tells them, "is *Snow*. It is snow inside the triangle." The students have yet to learn that their admirably remediable brains are as vulnerable and, from the point of view of many, dispensable, as the dime-store water domes inside which snow may be made to fall on a whim. They have not yet felt the chill in their skulls, the increasing numbness. Probably none of them has ever been a patient on a psychiatric ward.

Getting ready to go inside, I heard voices from the yard next door. Children were constructing a snowman. "Merry Christmas!" I shouted. Three children, two belonging to one family, the third to another. The girls are sisters. Last summer, Cheryl wanted to play Wedding, and made Jason marry her little sister, Trish. Every day for a week, Jason and Trish got married. Then they got a divorce.

All three waved at me, their mittened right hands like three red stars in the fast-falling night. A certain tenderness in the night's cold touch told me there'd be more snow by morning—not "the snow that is nothing inside the triangle," but very substantive snow in the elongated rectangle that is my sidewalk. I had just rehired my favorite teenager to shovel my sidewalk—he'd been in Japan with his parents, who were on sabbatical.

Whiffs of marijuana greeted me at the door, slinking down the stairs like a genie. I threw the packages into the hall closet and raced upstairs. Babette was lying in bed singing to herself. I recognized the lyrics from "Borderline": "Feels like I'm going to lose my mind / You keep on pushing my love / Over the borderline." She couldn't carry a tune and she was singing at the top of her lungs. She had her eyes closed and her hearing aid was on the dresser.

I crossed the room and removed the cigarette from between her fingers— something I had done that night with her father, only that had been tobacco, thinking *If I weren't here, maybe he would have burned the house down*, thinking *I'm not good for nothing; I'm good for something*. Maybe there was an inherited predisposition among members of the Bryant family to pass out with lighted cigarettes between their fingers. God help us. I should ask Cliff the geneticist. (I should not.) "Hey," she said, her lids snapping up like window shades, "what do you think you're doing?"

"I should be asking you that!" I said. "Who the hell do you think you are? Do you know what you could be doing to the baby?"

"I don't care about the baby!" she screamed. "I don't want it! I don't care about you! You don't care about me—all you care about is this stupid baby! I hate being pregnant, I hate it, I hate it!"

My dog went downstairs to his "house"—the traveling case I kept open for him in the kitchen. He escaped from dissension into it, curling into a small furry ball, but he could barely turn around in it. He kept his big red rubber ball in there, and a much beloved tuna fish can. When the world was too much with him, that was where he went to get away from it.

Babette had sat up on the bed when she screamed at me and was still crouched there like a cornered animal, beating on the bed with her fists. She stopped.

I thought, looking at her, that the baby was like a piece of furniture, too big for such a little girl to carry. I picked up the hearing aid from the dresser and sat down on the bed with her and pushed her long hair back over her ears. Sometimes I thought she could have been me—a family resemblance in the chin and cheekbones. She was so frantic for a man's love that she'd sacrificed her childhood—at thirteen, the experienced woman, the little mother, the caretaker. My brother liked to think he'd always taken care of everyone else, but everyone else had always taken care of him, including her. Alcoholism is like a psychosis: It reshapes the world along internal lines. But the world has its own tendency to shift its center of gravity in accordance with perceived need, and so Babette, for example, had innocently conformed to her father's reality. We accommodate our madmen.

I fitted the hearing aid in her ear and smoothed her hair forward again. Her eyes were like a view of the Atlantic from Virginia Beach—she was like a mermaid, she didn't belong in this snowy north country.

"Babette," I said, stroking her hair, "I'm glad you came to stay with me even for this short time. Having you here has made me happy. I can't tell you how happy."

She was picking at a scab on her arm. "Yeah, well," she said. "Just because I have a baby inside me doesn't mean I'm not me anymore."

"Is that what Roy thought?"

"Who knows what Roy thinks. Roy sucks."

"Do you feel good enough to come down for supper?"

"I guess," she said.

My dog crawled out of his house to usher us into his kitchen. He put his front paws out on the floor in front of him, raised his rear end, and stretched from one end of his body to the other, getting all the kinks out. Then he wagged his tail for us. From the kitchen window, I could see the snowman glimmering whitely, a sentry for the neighborhood in the night.

I had hoped Babette would get interested in my fourteen-year-old snow shoveler. He was clearly fascinated by her. He was a toothpick six and a half feet long, a junior varsity basketball player, good-natured and ultranormal. His brown face was like a flag for me when I saw it in my yard, it made me renew my allegiance to young people. But Babette had ignored him—she was hopelessly in love with a man who had never existed for her: her father. She thought she would find him in somebody sexy and charming, somebody who could control her the way her father controlled the world. Freedom was not for her—her pubertal hormones had brought her a lust for romance, which is finally the urge to see oneself as a hero or heroine, the focus of the family. What an old theme that was—the glorification of the self through averred powerlessness and servitude.

I turned on the radio. Garrison Keillor's soothing voice filled the room, became the medium in which we ate supper. Milk, protein, vegetables. I thought of Wanda and her short-wave vagina.

Babette was right.

I had begun, in spite of myself, to feel that the baby-to-be was in some sense mine. But it was her baby, and she planned to have it in Georgia. What she didn't know was that I'd also begun, in spite of myself, to feel she was mine too. Especially when something struck us both as funny, and we collapsed into shared laughter, I would suddenly catch my breath and think, *This is just like a family. It is!* We smiled at each other. There were days studded with such pleasures. A goldfinch flew past the kitchen window like a zipper on the blue dress of the sky.

On Christmas morning, Babette opened her presents with gratifying glee. My dog poked his nose into the pile of used wrapping paper, wondering where his present was. I gave him a porcupine that squeaked when he worried it with his teeth, a rawhide bone.

The lights on the tree were like musical notes you could see. The blue ones were the deepest, the left hand. The red ones were middle C. The white and yellow lights were the treble clef.

Babette handed me a small box wrapped in tinfoil. "This one's for you, Aunt Nina," she said.

I jiggled the box next to my ear and smiled at her. I unwrapped it and lifted off the lid. A piece of paper.

I took out the piece of paper and read it.

"I didn't have any money to buy you a present," it said, "so this just a box full of love. Babette."

And now she was going home—in time to return to her old school after New Year's. She had been a warm day in a cold season, but she was not "my daughter." She was my brother's daughter, though he had not sent her even an empty box.

I am too hard on him he was my brother he gave me my vocabulary my first books Brendan Behan/Céline/*Krapp's Last Tape* said describe a different object every day the brick walk/an alarm clock read my poems read me. When no one knew how to handle me, my parents called him in. I was furious with my limitations terrified of failing to live up to what was expected of me justify our parents' lives make up for the way he had disappointed them life had disappointed them. I tried to be what all of them wanted, was angry at all of them for not letting me be myself, even he wanted me to love him the way Mother didn't I couldn't I don't I won't I don't have to incest is not love.

In the empty house that was like a broken violin string after Babette's departure I washed dishes, watched television. My dog invented a new game: He sat on the couch and pushed his red rubber ball to the edge, let it unsuspectingly sit there for a moment, and then nudged it over the edge. Then he leapt after it as it rolled across the rug. In this way, he played catch with himself. I called Janice to confirm Babette's safe arrival. Maureen called me to say she'd seen Alma and my brother buying cigarettes at the K mart. She said he was jaundiced and had an old-man walk and was bald on one side of his head because he had a habit of pulling his hair out when he got drunk. Alma looked like *Frankenstein's Widow*—the bride after fifty years. The countess had sent a postcard, which had come to Maureen's address; evidently, my brother had not told her about his new alliance with Witch Alma. Maureen was sure the wives were gathering and would ride on her soon in a furniture raid. She had moved all my brother's things to the garage and was threatening to have a sale if he didn't pay her soon. She had figured up how much he owed her for meals, cigarettes, booze, general wear and tear on the house, and let's not forget her labor. He had treated her like a servant she said and he would pay through the nose. As she talked I watched the dog. After a while he grew tired of his game and went to sleep on the couch, resting his muzzle on his front paws. He is so doggy—my canine lifesaver, since he rescued me from a black hole of depression, the phenomenon that occurs when a mind collapses under its own weight of despair, setting up such intense negative energy that it completely absorbs itself. What a farce life had been then—a comedy of trial-and-errors. I remembered a night I had called the hospital to see if I could admit myself to the psychiatric ward. I talked with a nurse on the floor. She asked me for my name but I refused to give it to her—I don't know why I wouldn't, maybe I was crazy.

"You have to have a doctor's referral," she said.

This was before I had even one doctor, much less the troopship of psychiatrists I was to acquire in the hospital, or the self-important short shrink who succeeded them. So I said, "I don't have a doctor." I had thought a hospital would be a good place to find a doctor.

"Then you can't be admitted," she said. "You have to be admitted by a doctor."

"This is crazy," I blurted out. I wanted in!

"How dare you talk to me like that!" she said. "If you think you can talk to me like that, you're crazy!"

"That's what I'm trying to tell you!" I yelled. "I'm crazy, so please lock me up!"

"We can't do that without a doctor's referral!"

I listened to the echoes in my room. My voice was bouncing off the walls. So was I. So was the nurse.

I tried to reason with her calmly. "Suppose I cut my wrists," I said. "Then would you admit me?"

"You're playing games with me. I don't believe you. You're not going to cut your wrists."

"I'm not playing games," I said. "I'm—"

I was going to say "desperate," but she hung up on me. So I went into the bathroom and cut my wrists.

I was surprised it didn't hurt. It only stung a little, so I cut deeper. It still didn't hurt. I was starting to drip into the sink. Bright red beads on porcelain—a song, almost.

I couldn't do this to my dog. I couldn't do it to my friends; in my depression, I thought their lives might have been nicer without interference from me, but I had too great an awareness of their love and generosity to imagine they would not be overwhelmed by guilt and responsibility, if I killed myself. I couldn't send an SOS this way—it would be manipulative (I felt a residual sympathy for Wanda's husband), and besides, I had too much pride. I decorated the shallow cuts with Band-Aids. To the best of my ability, I would be my own doctor. (A decision I should have stuck to.)

When my brother died, his doctor called me even before Alma did. It was April. The snow had begun to melt—a medley of streams harmonized all over town. Walking to work I skipped over rivulets, like skipping over cracks to keep from breaking my mother's back.

My parents were too ill, too ill and much too frail, to return to the States for his funeral. They had not been back to this country once since leaving it. Maybe I felt a little like a vice president, sent to stand in for the president. ("You die, we fly," Bush's staff joked.) The time zone my brother had now entered was the farthest away, sad to cross. If I had been bored, I also wanted to cry.

I flew from Madison, Wisconsin, to Madison, Connecticut (the airport is actually in New Haven), and checked in at a motel. Because of Alma's heart condition, she couldn't put people up—and there was not only me to contend with, there were Carlotta and Andrea and Janice, and even Maureen, who was not going to pass up the chance to dance at my brother's funeral.

At the funeral home, I awaited the wives. We all got in the day before, because the service was scheduled for the morning, and signed on, as it were, at the funeral home. Andrea was the first to arrive. She glided in on celestial runners, a small blond sled toting forgiveness, ready to "share" her feelings with us. She encouraged me to cry. "You have to let it out," she said; "otherwise it'll just fester." I thought of telling her what festers—forced secrets, rage you have to lie to yourself about in order to protect your faith in someone's love for you. (I even thought about telling her that Christ on the cross accusing his father of forsaking him was the very heart of the passion, without which the story could not live. It was Easter week, and this was on my mind.) She slid on her slender, delicate blades of feet over to Alma, who was all in black, from her dyed hair to her textured hose.

Carlotta came next, swinging her elegant portfolio like a baseball player warming up in the bull pen. "Nina, my dear," she said, "how are you? Such a sad occasion—but rather fun, too, isn't it? Your brother would have enjoyed it." And she was right, he would have. Carlotta's lipstick was the color of a house burgundy. She shook my hand as if I had just agreed to invest money in her mutual fund.

Maureen appeared on the scene next, in silk slacks, a turtleneck sweater, and a raccoon coat. The silver threads among her gold were highlighted with rinse. She crossed the room to give me an exaggerated hug, avoiding Alma but playing to her. "It's so good to see you again," she exclaimed in her gravelly boozer's voice. "You'll have to come to my garage sale while you're here!"

"You have no right to sell his things!" Alma said from across the room.

The funeral director gripped Alma solicitously by her arm and moved her closer to the casket.

In that casket lay the body of my brother, which I had been acquainted with as intimately as had these women, as with the night, though none of them knew that, thank God.

The last time I had seen him alive, on a previous visit here, he had sat at the piano in Alma's house and lightly played a five-note tune. "This is what's in my head," he'd said. "It's been in my head for a year now. I can't make it go away. It's always there."

In profile, hunched over the keyboard, his younger self was visible, as if the past were the present in silhouette; as if, from the right angle, you could make time disappear—a simple matter of perspective. Such forcefulness he had possessed, wit that carried the day!

"Why won't it go away?" he had asked, removing his hands from the keys and placing them carefully in his lap.

Was he making this up, writing this scene on the spot? Was this an improvised piece of stage business, or did he truly suffer from a motif that had woven itself through his mind like a thread, until pulling it out would have been dangerous?

I was constantly obliged to deal with questions like that, responding with the expected irony to his statements as if I understood what he was talking about when actually I didn't have any idea how much to believe, what was real and what was a joke. From the time I was two, he had treated me as if he assumed I knew what was what—did he really think I did, or did he enjoy the bind this put me in? I tried to be "the one person who understands me." I feel exhausted just remembering how much work it was for me to keep up with this pretense.

"It hates me," he had said, playing the tune again.

"Why do you say that?" I asked.

"It won't go away. It won't leave me alone."

"Maybe it won't go away because it loves you. It wants you to stay alive and finish it."

He laughed. "You never miss a chance, do you," he said.

I said, "Because I care about you." And I did. My dear brother, handsome, charming, a verbal acrobat and physically a daredevil—he had been a flying young man on a steel trapeze, out-Plimptoning George Plimpton, skywalking the blazing girders above New York, elbowing death aside. He couldn't be as relentlessly selfish as I sometimes now suspected he was. Could he?

And even if he was, was that a reason to stop caring?

"I wish I knew where it comes from. What it means." The tune.

"Why does it have to mean anything?"

"It's in my mind, isn't it? It must mean something."

"There's a lot in your mind that's pretty meaningless." This time I laughed.

"God love you, Nina," he'd said, pleased, and closed the lid on the keyboard. "I do."

It had been a gray day, the faint diffused sun like a ceiling chandelier with the dimmer turned on. At dinner I noticed that his eyes had sunk back into their sockets like two rabbits going underground or dogs slinking off to their corners to die.

Once, the look in his eyes had been so penetrating that it had been almost a sexual metaphor. Look, I said to myself, how these women had been attracted to it and were still mesmerized, compelled to congregate in its memory.

I felt someone tapping on my shoulder as I were a door. I turned around to greet Janice. She was carrying a baby. "Here," she said, thrusting it into my arms. "It's all yours."

It was the tiniest baby I had ever seen—humanity in miniature. A round head with fuzz on top, worried little eyebrows, big blue-green eyes, a nose like the tip of a thumb, mouth like a musical whole note, chin like a parenthesis—all of it wriggly, especially the wet, protoplasmic bottom. "There are Pampers in here," Janice said, setting on the floor by my side the large carryall that had been hanging from her shoulder.

Janice was wearing a purple dress with a wet spot on the front like a map of Georgia.

"Where is Babette?" I asked.

"Where do you think?" Janice looked disgusted. "This time she hitchhiked all the way to California."

"The Promised Land," I said.

"Yes, well, I promised I'd kill her if she ever dares to come back after this cute trick. She left this with me." She gestured at the baby in my arms.

I could hardly breathe. I was holding what I had wanted most. The baby in my arms was like a liquid that had been poured into a hole in my soul. What I'd hoped for, felt guilty about hoping for, given up hope for—all this was now all at once incarnate, it had shape and substance. I wondered if I was holding it right. The head was in the crook of my left arm, next to my heart, and my right arm supported its bottom and back.

At that point the baby, which had been seemingly engaged in listening to our conversation, began to bawl. The funeral director came over to me and said, "Madam, I will have to ask you to take your baby into the next room."

But Alma was approaching too—and Maureen and Andrea and Carlotta. Like mother hens they flocked around to cluck at the baby chick. Maureen, who had raised five children of her own, put the baby on a table and changed her diaper. It was a girl.

"I can't take of her," Janice said. She was standing next to me. Her voice came and went in my ear like a tide. "Listen to that racket! Eugene just won't tolerate it."

In Wisconsin, Janice would have been legally responsible for her granddaughter until Babette reached eighteen. As I often have, I thought, To hell with Wisconsin law.

"Are you serious?" I asked.

"I wouldn't have made this trip if I weren't," she said. "You think I'd come all the way up here just to see your brother buried?"

"What's her name?"

"She doesn't have one. Babette couldn't make up her mind. She's Baby Bryant on the birth certificate." She reached into her purse and retrieved the birth certificate, as if she were handing over her puppy's AKA registration papers. "I figured that if I actually showed up with the baby, you wouldn't be able to say no."

Maureen picked the baby up again and transferred her back to my arms. She fell asleep almost instantly.

A baby in my arms.

Had my brother had this outcome in mind all along? Was this his way of making amends to everyone, of "taking care" of everyone—and also possibly his idea of a joke? Would Freud have laughed? Probably not, but so what: None of this mattered to the baby, who was holding my finger in her small-scale fist with such firmness that I figured she was destined to be a flutist. She had the requisite lung power.

Janice had brought a thermos inside which you could fit a bottle. Hot water kept the formula warm on the plane, so the baby could swallow when the plane took off and landed, to pressurize her ears. I gave her the bottle now and took her back with me to Maureen's house for dinner.

While we talked, the baby slept in a cradle Maureen brought down from the attic. I liked Maureen best of the women—I felt more comfortable with her.

She had a house old enough to have been officially designated a historical landmark. The sky through the leaded windowpanes was lavender.

She was holding a Bloody Mary. The drink was like a red rose in her hands. "You'd better see your lawyer as soon as you get back," she said.

"I will." My lawyer would be happy for me—he knew how much I had wanted a child.

"It's very important," she said, "to know the law. Your brother was damn lucky I didn't sue him. But I made sure I'm going to get at least a part of what's coming to me. Five cents on the dollar is better than nothing."

"Oh Maureen," I said, "you aren't really going to have a garage sale? Who's going to buy that old furniture?"

"Let me show you something."

I followed her outside to the garage. Her car was parked in the driveway. The smoke from the fire we'd been sitting in front of rose from the chimney, like a dark wide-winged bird. She raised the garage door and yanked on a string. The overhead light came on.

There was my brother's life, all crammed into one room: not only furniture, but his books, his paintings—his own and the ones he'd collected—his records, his manuscripts.

"I'm going to sell the records for a nickel apiece," she said. "He always acted like they were so bloody valuable, but my son says they've been superseded by tapes and discs."

Kreisler, Oistrakh, Casals, Landowska, Horowitz, Ashkenazy, Claudio Arrau. Christoff singing Godounov. Heifetz. Glenn Gould. Erica Morini. Myra Hess. So many years of listening, of finding in those performances a touchstone for his own life. Beethoven by the Hungarian Quartet, the Budapest, the Amadeus. Many of these records were irreplaceable. There were even some 78s that had once belonged to my grandfather.

"I'll buy them," I said.

She looked at me suspiciously, as if thinking maybe her son was wrong and they were worth something after all. "What would you want with them?" she asked.

"A remembrance," I said. I was looking at a facsimile edition of *Moby-Dick* that had been given to him by his students the year he taught at a private school in New York. When I was fifteen I had copied the last paragraph of *Moby-Dick* into my spiral notebook. Melville had been one of the writers my brother and I both loved. We differed on many others, but there were some, like Melville and Shakespeare, who had given us a private language, a shorthand—the briefest of allusions could communicate volumes between us.

Dust was settling on his paintings, stacked at the back of the garage, the first paintings of his young adulthood and the troubled, slashing paintings, crowded with anger, black with hate, that he'd done after Janice left him.

His manuscripts were in neat blue boxes. I started to open one and then couldn't—I felt as if I were raiding a tomb.

It was as if the garage were a pyramid; these were my brother's worldly possessions and representations, which were meant to go with him into the next world. There he would reread the books that had helped to define him. The shades of the great musicians would tremble in the breeze like lyres; the light, thrumming wind would play them as if they were their instruments. When he looked on his paintings, he would see again the life he had lived, the colors and mutable forms of the landscapes he had lived it among. His words would have a faint mustiness about them, like a mummy. The bond would crackle like papyrus as he piled up the read pages in the top half of the box.

Suddenly I felt as if I had been lured into a trap—as if the door were about to drop shut, cutting off air. I saw myself as my brother's handmaiden, sealed in death, his property in life and the afterlife. I darted from the garage.

Maureen put her arms around me. "I didn't mean to upset you," she said. "Come have another drink."

In the clouds blowing across the sky, I saw my brother, his face bending over me as if I were a text, the moon his racing boat.

In the motel the baby slept beside me while I lay awake remembering my brother. She woke at two and I fed her some formula I had made up at Maureen's house and kept warm in the thermos. He is dead he is like a record I can't listen to ever again never again irreplaceable.

At the service, the women were scattered among a larger crowd, but when we went to the cemetery, the crowd thinned again. It was a warmish, sunny day. A high wind knocked the leaves around but closer to the ground there was a layer of stillness.

At the far end of the cemetery there was a dark snow-spattered pine glade, but where we stood, spring had come. Somehow the efficient funeral-home director had unobtrusively translated the flowers from the chapel to the gravesite, and the small green slope of the hill was a chorus of color—lilacs, jonquils, shy crocuses, tenacious forget-me-nots, and Easter lilies. The lilies were like church bells, a carol of lilies.

The women were individual songs: Andrea a bit on the shrill side despite her extensive analysis, Carlotta contralto, Alma a dirge, Janice a clear soprano though she sang only for Eugene, Maureen the spear-carrier. I held my baby, my little grace note.

In the bright air we listened to the minister's words roll out, round as marbles. As he said them, a black limousine appeared at the gates, moving slowly toward us like an epiphany. It stopped a few feet away and a chauffeur got out and opened the back door. A veiled figure emerged. She was in sable and high heels. Her gloves were black, disappearing under the coat sleeves. A diamond bracelet circled her left wrist. She wore a hat that tipped over her face like a bird swooping down on a fish. The lace veils shielded her from our gaze as effectively as a helmet protects a beekeeper from bees.

She walked over to us, her high heels sinking on each step into the tender mossy grass. When she reached us, she stood unmoving while the minister finished speaking. I wanted to see what she looked like but the veils were impenetrable. Black dots covered the lace like moles. No matter how hard I looked, I couldn't see her face.

I nudged Maureen with my elbow. "Did you cable her?" I asked in a low voice.

"Why not?" she whispered back. "I had her address from the postcard. I thought we should have the whole gang here. Serves Alma right."

The minister glanced in our direction. The woman had taken a long-stemmed rose from under her coat, where she had been holding it next to her body. She stepped forward and placed it on the casket. Alma started to go over and take it off but Carlotta held her back. The woman turned and began to walk away.

"I thought you said she had a face-lift," I said to Maureen.

"Two. That's what he told me."

She had covered the distance to the car and was now entering it while the chauffeur held the door for her. The engine started.

We stood on the hill, watching the limo pull away. It went into reverse, turned, and headed back down the road, putting on speed as it nosed out onto the highway on the other side of the wrought-iron gates. The countess was gone for good. We were still stuck in our lives; my brother was stuck in the ground. But for one unforeseen, transfiguring moment, the Hungarian countess had appeared before us like the stranger on the road to Emmaus, and her coming and going had brought us face to face with possibilities we had barely dreamed we could realize.

I nuzzled the baby's neck, her skin as soft as a double-ply tissue. Twenty years ago, even a year ago, I could not have dreamed this day, but that, I now saw, was part of the point. The point is that if you knew something was going to happen, it wouldn't be a miracle.

NOT THE PHIL DONAHUE SHOW

This is not the Phil Donahue show; this is my life. So why is my daughter, who is twenty years old and, to me, so heartbreakingly beautiful that I think that for the sake of the health of the entire world and probably universe she shouldn't be allowed out of the house without a cardiologist at her side, why is my daughter standing in my doorway telling me she's a lesbian?

She hangs in the doorway, her face rising in the warm air like a bloom in a hothouse. (I have been cooking.) She has chin-length blonde hair, straight as a pin, side-parted. Her skin is bare of makeup. Her blue eyes are like forget-me-nots in an open field. She has a superficial scratch on her cheek, a deep resentment that pulls her head down and away from me.

I'm standing here with a wooden spoon in my hand like a baton and I feel like there is some music that should be playing, some score that, if only I knew it, I ought to be conducting.

If I say it's a phase, that she'll outgrow it, she'll peel herself from the wall like wallpaper and exit, perhaps permanently, before I can even discern the pattern.

If I say honey, that's great, nonchalant and accepting as history, I could be consigning her to a life that I'm not sure she really wants—maybe she's just testing me. Maybe this is just a phase.

I can't help it, for just a moment I wish her father were here. I want him to be as shocked and stuck as I am, here in this blue-and-white room with steam rising from the stove, enough garlic in the air to keep a host of vampires at bay. But I remind myself: He would have been glad to be here. I am the one who walked out on him. As Isabel, in her posture, her sullen slouch, her impatient, tomboy gestures, never lets me forget. *Daddy would know how to handle this,* she seems to be saying, defiant as a rebel with a cause. *I dare you to try.*

It is five o'clock. It's already been a long day, which I have spent as I spend most of my days—nursing patients to whom I have let myself get too close. And sometimes I feel a kind of foreclosure stealing into my heart, sometimes I feel like an S&L, sometimes I feel overextended. But I'm always home from my shift at the hospital by four-thirty, while Ian stays later after school to devise lesson plans, tutor the sluggardly, confer with parents.

Now the front door swings open and it's Ian. He's taller than I, who am tall, so tall his knees seem to be on hinges, and he unlatches them and drops into one of the dining-room chairs. I can watch him over the dividing counter that connects the dining room with the kitchen, one of the results of our renovation last summer. Isabel has not moved from her post in the doorway (there's no door) between us.

"Hi, Shel," Ian says to me. "Hi, Belle," he says to my daughter. "Nice to see you."

He wants so much for her to let him enter her life. He has no children of his own—he wants to be, if not a second father, at least a good friend. "Shelley," he says, "what are we drinking tonight?"

"Isabel has an announcement," I say, waving my wooden wand. I turn around and start stirring, the steam pressing the curl out of my hair like a dry cleaner.

"I'm in love," I hear her say behind my back.

"Hey, that's great," Ian responds and I realize how unfair we have been to him, we have set him up for this.

"With a woman," she says.

Girl, I want to correct her. With a *girl*.

Marlo Thomas would kill me.

"Oh," Ian says. "Well, why isn't she here? When do we get to meet her?"

And I remember: This is why I married him. Because he puts people ahead of his expectations for them, even though his expectations can be annoyingly well defined. Because he doesn't create a crisis where there isn't one.

But this is a crisis. If she were *his* daughter, he'd realize that.

Entirely without meaning to, entirely illogically, I am suddenly angry with Ian for not being the father of my daughter. Why wasn't he around when I was twenty—her age, I realize, startled—and looking for something to do with my life, which I had begun to understand stretched before me apparently endlessly like an unknown continent, one I was afraid to explore by myself? Why did I have to wait for most of my life before he showed up?

We are seated at the table from my first marriage, now located under the dining-room window overlooking the leaf-strewn front lawn and Joss Court. It is September in Wisconsin, and the home fires have begun to burn, smoke lifting from the chimneys like an Ascension. The maple and walnut trees are a kaleidoscope of color; the bright orange-red berries of the mountain ash are living ornaments. Soon it will be Halloween, Thanksgiving, Christmas. Across the street, abutting Joss but facing Highland, is my friend Nina's house, in which I lived for a year while making up my mind to divorce Isabel's father. Directly across from me, behind Nina, lives Sophie, recently widowed. She pushes a hand mower, the last lawncut of the season before raking starts.

"You should go over and offer to rake for her sometime soon," I say to Ian.

"I will," he agrees, drilling a corkscrew into the unopened wine.

Isabel says, "I think she likes doing things for herself."

"I can still offer," Ian says. "She can say no."

During this conversation, a fourth party has been silent: Judy, Isabel's friend. As soon as Ian suggested we meet, Isabel raced out of the house and brought her back for supper.

Judy is not what I expected. For one thing, she's pretty—almost as pretty as my daughter. She has long wavy honey-blonde hair so perfectly cut it falls with mathematical precision, like a sine-curve, around her glowing face. She has this generation's white, even teeth, a kittenish face. It is easy to see why Isabel has fallen in love with her; in fact, I don't see how anyone could *not* fall in love with either of them—so why shouldn't they fall in love with each other?

Thinking these thoughts, I am swept by a sense of déjà vu. I have lived this scene before—but where? In another life?

Then I figure it out: not lived but read, in all the contemporary novels Nina lends me. Again and again, a mother is visited over the holidays by her college-going son, who arrives with a male lover in tow to explain that he is now out of the closet. Sometimes the father seizes this opportunity to declare that he, too, has all along been a homosexual. I glance at Ian suspiciously. He is in his gracious mode, entertaining the two girls with tales from his life in the Peace Corps, following the fall of Camelot. These stories now have the luster of legend about them; they are tales from far away and long ago. The girls listen to them, enthralled and cynically condescending at the same time, in both their lovely faces the question, *But how could anyone have ever been so innocent and hopeful?* And I am filled with the furious rush of my love for Ian, my heart pumping, powerful as hydrology, and I want to say to them, *That's the kind of innocence you learn, it takes age and experience to be able to shake off your self-protective defenses and give yourself over to helping someone else.* But I don't say anything. I just look at Ian, reminding myself that later the girls will be gone and we can indulge our heterosexual sexual preferences on the water bed, and he says, "Passez-moi le salt, s'il vous plait."

Ian teaches French at West High.

Two sky-blue tapers burn driplessly next to wildflowers I brought back from the farm a few weeks ago. The wildflowers have dried—it was a delicate transition from life to death, so shaded it would have been impossible to say exactly when death occurred: At what point did these flowers become what they are now?

The candlelight projects a silhouette of the wildflowers onto the wall; it polishes the real gold of Judy's hoop earrings, casts a mantle of light over Isabel's bent head.

I'm not losing a daughter, I tell myself, I'm gaining a daughter.

*

"They are children," I say to Ian in the kitchen, after they have vanished into the night.

I remember those college nights, full of adventure, philosophy, midnight desperation in the diner over coffee and cigarettes. I had two years of them before I decided to go to nursing school, where nihilism was not part of the curriculum.

I peer out the window as if the children, or my youth, might still be out there, in the dark.

Through the window, which we have opened slightly to cool off, comes an autumnal aroma of fallen apples, bitter herbs. Already, the birds have started south.

"Isabel's almost twenty-one," he says. "You've got to start getting used to the idea that she's grown up. She has her own life to live."

But when he says "life to live," I of course think of one of my patients, only a few years older than Isabel and like her gay, who, however, has but a death to die.

Noting parallels and contrasts to patients' lives in this way is, I discovered a long time ago, an occupational hazard of nursing, and I don't allow myself to be sidetracked. I just say, "That's easy for you to say."

He slams the silverware drawer shut. "No, it isn't, Shelley. As a matter of fact, it's very hard for me to say, because I know you're upset and you're going to take it out on me. It would be much easier for me not to say anything, but someone has to keep you from making a big mistake here."

He's right, but I don't have to be happy about that.

I'm elbow-deep in hot water—literally. I rinse the last dish and he hands me a dishtowel. When we remodeled this kitchen, we made it comfortable for both of us to work in at the same time. We both like to cook. When I think of Ian, I naturally think of spices—"a young stag upon the mountains of spices." Old deer, I have called him, teasing; old dear.

Sometimes he sits at the dining-room table, marking papers, while I make something that can be stored in the freezer for the following day, and as I scoop and measure, doing the Dance of the Cook, I look at him through the rectangular frame created by the counter and cabinets. He is a year younger than I am. He would have made a great British colonel, except that he would have liberated all the colonials, at the same time forcing them at gunpoint to call in their pledges to public radio. He is a born-and-bred Wisconsinite, and I love every contradiction his un-French mind so blithely absorbs. For him, I left a husband who was equally good-hearted but incapable of such contradiction, paradox, surprise.

"Maybe I'm not the one to do that in this case," he continues. "Call Nelson. Maybe *he* can keep you from going off the deep end."

I look at Ian; I pick up the phone; I dial. It rings. "Nel?" I say.

"Shel."

God, we were young. We were young for so long—longer than we should have been. We were still so young even by the time our daughter was born that we thought, amazingly, that the family that rhymed together would stay together.

"I need to talk to you. Can you meet me at Porta Bella?"

"In twenty minutes," he says. "Listen, I know what it's about. Everything's going to be all right."

"She told you first?" I ask. I can't help it, I'm hurt.

Nelson leans back in the booth, and the leather seat creaks. His white hair—it started turning white when he reached forty—looks pink in the red haze of the table lamp, a stubby candle in a netted hurricane shield.

At the bar, male and female lawyers and professors bump against one another, pushing, as if hoping to annoy someone into noticing them. When you are young, you're a sex object because you're sexy, but then you reach an age when you have to make someone aware of you as an object before it will occur to him or her that you just might possibly be a *sex object*. This is one of the places near State Street that the students tend to leave to an older crowd.

Nelson's pink beard looks like spun sugar, and for a moment, I remember being a child, wanting to go to the circus and buy cotton candy. My parents said no. It was the polio scare—people thought perhaps children contracted polio from being in crowds. No circus, no swimming lessons, no—

"It's hard on her, our divorce," he says. "I'm happy things have worked out for you with Ian, but you must realize she senses a barrier there now. There's not the same unimpeded access to you that she had."

Unimpeded access. Do I detect smugness in his voice, the way he drapes one arm over the back of the booth like a long, sly, coat-sleeved cat?

"Do you think she's doing this just to get back at me? Will she grow out of it?"

"I think it's the real thing, Shelley," he says. He smiles. "As real as Coke." He means Coca-Cola, I know. We are not the kind of people who would ever mean anything else, I realize, wondering if this is insight, boast, or lament. It could be an elegy. "I think she's in love."

He has brought his arm down, shifted closer to the table. Whatever he wanted to say about my behavior, he feels he has said. Now we can talk about hers. "She's still our little girl," he says.

"She always will be," I agree. "And she's *free to be herself.*" I start to tell him that I'm quoting Marlo Thomas, then don't. The guy has enough to deal with without his ex-wife quoting Marlo Thomas. "It's just that, well, weren't you counting on grandchildren someday?"

"I wouldn't rule out the possibility yet," he says. "A lot of lesbians have children, one way or another. I think she wants to have children someday."

He leans back again, the thick, pink beard like a strawberry milk shake glued to his face. "That wasn't the only thing I was counting on," he says sadly.

We wake to FM. Ian and I lightly touch our mouths together on the corner of Joss and Highland, walking in opposite directions to our respective places of work. All night I dreamed memories, dream-memories of being pregnant with Isabel. That swimming heaviness, that aquatic muffle. Followed by life on land.

All day at the hospital, I dispense meds, take temps, rig IVs. I draw blood, turn or ambulate patients, record BPs. It's an unexceptional day—people are dying. September sunlight, that last hurrah of brightness already muted by the foreknowledge of winter, slips across the islanded rooms, making watery squares of shadow on the white sheets of so many, many single beds, in all of which people are dying. Some will go home first; some will have remissions; some will live long lives; all are dying.

In the hall, I pass Nelson, his white coat flapping behind him like a sail, a tail. If he hurried any more, he would lift off, airborne, a medical kite, a human Medflight. We nod to each other, the way we did before we were married, while we were married.

In the fluorescent glow of the hospital hallways, his beard no longer looks like peppermint. It is as white as surgical gauze.

Gloved and gowned, I duck into Reed's room.

Reed has AIDS. He has been here before, during two other episodes of acute infection. This time he has pneumonia. This time, when he leaves here, he will go to a nursing home to die.

It seems to me that his single bed is like a little boat afloat in the sea of sunlight that fills the room. Reed lies there on his back, with his eyes shut, as if drifting farther and farther from shore.

"Reed," I say to call him back.

He opens his eyes and it takes him a moment to process the fact that I am here, that it is I. I believe the dementia that occurs in eighty percent of AIDS patients has begun to manifest itself, but it's hard to say. I don't know what Reed was like before he became an AIDS patient.

I pull up a chair and sit beside him. The skinnier he gets, the more room his eyes take up in his face. He winks at me, a thin eyelid dropping over a big brown eye that seems, somehow, just a little less sharp than it did the last he was here.

"Hello, Shelley," he says.

"I thought for a minute you'd forgotten me."

"I still have my *mind*, Shelley," he says, too quick, I think, to assume I mean more than my surface statement. "It's just my body that's going."

I don't contradict him. He knows everything there is to know at this point about his disease. He knows more about it than I do—like many AIDS victims, he has read the research, questioned the doctors, exchanged information. At the limits of knowledge, the issue becomes belief, and I figure he has a right to choose his beliefs. Reed believes he will lick his illness.

I look at the *body that's going*: He has lost more weight since his last hospitalization, despite a rigorous fitness plan. His cheekbones are as pointy as elbows. His brown eyes have lost some of their laughter. When I pick up his hand to hold it, it doesn't squeeze back. There are sores on his arms—the giveaway lesions of Kaposi's sarcoma. K.S., we say around here. I take his pulse, the wrist between my fingers and thumb not much bigger than a sugar tube.

"Reed," I ask him, "are you sorry you're gay?" I almost say *were*. As in *were gay*. Or *sorry you were gay*.

"Because of this?" He withdraws his hand.

"No. Just—if there were no such thing as AIDS, if nobody ever died from it, would you be glad to be gay?"

"How can I answer that? How can I pretend Eddie never died?"

Eddie was his lover; he died of AIDS two years ago, in California. Reed came back home, but his parents, small dairy farmers in northern Wisconsin, have been unable, or perhaps unwilling, to look after him.

He's not having trouble talking; his lungs are much better now, he is off oxygen, and he'll surely leave us in a day or two. I'll never see him again—this former social worker, still in his twenties, now dying more or less alone, whose gentleness is reflected in the sterling silver-framed photo portraits of Eddie and his parents and sister that he brings here with him each time and props on the night table, next to the telephone and water tray.

In my imagination, I try to read—Reed!—the dinner scene from the story of *his* life: His parents are seated at either end of the old oak table that has been the heart of their family life for twenty-five years. Would they place Reed next to his sister, across from Eddie? Or would they put the two boys together, facing their only daughter? The former, I think; Eddie is an outsider in this scene.

I know what they look like, gathered around that table, because of the portraits. Reed's sister is dark, a little overweight; she is the mediator, the one who tries to make all the emotional transactions among the family members run smoothly. His mother looks like a blueberry pie—dark and creamy-skinned, round-faced, plumply bursting out of her Sears slacks and top. His father is shy, turning away from the camera, turning away from Eddie not out of any dislike in particular for him but because he always turns, always has turned, away from even the merest implicative reference to sex, and Eddie's presence is an implication. And Eddie—Eddie's healthy. Eddie is broad-faced and big-shouldered, Eddie is the one who looks like a farmhand, who looks like he could do chores all day under a midwestern sun and drink Stroh's at night, fish for muskie and shingle the roof on Sunday. He does not look like he will be dead anytime soon.

I wonder how the family took it, how explicit Reed was or how much they guessed or refused to understand. Reed would have been sensitive about everyone's feelings, wanting not to hurt either his parents or his lover, wanting his sister not to be disappointed in her big brother but eager for her to understand Eddie's importance in his life. I wonder how Reed felt when, after dinner, they all rose from the table and said, not impolitely, good night, taking him and Eddie up on their offer to do the dishes, and retired to their rooms—not condemning him but also, not, not—what did he expect from them? he asked himself. Had he hoped they would embrace Eddie as their own, that they would feel, when they looked at Eddie, the warmth of emotion that sometimes suddenly welled up in him so intensely he could almost cry, a cup overflowing? When he turned the dial on the dishwasher, a red light came on like a point of reference.

While I am musing, Reed is busy fighting off an invisible force that wants to pull his mouth down, wants to yank tears out of his eyes. When he wins, his face falls into place again, at rest, the exhausted victor of yet another round in an intramural boxing match against grief.

"How are Ian," he asks me, "and Isabel?"

We are talking together in low voices, telling each other about our lives, when Dr. Feltskog stops in with a couple of residents following in his wake. They are all using universal precautions. This is a teaching hospital. He introduces them to Reed, explains Reed's situation, the presenting pneumocystic pneumonia, our methodology for managing the disease.

Dr. Feltskog finishes his spiel, and I am looking at Reed, trying to measure its impact, when one of the young doctors steps forward. "Reed," she says—even the youngest doctors no longer use patients' last names—"how do you feel?"

Reed winks at me again, though so slowly I am not sure the others in the room recognize it as a wink. They may just think he is tired, fighting sleep.

"Okay," he says.

The young doctor nods as if she understands exactly what he is doing: He has said that he feels okay because he doesn't want to burden them with details about how he really feels. It doesn't occur to her that maybe he just doesn't want to burden himself with the attention he can tell she is dying to give him.

"Now, Reed," she says, leaning over him so close it is as if he has no boundaries at all, leaning into his face, "we know you have feelings you want to talk about. It's natural. If you like, we can ask a staff psychiatrist to stop in to see you."

There is a silence in which I learn to feel sorry even for her—not just Reed, not just Isabel, not just Ian and my ex, and not just myself but even this jejune, over-helpful (and unconsciously manipulative), too-well-intentioned doctor in pearls and Hush Puppies, the white coat, though she doesn't know it, a symbol of all that she owes to women my age, who made it possible for her to do what she does, have what she does, have what she has—as I watch Dr. Feltskog register, on his mental ledger sheet, her lack of sensitivity.

To Reed, the suggestion that he see a psychiatrist means he really is losing his mind. It means he will be defeated after all: If his mind is not on his side, how can he combat what is happening to his body? It means he really is going to die before he has had a chance to live.

"I don't want a psychiatrist," he says softly, the tears he had beaten back earlier now overtaking him.

They leap to his eyes, those tears, and others to mine, as he says, with as much exclamatory emphasis as he can command, a look on his face like that of a child who has been unfairly trapped into protesting his innocence even after he knows that everyone knows he is guilty, "Why are you interrogating me about my feelings like this? This is not the Phil Donahue show! This is my life!"

When he says this, I lose track of which one of us is me. It seems to be *me* in that bed, it is *my* body going, *my* mind that's no longer to be trusted. This is the opposite of a near-death out-of-body experience, this experience of being in *someone else's* body near *someone else's* death. Those are my tears on his face, surely; surely, these are his tears on mine.

At first I think he has read my mind. As I begin to regain my ontological footing, I understand that, all over America, people are struggling to prove to themselves that their lives are more than television, that their lives are real, the real thing.

Assembled like this, we have all entered a world outside time, it is as if a collective catastrophe has carried us into a place of silence and immobility, we are a mass accident, a tragedy.

Thus: A moment of stasis, a moment like cardiac arrest, and then we all come to life again, a jumpstart, a fibrillation. And a fluttering, too, a fluttering is going on here: a fluttering of hands, of hearts, of eyelids too nervous to lift themselves all the way up. There is this swift, generalized occupation, and I have a sense as of tents being taken down and away quickly and quietly, a stealth of tents, and yes, now everyone has scattered and I am alone again with Reed. I think of all the things he might have said, the true profanity of his condition, and it seems to me that no words could ever be an shocking as "Phil" and "Donahue" and "Show," words that have brought America into this hospital room, the dream of an essential empowerment so at odds with the insomniac knowledge of our own helplessness, our midnight desperation over coffee and cigarettes.

"Please," I say to Reed, and I am intrigued to note how my voice supplicates, my voice, which is, really, pretty good at both giving and accepting orders and not accustomed to hovering in between like this, "get some rest now, Reed."

He doesn't answer. He turns his face away from me and I wait, but he still doesn't answer or look at me. I am left staring at the back of his head, the bald spot that is the tonsure of early middle age and was once the fontanelle of an infant, and I think—what else could I think—that I don't care what kind of life Isabel leads, so long as she gets to lead one.

I think of my beautiful daughter, her grumpy spirit caged by the circumstances of her own sexuality and her mother's, and of how it will one day— soon, I think—be freed, *free to be itself,* and how, when it is, her sweetly curved profile will disclose the inner strength I know is there, how her blue, blue eyes, deep and true as columbine, will sparkle with the triumph that integrity is.

Not that I wouldn't prefer things to be otherwise; not that I am exactly happy about my daughter's choice. I wouldn't go so far as that—not yet. But what I know, almost annoyed with myself for knowing it because I wish I could surprise myself, but then that is why I married Ian, isn't it, to be surprised, is that I'm going to. I love her too much not to know that the day will come when I will feel however I must feel in order to keep her in my life. This, I realize, was never in doubt, no matter how much I may have been in doubt. The issue always becomes belief.

But back out in the hallway I stop short, confused, almost dizzied, feeling I have lost my place in some book or other. They are paging Nelson—*Dr. Lopate, Dr. Lopate!*—and I remember how I used to call him that our first year together in Detroit. We were the same height, and I'd launch his newly earned title in a low whisper from the rim of his ear, a little raft afloat on the sea of ego. And he loved it, at least for that first year.

I find my way to the locker room and change out of my work shoes into Nikes. Walking home on Highland, I see that we are having what I secretly think of as a Code Blue sky—alarmingly bright, the kind of sky that can galvanize you. A sky like emergency medicine, needing to be attended to on the spot. So when I get home I call Ian at the school. The secretary has to go get him, of course, because he's in his classroom, grading papers. *Nous aimons, vous aimez, ils aiment.*

Elles aiment.

"Let's spend the night at the farm," I tell him. "I'll swing by and pick you up."

After supper we go for a walk and wind up down by Beaver Pond. The pond is as round as a smiling cheek, the setting sun a blush on it like rouge, and in the sky a thin crescent moon, the squinty eye of it, the shut eye of it, is already risen, as if it just can't wait, it has things it wants to see, it won't be kept in the dark any longer. Ian and I straddle a log, and we're glad, given the late-day chill, that we are wearing flannel shirts.

Let's face it, things are not exactly quiet out here in the country. Things are going on even out here. We can hear the beavers working away in a scramble against winter. Every so often, there's a crash or a cry, and no way of knowing whether the sound means life or death. There are so many creatures out here, deer and owls and just so many, and the prairie grass, and the abandoned orchard, and wildflowers.

Sometimes I think of the whole world as a kind of hospital, the earth itself as a patient.

There are days, now, when so much seems to slipping away. Even the things one tends not to think of, like the walnuts. The walnuts are slipping away, going off to be stockpiled by squirrels. The green of summer is slipping away, hiding its light under a bush or a bushel of autumn leaves. There are dreams that slip away in the middle of the night, losing themselves forever in some dark corner of the subconscious. There are stars that are disappearing even as we look at them. There are mothers and fathers and children, all of them slipping away like the fish in the pond, going down deeper for winter. And you reach out to hold on to your child, and she is slipping away, going off into some life that is not your life, and you are afraid to see her go because you know, you know how far it is possible to go, how far it is possible for things to slip away.

"You're thinking," Ian says. "What about?"

But I don't know how to say what I'm thinking, because it seems to me I am thinking of everything there is to think of and of nothing at all, at the same time. "I don't know how to put it into words," I confess. "You have to remember, I had only two years of Liberal Arts."

"I've often wondered," Ian says, "what the Conservative Arts would be. Anything Jesse Helms likes, I guess."

We hear a noise like a senator. "Did you hear that?" I ask.

We listen to two or three frogs bandying croaks back and forth. They're more subdued than they are during the spring, but they still have something to say. "There are throats in those frogs," I say. "Those frogs are talking to one another."

"In French," Ian says. "Frogs always talk in French."

I let out a whoop and get up from the log, but when I do I trip and Ian jumps up to catch me, and he holds me, and my face is buried against his left arm, and my ear is over his heart, which is making its own happy racket through the walls of his chest, as loud as a neighbor living it up.

LOVE IN THE MIDDLE AGES

O saeculum, O literae! juvat vivere!
—Ulrich von Hutten

There had been in her life a time, now historical, that was dark with fear and superstition: her fear; the superstitions of psychiatrists and psychoanalysts. This was in a place where winters were long and hard, the streets a sibilant soup of slush, sand, and salt, or treacherous with drifting snow, drizzle of ice sugar-glazing the leafless lindens. People were always turning away from other people to cough or sneeze into cupped hands. They lingered in coffee shops, the hot liquid in their throats like a medicine. Outside, cars skidded sideways to a stop in a ditch. Drivers exchanged license-plate numbers and the names of insurance agents wearily, as if they had been through this before, as if they had been canceled years ago and were now in syndication.

Winter in the year of our Lord 735. Snow is sifting into the moat, a thousand swans doing swan dives; it featherbeds the inner stone wall that stands near Lindisfarne, known as Holy Island, in the north of Northumbria in Bernicia. A stockade surmounts the stone wall, for those who would attack and lay siege to the court are many, including the Picts, and also the Mercians to the south.

The wind quickens, hurling itself against the stones like a lunatic beating her head against a wall. The falling snow glitters above the windblown water, phosphorescing, a final, brave flare-up. Touching down in the moat, snowflakes are snuffed out like candles.

To Nina, in this impossible place, there now came the suggestion of a new personal happiness.

Except that she refused to believe it.

Except that she was afraid to believe it.

Except that she was used to the way things were, her routine of child-minding, teaching, writing, and walking the dog.

But especially, except she was afraid to believe it.

Though Nina loved some things wholly, things such as art and life, always ready to put either before herself, men were another matter. She had been unconnected to any man for so long, now, that she did not believe connection was possible. And who would ask her out?

"Single mothers are the romantically challenged of the world," she liked to joke.

The first time he kissed her, he touched his mouth to hers and then stayed there, mouth on mouth, as if resting, perhaps taking a short nap. Perhaps practicing CPR. For a brief moment of alarm she thought he might have forgotten what he was going to do. It had slipped his mind that he was going to kiss her! He had planned to kiss her, but then he thought of something more important! Breathing, for instance! And then, given that pause during which her fear walked past itself and out the door, she felt her heart bloom, felt the rose of it warmed and open, and he kissed her and kissed her until she forgot everything she knew: her past, her phone number, her name, why she never slept with men anymore.

The king and queen sit side by side on the high seat at the top of the table. Their dinner companions raise bronze cups of spiced red wine, cheering and toasting from places on cushioned benches. Platters of cold meats and smoked fish and flat wheatcakes glimmer blood-red or gold in firelight flung on the table by torches ranged along the wall and logs crackling in the hearth. Through thin slits in the wall, all in the hall can see the snow fall, fall, fall, the sky strangely lightening as the day grows darker.

The night before, a new moon's horns had lain downward, frowning, and forecasting a month of storms and bitter weather.

Present at the table, but made to sit far down along the side, is the princess, who watches her distant parents—so kingly! so queenly!—as if they were in another room. (It seems to her that they have always been in another room.) Not present is the princess's brother—firstborn and heir and, it is rumored, a follower of Merlin—who is doubtless joyriding in a stolen car or drinking or in bed with one of the princess's friends from college.

She had met him on the Square in summer, during the Merchants' Parade. He taught in the history department. Like most academics, he was deracinated, a man for all locales. Pittsburgh, Charlottesville, Palo Alto had been some of the points on his trajectory, but weren't they all the same, intellectually homogeneous no matter how ethnically diverse, one big reading list? He had the pampered academic's exuberant desire to see the world benefit from his thinking. He was generous and ignorant, a middle-aged male in a preserve for middle-aged males, a place where middle-aged males grazed on grants or snoozed the afternoon away in endowed chairs, a place where they had a kind of mental sex in institutes (Esalens for the mind, these "Institutes for Research") and grew fat on footnotes—perpetrated by friends in other preserves—that cited the few articles they'd written. He was a wild beast who had never actually had to survive in the wild and therefore knew nothing of the world Nina had come from nor anything of his own capacity for destruction; he had confused destruction with deconstruction—he had confused death with anagrams!—and Nina was afraid of him. Yet when she tried to imply something of this to him, tried to sketch (but gaily, optimistically, as if she was, after all, talking about a very *slight* apocalypse) the disaster and despair she feared might be the result of any further meeting (there was history and then there was her personal history, which she was not about to repeat), he said, "You're very imaginative. I guess that's what makes you a writer. Do you want to go to a movie?"

In the ninety-nine-cent dark in Middleton he put his arms around her. Popcorn spilled down into the neck of her cotton men's shirt, but if she reached after it she'd look as if she was trying to cop a feel from herself. It was a movie from the eighties, about murder among monks. The screen was thick with symbology. Nina felt she already knew everything there was to know about sexual abstinence.

She shook his hand before unlocking her front door. Under the porch light his eyes were hazel, a nutmeat brown.

Inside the hot house—it could be suffocating in summer—she paid the baby-sitter, went up and untwisted her daughter from the tangled top sheet, and let the dog run out in back and then back in, and then went to bed, letting her skirt drop in a sighing heap on the floor, taking the blue shirt off, her young-looking breasts bare. And buttery.

Torchlight dances over the woven tapestries and embroidered wall curtains and causes the swords and armor hung on pegs to gleam, a metal-plate and chain-metal mirroriness. The king has been inspecting the strength of his hold against invaders. It is late in November, "the month of blood": In November, people kill their animals, knowing the animals cannot survive anyway because there will not be enough fodder to last the winter.

Gleemen play pipes and fiddle and harp for the pleasure of the king and his queen. And beneath the music run these whispered words, making their way from guest to guest: Winds had swept a monk out to sea on his penitential raft, and only the priest's prayers had drawn him back, as if by the rosary's rope, to safety. Cain's gigantic progeny had risen from the whirling water, seas sliding from their shoulders, drowning sailors. People had reported seeing dragons on the heath, fires starting up first over here, then over there as if blown about by the devil's breath. Demons had been observed having intercourse at midnight. Infant demons grew to full size in a single day and played evil tricks on unsuspecting monks, loosing the mooring of rafts on the Tyne.

He took her to dinner at l'Etoile, an expensive second-storey restaurant she did not often get to eat in. It was still summer. The lights from the capitol, which the window looked out on, were as soft as candlelight in the aquamarine of early evening.

They talked about their jobs and former marriages. A waiter whisked glasses and plates away, returned with others. Nina listened as Palmer described his ex-wife: She had been beautiful, accomplished, lesbian. He had doubted himself. He had slept with women—he would hang his head to say how many—confirming his manhood, reassuring himself, but he was past that now. He was HIV-negative. What about her?

"What?"

"Have you been tested?"

"This is so mortifying," she murmured, wiping her mouth with a linen handkerchief the size of her daughter's nightgown.

"You shouldn't be ashamed. There's nothing mortifying about a disease. Although, etymologically speaking—"

"No," she said. "It's not that. I'm mortified to admit I haven't slept with anyone in a decade. I don't think I need to go for a test."

"In a *decade*?"

She didn't look at him. "Yeah," she said. "Is that a surprise, or what. I was surprised!"

"A *decade*?" Oil from the dressed mushrooms had gotten on his chin, giving him a glow like makeup. "*Why*!?"

"I was too busy?" she asked.

His fork had stalled in midair. "But you're so pretty!"

She looked up at him and then away and then back again, flattered and confused, gratitude making her simultaneously bold and shy. "I think I took a vow of poverty, too. I mean, the University certainly seems to think I did, because otherwise they'd have to pay me a living wage. But don't expect me to be obedient."

You can be a princess and still be forgotten during the festivities in the Great

Hall. You can be there, among the company, and still know that on another level you have been banished—were banished before you were born.

Yet, looking down the long table at them, the princess is proud of her kingly father and queenly mother, of the way the whole realm pays tribute to her parents. Her face is rouged with the warmth of the fire, the wine, her own royal blood. She bends her head to take another sip, trying to hold the cup so as not to acquire, as has happened on other occasions, a red-wine moustache, and manages instead to dunk a strand of her hair in the cup. She already had broken ends, and now they are wet and clumped like seaweed and smell of booze. She adjusts her royal crown to hide the fact that she is having a really bad hair day—her parents hate for her to be anything less than a perfect princess! Of course, she thinks sadly, her mouth still fuzzed and grainy with the taste of hair and setting gel, she has to be careful not to forget she's not supposed to be anything more than a princess, either. God forbid she should outshine her brother, get grandiose notions about the throne, displace her mother the queen.

"I always wanted to write a comic strip," she said to him, gaily, optimistically. This was part of her strategy for letting him know that she was not so easily snowed, she was not a romantic—she was going to let him know this by telling him about her comic strip. "Not as a way of life. Just this one strip. In the first panel, there are two hilltops, and on each hilltop is a snail. On one hilltop there's a boy snail, and on the other hilltop is a girl snail. They spot each other and it's love at first sight.

"So they race down their respective hills, only they're *snails*. And the seasons pass: It's summer, autumn, winter. And they keeping racing and racing to each other's arms. And it's spring again, and summer, and autumn. And they keep racing. At a snail's pace! And finally, one day, they really do meet, down in the valley, and their love has lasted all this time. He's got a cane now, and glaucoma, and she has a dowager's hump, but they get married. The last panel is headed: *Happily Ever After*, and it shows two tiny tombstones side by side."

"Writers," he said. "You don't get out enough, do you? You should join my volleyball team. We play the poli-sci department on Tuesdays."

Also absent, absent forevermore, are many friends, taken by plague. The princess has seen how they die: the skin blackening as if there is an eclipse of the blood, the painful, grotesque swelling, all the body's estuaries filling with sluggish fluids. Lymph nodes in the armpits and groin blown up like pig bladders.

And then that blackening, as if the skin were charred by burning fever. People with plague cried out, tossing on straw pallets all through the night, falling silent by morning. But the worst thing, thinks the princess, is the babies. She can't understand why babies should have to suffer like that. Babies, she thinks, all babies everywhere, should wear teensy crowns and romper suits, and when they get a little older they should be given velveteen dresses, and seersucker play-outfits and OshKosh B'gosh snap-on overalls, and be hugged and cooed to and get their chins chucked a lot and have the run of the court. And if they fall down, their mother the queen and their father the king should be there to put a Band-Aid over the sore spot and kiss the hurt away.

The reason the crowns have to be teensy is so they won't make the babies' heads lie uneasy.

Palmer wore her down. He wouldn't be put off. Nothing scared him—not her being a single parent, not her being in the public eye (of Madison, anyway), not her incredibly complicated past, lived in several countries (and a few psych wards, too). She thought sure the snails would do it, but he just smiled at her, a smile that squeezed his eyes into the canoe shape of Brazil nuts. There were lines in his face like snowmobile tracks, coming or going, depending on how he felt.

The more good-natured he was, the less she trusted him. What man ever pledged himself to a woman on the spot? In the Middle Ages, all right, but this was some fin-de-siècle folly. He might be a historian, but she could see what was in store for the future—the female graduate students; the return of that old sorrow of discovering she was not, after all, first in anybody's thoughts. She saw the emotional distance that would gradually develop, as if the house itself were expanding, the bedroom miles from his study, her study, how he would come home one day—in a year, five years, twenty—and ask for a divorce, his voice breaking a little as if he were going through puberty. Which would be pretty much what he would be doing. In a year, five years, twenty, he would take back his books and exercycle and say he really hoped they would still be friends. After he left, everything would go back to being exactly the way it was now, except that her heart would have stopped, when he said he was leaving her, just long enough for a little more brain damage to take place. She was already concussive with rejection! That's why she would be bursting into tears for no good reason—she'd have lost control over certain bodily functions. She'd have trouble breathing, the work of it almost more than she could bear. Give this woman an oxygen tent! She should go home and make out a Living Will, right now. For a time, she would be irrational and in pain, the bones of her body bright and cold and snapping off like icicles, and at night she would crawl around in the cave of her own cranium, that unknown, dank, cobwebbed place. All this, while her daughter needed her—needed her to praise a scribbled drawing or button the top button on the back of her jumper or arbitrate a dispute between Teddy the Bear and a mob of plastic dinosaurs. No, Nina could not have this. She refused to sleep with him.

"I can wait," Palmer said. He looked at her thoughtfully. "Maybe not a decade. I don't think I can wait a decade."

Monks on rafts may be frightened by whales or evil spirits rising from the sea floor; a son of Cain can raise a full-blown gale merely by seizing a monk by the hair and twirling him like a top.

Cormorants, shags, gannets, and guillemots are birds of the shore.

Monks of the time carry gospel books. Living in large groups, monks are in constant danger of infection transmitted by communal cups. Infectious diseases include smallpox, tuberculosis, and bubonic plague.

Stained-glass windows shatter light from church lamps, splintering it into stripes that paint the cornfields and countryside, sheep fells and cow byres. An angel approaches the boy Cuthbert, who later becomes a monk, and advises him to treat his swollen knee with a poultice. "You must cook wheat flour with milk," says the angel, "and anoint your knee with it while the poultice is hot." On another occasion, Cuthbert sees an angel whisk a soul off to heaven, and the soul appears to be in the center of a fiery orb, like a small wax figure in a paperweight.

The princess, a studious sort, has made herself a kind of home office behind a folding screen. She convinced herself that if she hid behind a folding screen her brother would not know she was there, or would forget to pay attention to her. Her brother the prince, who has absorbed all the Continental ideas of existential absurdity and artistic freedom from psychological and social convention and keeps telling her she is the only person in the realm who has ever understood him. Which confuses her greatly, because she doesn't understand anything, especially him. Most of all, she does not understand why her brother said it is a tragedy that they can't get married. And she does not understand why, on one hand, he said this, and on the other hand, he sleeps with her girlfriends from college.

At two o'clock every afternoon during the summer Nina walked over to Mrs. Kendall's house on Kendall Street—though, as Mrs. Kendall was fond of pointing out, she was a Kendall by marriage and her ex-husband's family had been from South Dakota anyway so God only knew where the Kendalls were that Kendall Street had been named after—and helped her daughter gather up her day's output of drawings and collages and cardboard cutouts and brought her home. Today Tavy was baking Play-Doh in the pretend oven. "What kind of pies are these?" Nina asked her, saying "yum yum" and poking a finger in one.

"They're not pies," Tavy said.

At this age, Tavy had long, straight, brown hair with bangs; eyes that some-times seemed like cameras registering everything on a film not yet developed; and the cheekbones of her mother Babette, her great-aunt and adoptive mother Nina, and her late great-grandmother Eleanor—cheekbones already celebrated by three generations of men. She had on a pale yellow blouse that was like a slice of lemon and a skirt the smoky color of Darjeeling. My little tempest in a teapot! thought Nina. "What are they, then?" asked Nina. "Cookies?"

"Turd tortes," said Tavy.

After dinner—meat loaf, not turd tortes—Nina sat on the front stoop of her house with Tavy and their little dog. Tavy held Teddy the Bear in her lap. It was a beautiful, clear night, just late enough in the summer to grow dark before Tavy went to bed. The sky was cobblestoned with stars. Headlights hurried by in pairs, as if they were on their way to an ark somewhere. "Tavy," said Nina, "do you want to tell me what's bothering you?" She smoothed Tavy's hair back behind her ears. "You seem angry about something."

Tavy tried to smooth the little dog's hair back behind his ears. "Mommy's being silly," she told him.

Nina said to Teddy, "Well, Teddy, if Tavy won't tell me what's wrong, how am I ever going to make it right?"

"Teddy can't hear you," Tavy said.

"He can't?"

"He's just a *bear*," she said.

"Can he think?"

"I didn't say he was stupid!"

"Then what is Teddy thinking?"

"He thinks you should marry Rajan. He doesn't think you should marry Palmer."

"Don't you like Palmer?"

"He's okay. But Teddy likes Rajan better."

"Honey, Rajan is married, to Lucy, remember?"

"She might die. She could do like Grandma and go to a foreign place and get old and die. Then you could marry Rajan."

"I'm sorry, sweetie," Nina said. "It doesn't work that way."

"I don't see why not," said Tavy, leaning heavily over Teddy, her chin in her hands, her elbows on her knees, her feet in their brown wide-strap sandals planted firmly on the chipped and cracking concrete steps that cost too much to replace.

In her home office in the castle keep, she keeps her personal library. Donatus on the grammar of Latin; De Arte Metrica, *with its study of poetic scansion; Isidore of Seville's* Etymologiae, *Pliny's* Natural History, *the poets Sedulius, Juvencus, and Paulinus of Nola. (Perhaps she borrowed some of these books from the local monastery and has never gotten around to returning them.) During the winter, scribes' scrivening slows down; their fingers freeze up like the pistons of old cars and stall on the page.*

The monks smear resin from cedars on the books; otherwise, worms make holes in the vellum and binding boards and swallow words, and to no purpose for who ever heard a wise worm? Precious and semi-precious stones stud gilt bookcovers worked in intricate designs. The princess glances out the window—moonshine makes a glow of frost, the whorled crystals a wavy pattern on the pane: frost-stars and frost-mountains. She hears wolves howling in the distance. There were travelers who walked a hundred miles to find books for their libraries; they carried the books in satchels, these backpacking librarians. They were sometimes eaten by the wolves.

Everyone has gone, settled down in some secret corner on a straw pallet or featherbed or sprawled on a cellar floor. The princess pores over her books.

This is what the princess has always done. She has always pored over her books.

A chill wind wickedly wriggles its way in around the edges of the frosted pane. Wax pools at the base of the candle and hardens; she chips at it with her nails. As she reads and writes, she stays alert to any sound, any shift in shadow—whatever might tell her that he is near and waiting. If her brother the prince is going to rape her, she doesn't want to be taken—taken!—off guard. She tells herself she is nothing if not regal. Even raped.

Nina and Shelley and Jazz stopped to have coffee and cranberry muffins at the bookstore. Palmer and three of his volleyball cronies were already there in a corner, a guitar trio with concertina accompaniment, knocking out "Whiskey before Breakfast" and drinking Blue Nun white wine.

Maybe some of the customers were playing *taefel*, rolling the dice on the table, the cubes spilling out of a pewter cup. Once, rosaries were made from dried roses, were bracelets or necklaces of rose petals, were a rose garden of prayer. Hence: the name of the rosary.

Nina, Shelley, and Jazz took a table up front by the high churchlike windows. Jazz was saying, about someone in her department, "I think he lives on some other planet."

"Yes," agreed Shelley, who knew Jazz's colleague outside the University, "but I always found it an easy flight to that particular planet."

"Well, he's moved on into deep space," said Jazz.

Nina was listening to her two girlfriends, one older and one younger, and watching their expressive faces, one white and one black, and feeling the secret warmth of her involvement with Palmer. How astonishing it was to feel, after being so long alone, this sense of an invisible but ideal geometry, as if he and she were dots that knew their destiny was to be connected in a picture that would come clear. ("But when?" he had asked her again that weekend, the snowmobile in his face returning, crisscrossing the skin around his eyes. "Connected when?" And she said, "It's this chastity belt. I seem to have lost the key.") Even with her back turned to him, she saw him with one leg outstretched and the other propped on a footrest. She could almost feel the consoling softness of his sweater—the raveled sleeve of care knitted up in a cable stitch by Bill Blass—and his chest like something strong that she could lean against, a wall. She had thought this affection for manliness, for a man's way of being in the world, had died out in her, was a thing that had been catalogued and stored in the museum of herself, an artifact of feeling. But here it was, pulsing with contemporaneity. She thought he was beautiful, and she thought this very much in the same way she had once thought Bobby Kennedy and Dirk Bogarde were beautiful.

Jazz said, "Excuse me a bit, ladies, while I jive and jam," and went to sing with the guys.

With only the two of them left at the table, Shelley—who sometimes ran into Cliff, a geneticist, at the hospital where she worked—said to Nina, "He sure beats Cliff."

Cliff, not Rajan, was who Nina had been going with before she stopped going with anyone, ever. "Cliff doesn't even seem real to me now," Nina said. "And it's not just because it was so long ago. My ex-husband, for example, was longer ago, and he still seems real. But not Cliff."

"Some men really are unreal," Shelley said. "Oh! But, anyway, I mean, you know what I mean."

"You mean that some men don't leave a mark on the world. They don't go down in history."

Jazz's voice climbed over the music like a bird that flies in through an open window and out another, a bird like a famous metaphor for life.

"They can be all the rage for a time, though," said Shelley.

"Oh my God, tell me about it. A miniseries. Foreign rights sold to eleven countries. Paperback tie-in." Nina frowned, remembering Cliff's brief appearance on her bestseller list, the rave reviews she had so uncritically given him at the beginning, his Avedon-should-photograph-it profile, elegant and arrogant.

"What I think," said Shelley, "is that it's time you went back to the classics. Palmer looks to me like literature that lasts."

At high tide the horizon is a silvered blue; at low tide it is gold, as if an angel had tipped his wings toward the earth. Cuthbert, on the verge of starvation, was saved by two freshly cut and washed wedges of dolphin flesh that appeared before him as on a plate of air. A pair of dolphins frisked in the distant sea, each lovely and whole except for a missing triangle into which one of the wedges would fit. They seemed to have delivered themselves to him, willingly, unnetted with tuna, a dolphin-pizza delivery service.

Boats are wrecked on whales, nosed into disaster and salvage, or sunk by small forms of marine life that pierce the sterns' covering of tanned ox hide. Survivors often enter monasteries, devoting the rest of their lives to worship. Monks on rafts, affrighted by whales, may paddle and pole furiously, churning the sea into a beerlike froth. Everyone has something to do—the wheelwrights, the mason, the blacksmith, the baker, the brewer, the cook, the beekeeper, the weaver. Prostitutes advertise their calling with handworked linen and luxurious brocade on their beds. Soldiers are armed with swords, spears, and axes; some turn the skulls of their slain enemies into drinking cups.

Every age has its customs: When a dead rat is discovered in the cook's flour, the cook pitches out the carcass and brushes away a bit of the surrounding flour but uses the rest without a qualm. Frequently, women who have been wives leave the secular life for the monastic when they become widows. These are some of the customs of the age.

Meanwhile, strewn among the princess's books are her personal effects: combs and needles, buckles and pins and brooches of bronze and bone. She wears a bracelet of blue glass beads.

She writes on goatskin, using a goose quill pen dipped in black ink that smells as sweet as perfume. Riddles, puns, and codes are much admired by the people of the time.

When her brother the prince comes into the room, he is laughing but in a way that seems, to her, mocking. He has sucked in his cheeks and raised his eyebrows and pursed his mouth in a skeptical moue and he looks like James Dean but a brighter, harder version, a movie star who reads books. A movie star who reads books by Nietzsche. He shoves the screen aside and lies down on her bed; perhaps she hopes that if she does nothing, nothing will happen. He is talking about their parents, the king and queen—their parents' failures and the contempt he is forced to feel. Again, a wolf howls. The candle has burnt almost to the end, its nub swimming in a hardening sea. The princess feels as though she has forgotten how to breathe. She feels clumsy, stupid, inanimate. She can't move. He rolls on his side and reaches out a hand, grasping her by the wrist. "Come over here," he says, "so we don't have to talk so loudly. We don't want to wake anyone." The world (which, she knows, everyone knows, is round, though everyone also knows that no one lives on the underside) has shrunk. It has gotten ever smaller, and now the princess sees that she is trapped in the middle of it, a world the size of an egg, a burning egg. A burning egg that scorches her ovaries, that turns her womb to ash. Her cauterized, useless womb. He doesn't kiss her. He just makes another quarter-turn until he lies on top of her. Her crown slips off and falls behind the pillow. He undoes the brooches of bone, of bronze. Her blue-bead bracelet slips from her arm, a sly little animal escaping like a salamander beneath a rock. It lies on the bed, a kaleidoscope on the tapestry and scallop-edged linens.

When she had been a very young princess, say, five, her parents had told her that if she could kiss her elbow she would turn into a boy. She had tried and tried, all the while being terrified she might succeed. She liked being a girl, she really did! She wanted to grow up and have lots of royal babies. But already she knew that it was better to be a prince. It was safer. Princes had things easier. They earned bigger salaries for less work. This, too, was a custom of the age.

With all these conflicting opinions swirling around her, Nina often felt as though she could not see where she was going. Was she, that is, going to go to bed with Palmer?

She still didn't trust him. Why her? she wanted to know. And why was he so set on marriage, which, even if it made a new sense in parlous times, re-mained a radical step?

"You've heard of the end of history," he began. They were in her living room, dog and daughter sleeping overhead. An ambulance raced past the house to the hospital, its air-raid siren like a blitzkrieg. A semi rumbled past, shaking the house on its foundation.

"I have," she admitted. Academics loved these catch phrases, the undan-gerous electric shocks of them, the semiotic therapy of them, administered to lift the black cloud of scholarly depression, give a drained brain a charge. The death of God, the authorless text, the end of history—you made a conjunction of a contradiction and the Guggenheim Foundation prostrated itself in admira-tion. But this had nothing to do with ideas; it was all grammar, as Donatus had known.

"I saw it," Palmer said.

Nina was wearing jeans and an oversized dark brown sweater and a Hill-ary headband, also brown, and white socks. She was sitting on the rug. She stretched out her legs so the bottoms of her feet could feel the fire Palmer had built in the hearth. She could make a joke now, or she could be serious. She decided to be serious. "What do you mean, you saw it?" she asked, hoping she was not about to find out that Palmer was, after all, weird. But if he was, after all, weird, that would explain, wouldn't it, why he'd said that he loved her!

He got up from the floor, sighed heavily, and threw himself into the Green Bay Packers chair, which was worn thin where her dog had, day after day for thirteen years, pawed in a furious flurry and then wound himself up like a clock before settling down to nap.

"I was walking home from school along the lake. It was a typically brilliant October day, the sky buffed to a high sheen, the leaves golden and flashing and the lake silver and sapphirine, everything lit, as with drugs, and shining. I was looking, you know, truly looking, thinking about what I was seeing and finding the words for it. And then it just stopped." He rubbed a hand over his forehead. "It just stopped," he said. "It didn't get dark, it was all still glowing, glints in the lake like fish, but these fish of light weren't moving. They weren't even bobbing. Nothing was moving, because everything was just repeating itself. The wind blowing and the waves breaking on the shore and the people jogging and the airplane, I remember there was an airplane, getting smaller, and all the other stuff—everything that was happening had finally happened too many times and now it didn't count anymore. It was pure repetition, and repetition is the opposite of history."

Nina, who had recently been experiencing flashbacks in which she remembered not just that her brother had come into her bedroom (she had never forgotten that) but how she had felt when he did, looked into the fire for a reply. The woodsmoke smelled cedary and dry, like a shelter for birds in the snow. She imagined her heart glowing like a little fire, the way she warmed to Palmer. Maybe even the way she was getting hot for Palmer! But her daughter was upstairs.

"History is over," he said. "Done with, used up, finished. Don't you see?" he begged, and there was, she saw, in him a kind of contagion no matter what the test had said. It could be a sickness unto death, but she knew a cure for it. "On the tomb of Bruni in Santa Croce are inscribed the words *History is in mourning. All we have now is fiction*," he finished. "On the other hand," he added, "maybe I'm just having a midlife crisis. I believe it would be my third."

"From a parent's point of view," Nina whispered, knowing that tenured professors had seldom heard a parent's point of view, "repetition is not the end of history. It's the beginning of history. Every child is the dawn of time."

The blue-bead bracelet slips from her arm, as if fleeing. . .

Nina went on: "What you saw was the world in *imitatio*, the photocopied world, the world that is merely a shadow cast by a larger reality. But what you *didn't* see is the *smaller* reality, which can be mistaken, at first, for a duplication but then reveals itself as essentially and eternally itself. You certainly don't have to be a parent to see this smaller reality, but being a parent may make spotting it easier. It's what children are—smaller realities. It's too bad you and your ex-wife didn't have any children."

"Thank you," Palmer said. "I knew you would save me."

"Who *are* you?" Nina asked, feeling as if she were remembering the words to an old, old song.

She held her breath; she could not imagine what she might have to offer him that he couldn't find more of, and better, elsewhere.

His thighs pulled against the cloth of his pants as he sat, legs athletically apart, in the Green Bay Packers chair. A sunburst of creases radiated out from the upper inseam of each pantleg. She looked away. "I had a vasectomy," he said.

"You and who else?! Every man I've ever known in this city has had a vasectomy. This is a city of vasectomies! I wonder why?"

"My wife didn't want kids. Look," he said, "if you don't marry me, it's the same as if we'd never met. Or it's the same as if we both had Alzheimer's." He placed his hands on his legs, cupping his knees in his palms as if hanging on but all he had to hang on to was himself. Or maybe he'd gotten mixed up and thought he really was a Green Bay Packer and was crouched to block and tackle. He looked so defensive, Nina thought, and so vulnerable, too. "I don't want to be forgotten," he explained. "Not again. I need to live with someone who is not going to forget who I have been to her." He let go of his knees, turned his palms up. "I can't keep doing this over."

"Tavy's the one you have to persuade." She was still whispering, as if not saying it louder would keep it from being too true. "I can't marry you if Tavy won't let me."

The bracelet is sliding from her arm, pale-blue beads spilling like ampules over the coverlet and onto the floor. . .

After the fire burned down, he left and she went upstairs to undress for bed, but first, as she always did, she glanced in on Tavy. Tavy looked like a pinwheel in sleep, arms and legs flung in four directions, her soft blue nonflammable flannel nightgown in a windmill splay. The little dog was sleeping beside her, on his back, all four legs in the air.

It was well into winter now, the medicine cabinet in the bathroom cluttered with half-used bottles of cough syrup, cards of twelve-hour time-release Contac punched out except for one or two remaining tablets, the basement laundry sink plugged with lint from months of washing Tavy's thermal undervests, the maple floor scarred with salt near the front door. Municipal snowplows packed the snow in at the entrances to driveways so citizens couldn't get out without shoveling all over again. Four-wheel-drive vehicles splashed mud and grimy snowmelt on passing pedestrians, who, in down parkas, looked bulked up, as if they were on steroids. This was life in an unfriendly clime. It hardened you, toughened your character, caused you to blow your nose and fix yourself a cup of hot cocoa to take to bed with you, where you lay propped up against a pillow, dreaming, a little bit feverishly, of a wedding even at this late date, this date late in the millennium.

The bracelet drops from the bed to the floor, glass beads shattering bluely, a waterfall of pale beads. . .

Nina talked to Tavy. Tavy listened. Then Tavy wept. She wept from somewhere deep inside herself, her small back bent and heaving, the flexible spine outlined under her pullover, shoulder blades trembling as if something were pushing against them to get out—something like wings. When Nina put a hand under Tavy's chin and turned that fierce face toward her, it was a whole small area of turbulence, a storm, a tornado watch. Tears blurred Tavy's eyes and dripped down her cheeks, her nose ran, she swallowed tears and hiccupped, she used the back of her fist to wipe the tears from her face but more kept coming.

Already Nina could see the beautiful young woman her daughter would grow into, and she worried, knowing that beauty is often perceived as a form of power and that people seek, therefore, to prove their own superiority by subjugating it. (How many times, Nina remembered sadly, had men—in the days before she began to live like a nun—slept with her merely to establish for themselves the fact that they could. And each time, of course, she remembered ruefully, she had thought they loved her, and she had waited for them to ask her to marry them but they never did.) "Sweetheart," she said, beginning. But what she wanted to say was, *Get thee to a nunnery.* "Sweetheart," she said again, "do you really miss Rajan so much? We hardly ever see him anymore. Palmer is the one who does things with us now. And Palmer likes to do things with us. He cares about you very much."

"Is he going to live here?"

"I don't know. Maybe. Or maybe we'll all move to a bigger house. Would you like that?"

"Do you love Palmer?" Tavy asked.

"Well, I—"

"Do you love him more than you love Teddy?"

"Well, I—"

"Do you love him more than you love me?"

"Oh no! Never never never!" Nina cried, amazed to realize what grownup fears a child can harbor. Or maybe she meant, What childish fears a grownup can harbor.

She is falling, too, slipping out of time and shattering into all her selves, so blue, so blue. . .

Nina had noted that the older she got the faster time went. She had a metabolic explanation for this: When you were a kid, you had so much energy that your internal mechanism was going faster than real time, so real time went by slowly. But as you got older, you slowed down inside, your brain, your nervous reflexes, even your heart—which became cautious and invalid, an old lady holding on to the wrought-iron railing for fear of falling on ice and breaking a hip: that was your heart—and now time sped by you, you couldn't keep up with it. Eventually it outstripped you and was far up ahead somewhere, out of sight.

You had been left behind forever.

But that wasn't the whole story. There was a Darwinian advantage to the way time worked. If time didn't go by faster and faster as you got older, you would always be in mourning for those you had lost—your parents, your alcoholic brother, your ex-husband who died too soon, before you both had a chance to turn ninety and meet again and get married all over again and get it right this time, the way it was meant to be. As you got older, the movie stars started to die, the politicians who had shaped your world, the writers who, even if you'd never met them, had been a part of your literary landscape. And the friends, too, including the girlfriend you'd been twenty-two and on lunch break with, and including the handsome male friend you'd gone to Luchow's with and laughed with all one afternoon while the band played polkas. They were gone too. If time were still as slow as it had once been, you couldn't endure it, feeling the pain for a thousand years every day. But time wasn't that slow anymore; it had gathered up enormous speed. It was only yesterday you broke for lunch, only yesterday your family were alive and problematic, only yesterday that you had been a new wife, shy and scared and deeply in love with a man who would break your heart before he died. Time had changed so that the past was almost present. It was the only way the fittest were able to stand surviving. Nina called this her Theory of Evolution.

*

Inside the fiery orb that was the size of a drop of blood the princess lived in a miniature village, where the huts had thatched roofs and there was a well in the town center, and there were neighbors and livestock. And then soldiers bore down, out of the hills, setting fire to huts and lopping off heads and arms and legs, and burning the cows and horses locked in barns. She felt her wine-dark hair burst into flame, the seed pearls sewn into her gown glowing red hot, like miniature coals. She felt herself gutted, nothing left to her but bricks and roof beams, a smudge of ash, a last smoulder of smoke. This was what it was like to be raped and pillaged, the Bosnian minority of yourself driven out and made a symbol. A symbol of something.

A grammar of contradiction.

History deconstructing itself.

She felt despair and recognized it as destiny, a sad song she was born knowing the words to. It rang in her body like a death knell, or the theme music for the nightly news. Wars and death, wars and death—they had happened before. By the time her brother was lying on top of her, she felt cynical and exhausted, as if this was old news, something that had already happened. That was the nature of doom—to be a rerun, repetition, the end, the forever-fated end. History? What history? There had never been any history, only a screen with moving pictures.

But there had been a time—she remembered now, weeping from deep inside herself, her back bent and heaving as he rolled off and she turned on her side away, shoulder blades trembling as if something were pushing against them to get out, something like wings—a time before history. It was so long ago; it was when she was younger, even, than Tavy was now, when everything still remained to be discovered for the first time. Tears burned her eyes. The betrayal at the center of her life was like a trap into which she kept falling, over and over. She had become a prisoner of expectation.

As if her brother had cared. As if anyone had cared. Her mother the queen and her father the king—they had had their minds on matters of state. She knew better than to bother them. She knew that as long as you still had your arms and legs you had nothing legitimate to complain about.

As if her brother had ever cared. He had confused her with anagrams, a game.

The students stuck such sweet suck-up notes into their end-of-semester folders. *Professor Bryant, I really liked your class.* Or, *Dear Professor Bryant, I feel I have learned a lot.* Nina tried to harden her heart against these not very subtle pleas for attention, but her heart grew soft anyway, the cheese spread of it, the cream cheese and crackers of it. Perhaps she was a woman with a deep need to be entertaining, to bring out food and drink and serve her friends.

Palmer was at the same table, reading blue books from his Honors section. After a while he capped his pen, put it down on the table, leaned across to her, and said, "Let's make history." And after he said that, he rose from his chair and held out a hand to help her out of hers, and he led her, chivalrously, upstairs to her own bedroom, and she followed.

But she was afraid!

But she was afraid not to follow.

But especially, she was afraid, and she mumbled, "Tavy—"

But he said, "Tavy is sound asleep. Kids can sleep through anything. And she might as well get used to my staying here."

"The dog—"

"That's an old little dog, believe me. He'd rather sleep than watch us have sex."

"He's never had sex."

"Wake him up!" Palmer said. "Let that old dog turn a new trick!"

Nina looked at Tavy's closed door, and part of her wanted to open it and look in on her daughter: *'Night, princess,* she would say almost aloud, brushing Tavy's hair off her forehead. But another part of Nina reminded herself that her daughter had gotten over her cold, and also over her hurt, and would be okay.

As they entered her own room and shut the door behind them, she looked out the window and saw that fresh snow had fallen, arborvitae wearing long white gloves on their limbs, like women at the opera. Frost-mountains sloped down the windowpanes into the valley of the sill. He lay down on her bed and, still holding her by the hand, pulled her down next to him. She was too embarrassed to look at him and ducked her head against his chest. He gripped her head with a hand on either side and lifted her away from him and looked her in the eye. It was like alchemy, the way the base metals of her brain became as bright as gold. She felt, suddenly, rich, as if she were the most fortunate woman in the world, and she wanted to give everything to him.

He undid the buttons of her shirt, the zipper of her jeans, the hook of her bra, the catch of her bracelet. Pale-blue glass beads sprawled like a rosary on the quilted comforter. Monks lost at sea could be tugged back to shore by people praying, if they prayed well enough.

There was always that fine print.

The wickedly cold air—despite the rope caulking! and Madison Gas and Electric made heating seem like something only a king could afford!—made her tingle, or maybe that was his hand. He got up for a moment and, in what seemed like a single swift movement, divested himself of sweater, shirt, slacks, socks, shorts. His naked body, white from months of winter living, was like a statue in Florence, hard-smooth and cool-warm as marble, a masterpiece, the human form in all its democratic beauty, freed from preconception and dogma. "You must work out a lot," she said weakly.

"Not really," he said, lying beside her again. "I just try to ride the exercycle every day." He kissed the dainty wrists and ankles that proved she was a real princess, the vein in the underside of her wrist where blue blood ran (she knew from a grim night long ago) ruby-red. She smelled his disinfectant smells of drycleaning and deodorant, toothpaste and soap, a slap of shaving lotion, a flourish of cologne, going down, down, down through all the layers of discovery to the Trojan base.

"You have an exercycle?"

She felt surrounded by him as by a Parthenon, a Colosseum. She put her hands on his shoulders, the rounded bones of them like amphorae, or well-wrought urns. A decade! she thought, disbelieving. Almost! As if she were encountering, in a way that would compel her to rethink everything she had been taught, an idea of antiquity, a belief in the dignity and excellence of Man, she caressed his neck and arms and calves. Touching him was like relearning some knowledge she had had and lost, knowledge of the world as a place that made sense. A place that could be studied, a place in which she could study without fear of interruption. A place like a science, rational and with laws. She felt his back under her hands like a revival of classical literature. She felt him in her like a kind of wisdom, humane, not dictated by the powerful God of superstition.

The next morning she woke late, Palmer already downstairs in the kitchen, with Tavy, pouring dry dogfood and cereal into bowls. She got up and threw on jeans and a T-shirt. She stopped to look out the window, before she left the room, and saw that spring was on them, or almost on them, like a new age. The snow was melting, and the sun shining like the Renaissance.

ART AND ABERRATION

Divine aberration: a small apparent displacement in the position of a heavenly body caused by the motion of the earth and the finite velocity of light.

It began with the letters. They turned up at the house, or at the school where we teach creative, as English departments are pleased to call it, writing. After a while it seemed as though the letters were following us. The letters were not, originally, something that happened in the normal course of a day. They became quotidian. We were put on our toes by the phenomenon, yes—we became alert, even apprehensive. We half expected to find these letters materializing out of the cold damp sleet-bearing air. We would plump up the pillow at night to find one underneath—the tooth fairy's literary cousin. We would discover the letters in our coat pockets. We would go to a restaurant and order steak and be served letters. None of those things happened, of course. The letters arrived only through conventional channels, each with the same return address in the upper left-hand corner, but it is important to understand the way in which they began to dominate each day as it was lived. The letters demanded attention. There was no possibility of ignoring them.

***

We live currently in the Fan District of Richmond, Virginia. It is an area of old townhouses, some renovated and some in pretty bad shape, that fans out: only two blocks wide where it begins, it spreads out to include more and more streets. Hence the name. Our house is three storeys high. It is made of brick. No two windows are shaped alike. We have owned it for two years now. Richmond is our hometown, and we are glad to be back after living elsewhere for some years. The pace of the place is right for us. When life moves too fast, there is no time to catch it on paper, and we are eager to catch life on paper.

Richmond has other attractions besides the livable rhythm. In spring, the city's median strips bloom pink and white and yellow, with azalea and mimosa. Hydrangea and lilac grow in people's front yards. In summer, the sun is gay. In winter, snow floats serenely down from the sky, lit by streetlamps, past the elegant and inelegant townhouses, and we are charmed. At Christmas time, there is a lighted candle in every window. It is the whim of the city council to advertise our city as the "city of candlelight." We do our share with candles in our own variegated windows. We would never let it be said that we are deficient in civic pride.

But—the letters.

***

They came well-spaced apart at first. Then they came at weekly intervals. Now they arrive daily. Each of them is masterfully cruel.

We were talking with a colleague about the letters. "Don't even think about them," he said. But that's easy for him to say. How could we not think about such blatant intrusions into our life? Letters, simply by virtue of being letters, require replies.

Yet to answer them would have been demeaning. It would have meant acknowledging the relevance of the criticisms if not their truth.

And yet, and yet—we were compromised in the mere opening of the letters.

***

Now, a scene, this scene: A woman is sitting at a table in front of a window, writing—a letter? a story? A story. Snow has piled against the windowpane in a pattern like tie-back curtains. Outside, the sun is shining ecstatically. Inside, the woman continues to write. A dog barking in the street punctures the silence in the room, as does the scratch of the woman's pen moving across rough yellow paper. On the right side of the table, next to her elbow, is a coffee cup; a spoon is making a brown stain on the table where it has been idly set aside. On the side of the table that is flush with the window, a jonquil sits in a jelly glass, stem snipped short for balance, the flower head bright and pert. But now the sun has moved so that it is in the woman's eyes, and she stretches out of her chair to pull the shade halfway down the window. Her attention is caught by the dusky quality this sudden rearrangement of sun vis-à-vis earth lends to the light that lies across the table like a tablecloth.

***

At first we had certainly *tried* to ignore the letters. But they refused to be ignored and in retaliation became more precise. They moved beyond the realm of professional concern to the personal. They tried to revise our understanding of ourselves in the pitiless light of their evaluation. We refused to be intimidated. We insisted on our right to interpret the past according to our sense of its movement into the future. Nevertheless, the letters continued to come.

***

The woman writing gets up from the table and moves across the kitchen to the gas stove. While she is boiling water, the telephone rings. She leaves the kitchen to answer it. When she returns, her face is changed: Delight has raised her spirit; she feels like Lazarus, newly returned, newly filled with oxygen, energy pumped into her lungs like air. She takes the pot of boiling water off the stove, fills her coffee cup, and sits down again at the table, using the same spoon to stir. Because of the phone call, she is seized with pleasure in the performance of all these small actions.

***

We composed an answer. Dear Sir, it began. *With regard to certain recent letters. . .*

***

The woman has her right eye squinched to the eye of a telescope in the dome in the backyard of a friend's house. The friend is male, married, about forty. His wife is in the house and knows that her husband is at this moment extending an arm around the younger woman's waist. The younger woman rejoices in the pressure of the man's arm; she finds it reassuring, stabilizing. The night is cold and both the man and the woman are wearing wool coats. The woman can feel the coldness of the concrete floor under her boots' soles. The wife is watching television in the living room. When the pair come back in, she will pretend nothing is wrong, nothing is amiss. They will both know that it is a pretense, and they will know that she knows they know. The wife is not amused by these moments of irony but neither is she overly concerned. She has long since given up caring. She tells herself.

***

The next letter made no mention of ours. It was, if anything, even more specific in its objections. We wondered if the police could arrest their author on general grounds of harassment, but we were too ashamed of the letters' charges to show them to anyone.

Each day became an ordeal.

***

Night was a sheet of carbon paper. Daylight—thin transparent onionskin.

***

The letters made no insinuations, innuendoes—that was not their style. They did not involve themselves with questions of relationship, affinity, love or hate. No, their objections were aimed at the target points of character, talent, and appearance.

***

At this point, into the story enters a new figure, a man of about thirty, a man with an acne-pitted face, a man with an automatic rifle.

***

The wife wakes out of a disturbing dream and rolls over to look at the clock on her side of the bed. 5:00 A.M. It is too early to get up, too late to go back to sleep. She gets up. She had been sleeping in her robe. It has become an old friend to her; she thinks of it as her security blanket. She slips into slippers, shuffles softly into the kitchen, and gets a beer from the refrigerator, opening and closing the refrigerator door as carefully as she can. Her husband will sleep for another hour, her son for two more hours. She pulls off the tab and drinks from the can. The sky through the window is barely beginning to lighten. The hum of the refrigerator is like a mantra. In her red robe and slippers, the wife is a focal point for the whole room. She begins to cry.

***

The man is lying in bed, awake, putting off getting up and facing his wife. He is sure she is crying. He knows she will have started on her first beer of the day. The bedroom faces the east and the blinds are drawn; he can see nothing in the room but everything in his mind's eye. He is thinking about the woman he is having an affair with. She would like for him to get a divorce, marry her. He is afraid of what this would do to his wife. He feels he must somehow be the cause of his wife's drinking and that he has a responsibility to take care of her. He wonders what a divorce would do to his son. Maybe nothing. Maybe his son would welcome the event. The house has not been a happy one for a long time.

The man knows he is not going to get a divorce.

***

As for the problem of the letters, when our reply had no effect, we wrote again, making a suggestion: We offered to meet with the letters' author.

***

The man is in bed again, but now it is not his wife's bed. It is 10:00 A.M. on a Monday morning. He does not have to be at work because he owns his own business. At the same time that his secretary is on coffee break, he is touching his mistress's hair, kissing her eyelids, drawing her closer. The sheets and pillow-cases are navy with an Oriental floral design. He has told his mistress that the inside of a woman's thighs is the softest spot in the universe. Entering her is like going down to darkness and death. When he comes he feels resurrected.

***

After dinner that same night, the man steps out into his backyard to view the sky through his telescope. Cassiopeia is in her rocking chair; the Great Bear, hibernating, sparkles brightly. He enters the dome. This time his mistress is not with him. He adjusts the focus. The craters of the moon come into view, the lunar seas. The man's telescope gathers this far-flung light and transmits it to his eye. Before he goes in, he gives the telescope a loving pat. Both his wife and mistress refer to it in a patronizing way as his "hobby." He thinks of this small domed shell with its oblong slit for the long tongue of the telescope as a place of refuge. When he was a kid, he was enamored of Galileo and read everything he could find about him. His own son has no interest in astronomy. His son's thing is motorcycles.

***

The man with the automatic rifle is cleaning it, oiling and polishing it. He feels as if he is caressing it. He is doing this sitting on the side of the single bed in a room on the South Side.

***

The wife is watching reruns of "The Brady Bunch" on television. Her son is playing old Grateful Dead albums on the stereo in his room upstairs. She yells at him to turn the volume down, but he can't hear her over the noise. She swears and sits down again in front of the TV. She promises herself she will wash her hair tonight. Her hair is red; it has always been her best feature, but now she has to dye it because it has started coming in gray. Her red hair. The night she met her husband for the first time, seventeen years ago, she was wearing a black leather jacket, a black turtleneck sweater, a black skirt and boots. Her red hair, no gray in it then, glinting like copper, stoplight saying Go, spilled over her black-clad shoulders and black-clad back, and she knew red on black spelled temptation and danger. She had been wild and sweet, a belated beatnik, and now she is a middle-aged, middle-income suburban housewife and not-so-secret drinker. There are finely etched cross-hatchings on the pale skin of her face, and she wears glasses, medium-sized glasses with narrow translucent red plastic frames.

***

To continue. We received an answer to our answer. Really, it went beyond all tolerable bounds. There was a limit to what we could be expected to take.

The temperature had dropped, a nasty dive. The radiators in our house hissed. The house itself creaked from the cold. We made a fire, but even the fire seemed uncooperative, sullen. It kept dying out.

***

It is now Tuesday. The man is at his place of business, talking with his secretary. He is asking her to look up a certain file containing correspondence with a certain firm. When he retreats to his private office, he discovers that he is agitated, on edge. He cannot imagine why he should feel so jumpy. Then he realizes that his secretary is wearing the same perfume his mistress uses. This fact, that his mistress exists in a context of other women, that she buys and uses a product that thousands, perhaps millions of other women buy and use, profoundly upsets him. He feels he cannot afford to think about this.

***

The woman who was writing is now not writing but cleaning house. She derives a great deal of pride and emotional comfort from this house. Also, it is very near the place where her lover works.

***

The wife remembers the first house she and her husband lived in. They rented it from an elderly widow who had moved into an apartment complex. The wallpaper in the bathroom was hideous, with red, pink, and orange stripes, but they were afraid to hurt the widow's feelings by changing it.

When the baby came, they moved into a bigger house. This time they bought it. The wallpaper in the bathroom was fine, but they changed it anyway.

She had loved the new house before they moved into it. Then it had become something different, unfriendly—alive, an organism. It had fed on her. It grew warm and shiny and vital with her life-energy, and she had sensed herself growing colder, dull, angry. When she tried to explain this to her husband, he told her to get a job, get out of the house, do something. But what could she do? She had a baby. Now she has a teenaged son and her husband has a mistress. There is tit for tat somewhere in that. Tit for tat. She laughs.

***

The mistress would like to have a baby. Time is rapidly running out. She has tried to express her urgency to her lover, always keeping her tone light. Sometimes he goes away from her in his mind—she can tell. She can tell from his eyes, which are deep blue, from his face, which is worn, from his hands, where he displays his only sign of vanity in well-manicured, buffed nails. She is careful then to call him back with little jokes, asides, small indications of greater self-sufficiency. She knows he does not want her to be dependent on him, a drain. He already has a wife.

When she arrives at this last thought, she starts to cry, checks herself, and mops the kitchen floor. The sun is almost overhead, slanting through the window, its glare on the stainless-steel sink intense, demanding. Suddenly she feels weary and decides what the hell, the floor is all right without mopping.

***

We were describing the letters, how we decided to deal with them: head on. This time, therefore, we did not suggest. We simply announced that we could be found sitting in a certain restaurant at noon on a particular day. We picked a day some days away, in order to avoid conflicts with the letters' author's schedule, whatever that might be. We were unwilling to allow him to come to our house.

***

The New Year came and went. The candles were removed from their windows, the Christmas trees were stripped of their ornamentation and left on sidewalks for pickup, the downtown decorations disappeared. The city looked naked. No festivity about the town now! The starry nights no longer competed with the colored winking lights of Christmas, nor with candlelight. The earth had rolled farther along on its endless circuit, and the city was exposing its nether side, the grayish-whitish slush-brushed underlayer of the long turning year.

The sun came out, but still the snow refused to melt. Snow crystals scintillated among the massed dullness of snowbanks along the sides of streets. An exhibition of Chinese pottery opened at the Museum of Fine Arts. A new branch of the public library system opened on the expanding South Side; there was a brief ceremony and neighborhood reception; the mayor arrived late. Certainly nothing momentous in any of this.

A perfectly ordinary city, except in one particular: Unlike Moscow, London, New York, it happened to be where, at such-and-such a moment, *here* was.

It was now the twenty-third of January, a Wednesday.

***

The man who is loved by the woman who was writing is promising to drive his teenaged son to a motorcycle race track in Maryland next Sunday. The son is six-three, taller than his father, "and about three inches wide," his father likes to say. His father figures that being a participant in a supervised motorcycle competition is safer than being a sixteen-year-old automobile driver.

The boy is his father's most adored reason for living. Sometimes the father forgets this, but always the boy reminds him, merely by being, even by being a pain in the neck. Even the demands his son makes of him force him to recognize that it is exactly those demands that justify his own existence. He thinks there is precious little else that justifies it.

***

For the man who is a father is inclined to feel that he is a failure as a husband and a lover. He knows his wife and mistress cry when he is not around. He does not want either of them to cry.

***

Now:

***

The man with the automatic rifle has secreted the rifle under his overcoat. He has locked himself into a stall in the men's room in a downtown office building.

***

As in a rhyme, the woman who is married to the man who is the lover of the woman who was writing is sleeping next to her husband. She will wake early, restless, assaulted out of sleep by the twin desires that plague her, the desire to drink and the desire to stop drinking, a conflict that keeps her in perpetual turmoil, but for now she is sleeping, on her stomach, her right bare foot touching her husband's right leg, her left leg bent at the knee in childlike fashion.

***

The woman who was writing is also sleeping, in her double bed, alone. She envies wives, who sleep next to their husbands. She also luxuriates in the freedom she has, living alone, to be her worst self without reprimand. She thinks this must be the unhappiest restriction in marriage: being subject to someone else's approval or censure, having to look good, be good, do good all the time. She could never do this. She has said so to her lover, warning him against marrying her at the same time she pleads with him to marry her. He has told her that she doesn't understand marriage. She does not believe him.

***

The night watchman has made his rounds, and the man with the rifle is climbing the staircase of the office building.

At the top of the staircase, the man with the rifle breaks a padlock and steps out onto the roof. The night is extremely cold. He spends it huddled on the inside side of the door to the roof.

***

Everyone sleeps.

***

The sun comes out as if high-spiritedly in the morning. The temperature has soared to fifty degrees, a foresign of spring. By seven, the rest of the snow has melted away. The wife retreats to the bedroom, reclaims it for herself after her husband has left for work. Her son makes his own breakfast, grabs the lunch money his father has left on the kitchen counter, and leaves for school. His mother has not drunk her usual wake-up beer. She is pacing herself; she plans to do some shopping downtown today.

She makes up her face, pulls on skirt, sweater, stockings, shoes. Makes the bed. The silence in the house seems to emphasize the clatter in her own head—she feels as if she can almost hear her brain at work, thinking, gears grinding up for the day. She would as soon shut it down permanently.

The stores won't be open yet. She goes into the living room, sits down, picks up a book.

***

The husband is at work, finalizing the details of a contract with a subcontractor. He puts one party on hold while he talks with the other. The door to his office is partly open. He can see his secretary seated at her typewriter. She is wondering when would be the best time to tell him that he will have to hire a temporary replacement for her. She is pregnant and plans to stay out for at least a month after the baby comes.

***

The woman who was writing enjoys and prolongs the business of getting out of bed. She stretches her legs, turns on the bedside TV and listens to the news, and only then gets up. The bedcovers are rumpled. She stares at them for a moment, realizing she has never spent an entire night with her lover. Would she be less restless with him? More? She shrugs and gets dressed.

She pulls the kitchen window shade, lets it snap up. Sunshine plunges into the room, spilling over the linoleum floor like a wax.

She makes herself a piece of toast, eats a bowl of cereal, drinks orange juice, coffee. She is meeting her lover at noon. The morning seems long.

***

By eleven-thirty, the wife is on West Franklin. She discovers she has let herself drift into her husband's domain. She thinks briefly of finding a pay phone and calling him, suggesting they meet for lunch, then discards that idea as a bad one. He does not like to be called at work.

She has not actually bought anything yet; sometimes when she goes to town she comes home with nothing. But it is an achievement to have gone to town, to have spoken with salesgirls, moved among other lonely housewives, established for a while at least that the outside world is still there. She could use a drink.

***

The sniper is feeding the magazine into his M-16. He feels the sun's approach as he would any intruder's. He wishes he had brought shades, a cap with a visor. The sun ricochets off the rifle barrel, makes it look hot and sticky, the roof tarry.

***

The secretary is making her way into a crowded nearby restaurant, ordering a sandwich and soft drink to go. Waiting, she turns around and scans the restaurant. Her boss is here, in a booth on the side. She wonders if the woman he is with is his mistress—she knows he has one, has overheard whispered telephone conversations, sent flowers when he told her to. Taking a longer look, she approves of the woman's haircut, brown hair shaped in a pageboy, her face bare of make-up. She is too far away to see more than that. The woman in the booth looks up, catches the secretary's eye, her glance sliding away immediately, not recognizing that the woman at the takeout register is her lover's secretary. The cash register rings, bell-like. The secretary gathers her change, her order, and steps back out onto the sidewalk. It is now noon, and she walks slowly, liking the January sun's proleptic warmth.

***

It is a lovely day, the air full of the cool perfume of a spring day in the middle of winter. The secretary decides to eat her lunch in the courtyard that lies between the building she works in and the bank on the corner. She picks out a bench, takes her lunch out of the paper bag, unbuttons her coat but leaves it on. Above her, the sniper is trying out possible targets, fixing this person and then that one in the crosshairs. He has no intention of rushing, of hurrying over what he has for so long waited for.

***

The wife is trying on a dress in a boutique, one of the small stores on the fringe of the Fan District between the university and the downtown area. It is too young for her—too campy, too playful. The salesgirl asks if she wants it wrapped. She shakes her head no.

***

In the restaurant, we too were there. We had gone there to meet the author of the letters. We believed he would show up, if only out of curiosity, and he did.

We were calm, controlled. After all, we had had time too, time to decide what course we would follow, which responses we would allow him to notice and which we would keep to ourselves.

He did not look at all like the person we had expected. We had expected someone better dressed, with an air of authority, someone more commanding than that person facing us from the opposite side of the table. We were interested to know what this meant, this person's presence's being so plainly at odds with the voice in the letters.

There was an awkward lull at the start, and then we began to speak directly to the issue. We asked him what he wanted of us.

Greater significance! he said. More meaning!

We were ashamed, guilt-struck.

A deeper analysis of character, he continued.

We were full of remorse, and yet we asked how we could possibly have done any better than we had. We had done our best, we said.

Not good enough, he said, slapping his right hand down on the table top. He was holding a hot dog in his left hand.

He had gotten mustard on his tie—hardly the most dignified of figures. Yet he knew as well as we did that all power rested on his side of the table: We were the ones who had allowed ourselves to be scrutinized and judged. It had not been unavoidable. We chose to do what we did.

But it was precisely for that reason that we were so vulnerable. What we did mattered enough to us for us to have chosen to do it.

He was rubbing at the spot on his tie with a paper napkin he had wetted in his glass of water. While his head was down, we saw that he was going bald. This made us feel, however frivolously, surer of ourselves: He was as mortal and fallible and corruptible as the rest of us. We tried to hang onto this thought when he returned his attention to us.

Give up, he said. Quit. The world is already overrun with trivia.

We looked him in the eye. No, we said.

Well, that's a helluva note, he said.

Nevertheless.

All right, all right. It's your life.

Exactly, we said.

If you want to throw it away.

***

We said nothing.

I mean, he said, *I'm* not going to stop you. Jesus Christ, I've got better things to do with my time.

***

We doubt it, we said.

Aha. Sarcasm, the last line of defense for any writer.

We were realizing that what we had said could have been taken two ways, one against us. He was too stupid to catch the ambiguity.

Jonathan Swift? we argued. W. H. Auden?

Irrelevant. Objection overruled.

We decided to let him make the next move.

***

The sniper has placed his rifle aside again. He is experiencing the strangest sensation: He feels as if the sunlit air is water, and that he is floating dreamily upon it. He blinks his eyelids, trying to clear his head. His arms and hands seem limp, muscleless. Impotent.

***

The wife returns to the street. It is 12:55.

***

The wife's husband and his mistress rise out of the booth, put on their coats, and pay the check. While they are standing at the cashier counter, the mistress picks up two creamy mint patties at two cents each and glances at her lover, querying him with raised eyebrows. He smiles and tells the cashier to add four cents to the bill. His mistress gives him one of the mint patties and they both pop the patties into their mouths, slipping the balled-up tin-foil wrappings into their pockets. This simple action has much affected them both. They feel connected, alive, and for one memorable moment anyway, irresponsible.

***

It is 1:00 P.M. Only the son is not present at this next scene. It is he on whom the consequences of what happens now will devolve.

***

The sniper passes a hand over his eyes. He has resolved his intention, the purposive relation between himself and this place he is in. He picks up the gun, takes aim, pulls the trigger, and shoots.

***

The point is, the author of the letters was saying, some things are necessary, others are not.

***

We agreed. Our disagreement was only in deciding which was which.

An example, he said. Some writers of fiction are necessary, while others are not.

We disagreed.

Of course you would, he said. You would have to.

Not because of that.

What, then?

An example, we said, and we narrated a short story about a man, his wife, his mistress, his secretary, and his son. Then we got up to leave.

But the ending? he said.

Yes, we said. That's what you need us for. The ending.

A cheap trick, he said, scowling. A cheap trick. His complexion was bruise-colored, with a strong undertone of orange. He looked as if he was a candidate for a heart attack at some future date. He had those creases in his ear lobes that are said to indicate a weakness in that direction.

We don't care, we said.

***

The sun had moved behind a cloud, and it was winter again. Here we were, in the place we had started out from. We stood on the sidewalk, liking that melancholic mood. Then we went home.

***

Of course, we thought later, he made the mistake of taking us at our word. Maybe there was no ending, or none that we could tell. Maybe the ending was out of our hands as well. Who knew what ending a beginning might lead to?

We were ourselves only part of a larger story, whose ending we could not know, a denouement that would find us whether or not we could find it. Such is the nature of eschatology, or shall we say simply, the study of *last things*. The conclusion, lost to us in mystery, reveals itself in the act of self-knowledge, God's mind learning its own power.

II

ABOUT MY NOVELS, BEGINNING WITH THE FIRST

The novel I envisioned would begin as comedy and end in tragedy. It was to be a narrative Möbius strip, the twist seamless, central, and revelatory.

That was the idea, anyway. I would make sure each half of the novel contained the possibility of the other half.

I did not want to write a first novel about my childhood. I didn't feel ready to attempt a novel about my childhood. Although I did make use of more recent autobiographical elements, I was pleased when, after the novel was published, I heard from readers who assumed I, like Tennessee Settleworth, had attended medical school. To view the world from a perspective not one's own is one of the primary satisfactions of writing fiction as it is of reading fiction.

Novels often are read as if they were autobiographical or reportorial accounts, but the novelist doesn't just tell a story: she creates a world in which various and numerous characters interact with one another and the circumstances in which they discover themselves. In *Sick and Full of Burning*, the protagonist arrives at a conclusion about the extent of anyone's moral responsibility: Is she her sister's keeper? Yes, she decides, so long as she remembers that her first duty is to survive. The first duty of *all* life, she concludes, is to live. But her conclusion is contradicted by her behavior, which is contingent upon the narrative's events: Tennessee risks her life on behalf of Lulu and Cameron Carlisle. She is not prepared to die for someone else, but preparedness is not a relevant issue.

It seems to me that there are statements that can be made that are both contradictory and true. Must our moral responsibility to others transcend that to ourselves? I don't know how to answer this except by saying, "Yes and no."

The Old Testament, of course, says, "Choose life," and it is only by choosing life that we can encounter subsequent dilemmas. Do we possess free will or are our actions and even ideas and feelings determined by external or internal factors? I began to realize that I might be tracking a series or, more precisely, sequence of philosophical questions to each of which the only answer was "yes and no." To look ahead before returning to *Sick and Full of Burning*: In my second novel, *Augusta Played*, two characters, a young husband and wife, are equal and opposite forces, Augusta an embodiment of the idea of free will, Norman of the idea of determinism. A comedy that ends in divorce rather than marriage, this novel contains the contradiction that the marriage cannot contain.

My sequence of questions went astray with the third novel I wrote, for that novel was never published. In "Paula," I asked how, if we assume we act as free agents, we should act when our desires conflict with those of another. The extreme case, it seemed to me, would be murder. I wrote "Paula" during a period of depression and while carrying an impossible, debilitating workload, and the result was not publishable.

So there is a gap in the sequence, and my third published novel addressed what in my mind was the fourth question. *In the Wink of an Eye* (my title was "The Revolution of the World," but the editor vetoed that and supplied the published title), pursues this question: Choosing to live together, how shall we go about establishing a society that is just? Can a just society be founded by revolution? Again, the answer seems to me to be, obviously, "Yes and no." I think of *In the Wink of an Eye* as a political cartoon. It is not quite satire, unless Samuel Butler's *Erewhon* is satire, but something closer in mood to *A Midsummer Night's Dream*, which was, in fact, the novel's hidden model. (I felt gleeful about disobeying Northrop Frye's dictum that one ought not combine satire and fantasy.) *In the Wink of an Eye* is narratively a *reductio ad absurdum*, the contradiction in revolution spinning itself out and out, all the way into outer space. *The Lost Traveller's Dream*, which followed, was presented as a novel but intended as a book of interlinked stories. If I had thought of calling it "a novel in stories" I would have suggested that, but the publisher wanted to market it as a novel for the sake of sales. Against my better judgment, I agreed to add material to clarify connections. This added material did not really fit; it damaged the book—and to no avail, since the publisher sold almost no copies. Ironically, the book appeared in 1984, at the very moment short story collections began to be seen as marketable.

Indeed, as it became increasingly difficult for me to publish my novels, I turned to stories as a back door into publishing. (Another writer might have been content to write for her desk drawer, but I have always hoped for readers, the unread work seeming, to me, as soundless as the tree that falls unheard.) Nevertheless, I have preferred to develop my stories into book-length (or longer) objects rather than merely assemble them as collections.

The sequence of questions has thus by now been abandoned. I no longer concern myself with it, but because contradiction is basic to my understanding of the structure of the universe and mind, a reader might locate and trace a continuing line of inquiries. (In my next book of fiction, *My Life and Dr. Joyce Brothers*, billed by the publisher as "a novel in stories" but the first entry in what I think of as a long story cycle although a narrative arcs novelistically forward through the whole, contradiction is embedded in the figure of the child, who is, as various clues indicate, both "real" and a metaphor for "the child within.")

The one end of the thread, however, remains clear in *Sick and Full of Burning*. I have called attention to it partly to illustrate that the novelist's most direct and self-exposing relation is to the work as a whole, not to a character or characters in it, but certainly she cares about her characters, cares deeply and wants to know them as well as she can. Tennessee, as the book opens, has been emotionally hurt and is reluctant to invest her feelings in anyone. As the narrative progresses, she learns to love the handicapped teenager she tutors. As the book closes, she realizes that, having risked her life for someone, she has acquired the courage to risk her heart for her current boyfriend, Adrien. A few radical feminists thought the book's ending was too traditional, but when Tennessee calls Adrien in New Hope, Pennsylvania, her "new hope" is not necessarily for a future with him—that may or may not materialize, and in the meantime, she is still pursuing her medical studies—but for whatever life might thrive amid rubble and ruin, chaos and destruction.

That rubble and ruin, the apartment after the fire, are the outward sign of the inner devastation that is the underside of the first half of the novel. It is now uppermost. Yet Tennessee, at least, is stronger and braver than she was when the novel opened.

Finally, I would like to mention what I think of as "the sex scene." In the early seventies, novels by women (not that there were many in a literary world that felt it deserved congratulations for publishing any women at all) usually included a sex scene; I suppose we thought we needed to enter every territory that had been claimed by men. It seemed important to show that we, too, could get down and dirty. I felt a sex scene was almost mandatory, and I thought it would be both funny and telling to have it take place between a woman and technology instead of between a woman and a man.

Until the early seventies—if not until last week—men were assumed to know more about women than women did. A then-famous editor ("Ace Winters" in *Sick and Full of Burning*), rejecting a story of mine, explained that a woman could not think the way the character in my story thought. We were having lunch in the most expensive restaurant I'd ever eaten in. I remember smiling deferentially—it *was* his expense account—while frantically trying to fight my way through the illogic of his pronouncement. Another then-famous editor said to me, in the elevator of a building that housed the prestigious magazine for which he worked, "If you want to be a serious writer, you must not have children." A then-famous novelist challenged me to prove him wrong about my sexuality: "Since you refuse to sleep with me," he said, "I have to think that you are lesbian." We were in a diner on the Lower East Side; I think I'd ordered a grilled-cheese sandwich. Did he imagine I was concerned with what he thought about my sexuality? A then-famous publisher ("Maury Goldberg" in *Sick and*

Full of Burning) told me, over drinks at the St. Regis, "If you're going to write a novel, go home and start writing." At once, I realized that here was a man who *did* know something. Reaching under the table and gently removing his hand from my knee, I said thank you and good night, caught a cab, and went home. I was then living, as did Tennessee, in the small upstairs maid's-room in my employer's duplex apartment. I shut the door and began writing *Sick and Full of Burning*.

FROM *AUGUSTA PLAYED*

Norman

It was the season of second thoughts. Norman fretted over the lack of free-dom in the world, as he saw it. He felt constrained and irritable, like a child in a playpen. He walked up Broadway to Columbia, hunched over in his unbelted Burberry trench coat, bucking the chill wind, and if he appeared to be carry-ing the weight of the world on his shoulders, it was because he was carrying the weight of the world on his shoulders. You see, if every proposition had to be either true or false, then the proposition "It is true that Norman Gold will marry Augusta" *had been* true or false, but *not* neither or both, long before they'd met each other; from eternity, in fact. And the proposition "It is true that Norman Gold will accomplish a revolution in intellectual thought" was already determined, came with its truth-value attached to it like a luggage tag. Or if truth or falsity only descended upon a proposition at a certain time, like the Shechinah, the Light of lights, on Mount Sinai when Moses received the Ten Commandments, or over the Shabbas feast on Friday at sunset, what happened to the conditional tense? "If Norman marries Gus, he will (will not) accomplish a revolution in intellectual thought"—was that true, false, both, or none of the above? The clear sky seemed hard as ice, as if a well-aimed pick might chip off cubes of cloud.

Norman and Augusta

Norman and Augusta were married at City Hall on the last day of January, with Philip Fleischman, Norman's erstwhile blood-brother, and Phil's current girl, Dinky, acting as witnesses. Gus wore pale yellow wool, a navy coat, and bone-colored shoes and panty-hose, but the sleet turned the toes of her shoes black when the wedding party returned to the street.

"Right," Phil said, with a great air of taking charge, "who wants a drink?"

They went to Max's Kansas City, because Phil had a car and because he said Max's Kansas City was the place to go. Gus and Norman, as Upper West Siders, were both inclined to lose track of which was "the" place to go. Phil mocked himself for knowing the in-scene and blamed it on his profession, trendiness being an occupational hazard of counter-culture advertising, but the innocent glow in his round cheeks gave him away. For Phil, heaven was eating chickpeas in a crowded room with red walls screened by swirling smoke.

For Gus, heaven was being called "Mrs. Gold."

"Here's to Mrs. Norman Gold," Phil said, holding his glass high in the air. At that moment, the crowd standing next to their booth swung in their direction, an unpredicted surge of the human current, and connected with Phil's shoulder. The glass tipped, the drink spilled, and Dinky ended up with a lap full of liquor. During the confusion, Norman sprang his surprise on Gus: "Guess where we're spending the night," he said, whispering mysteriously into her ear. He named a hotel.

"You're crazy!"

"Bridal suite." His heart was full of love, overflowing like Phil's drink.

A suspicion entered Gus's mind. "Phil put you up to this, didn't he?"

"Phil," Dinky said disgustedly, "isn't capable of putting anybody up to anything. Or anything up to anybody."

"You don't even know what they're talking about," Phil said to Dinky. "Here, dry your own lap."

Norman said, "This conversation is getting entirely too gross for newlyweds. Gus and I are splitting."

"Where are we going?" Gus asked.

"You know."

"I don't," Dinky said.

"But I have to go home first. To pack."

"I packed for you," Norman said.

"The suitcase is in the car," Phil said.

Gus was not sure she liked this. She had thought she was getting married of her own free will, but it was beginning to feel as though she was being abducted.

Norman paid the check and they walked two by two back to the car. The wind was cutting a path down the street like a lawnmower made of air, whirring over the pavement. Dinky, a brunette model with exophthalmic eyes and a trick of wetting her lips with her tongue between words as if her speech might otherwise stall at her large, white teeth—it gave her a faintly oiled character, in keeping with the cosmetic and perfumery oils that surrounded her—said, "My skirt is going to freeze under my coat. Thanks to you, Philip. I'm going to get arthritis in my pelvis and be frigid for the rest of my life."

"If you ask me," Phil said, "you've got arthritis of the brain." He retrieved the suitcase from the trunk. "We could give you a lift," he said to Norman.

"No," Norman said, cutting him off quickly, hailing a cab. He wanted to be alone with Gus as soon as possible. Christ, she was his wife, and he hadn't yet had a second of peace in which to think what that might mean. It had to mean more than chickpeas in Max's Kansas City. All the way to the hotel, he was silent, thinking, his hand on Gus' bone-colored knee, a smile slung across his face in a wide loop like a lariat, smoke from his cigarette curling upward into his long lashes. Sleet coated the taxi's windshield, and with every sweep of the wipers, there was a thick whooshing sound that reached them in the back seat.

"Some weather," the driver said.

"Yeah," said Norman.

"You guys don't look like you're from out of town, if you know what I mean."

"We're not. And that's no guy," Norman said, jerking his thumb at Gus, "that's my wife."

"Hee, hee, hee," the driver laughed, drawing air inward with each long, harsh syllable. He never seemed to exhale. His back and shoulders, bent over the wheel, just kept rising, filling with heated air from the dashboard vents, the stink of gasoline and wet wool and cigarette smoke. Norman listened to the man's indrawn laughter and imagined the day when he would simply float through the roof of his cab, literally carried away by some joke.

Gus pulled at Norman's coat sleeve. She had been thinking too. The plan had been that they would return to her apartment, finish putting her stuff in boxes, spend the night, and in the morning, on the first of February, move her in to Norman's place. He lived on West Eighty-eighth, and like her, he had only one room, but his room was larger. She would have liked to keep her old room as a private studio, but they couldn't afford it, not with sources of income being cut off all around them. How could they pay for this? She tugged at his sleeve again, but he still didn't notice. In a fit of desperation, a kind of ontological claustrophobia, she said in a voice much too loud, "What about Tweetie-Pie?"

"Your wife has a lithp," the driver said. "Hee, hee, hee!"

"You," Gus said to the driver, "are an ass."

"Phil will bring him over in the morning," Norman said to Gus.

"I'm an arhth," the driver said. "Hee, hee, hee!"

That braying was still echoing in Norman's head after he and Gus—his wife—had been shown to their room and he had tipped the bellhop and shut the door and they had both thrown their coats on the settee in the first of the two rooms that composed their suite. He had managed to sign the register and stand upright without his knees buckling out from under him in the elevator, but he was sure the eyes of the hotel had been trained on him all the way. Now he and Gus were alone in a strange room and the quietness of it was overwhelming, appalling. Normally, being alone with Gus was an unself-conscious pleasure, but here, in this suite of rooms designed for Love with a capital L, every object in it invisibly labeled LOVE, Norman felt as if he'd been handed a sheet of instructions or a list of standards to be met. The settee shouted LOVE, the drapes shouted LOVE, the bed in the next room shouted LOVE, all in a disappearing ink visible only to the infra-red eyes of people in the know, the throbbing outlines of the letters pounding against his informed retinae.

"Take a look at this," Gus said, calling from the bedroom. "One of us, me I guess, is supposed to take a bath in this bathroom in here, and meanwhile"—she left the bedroom and walked back to the sitting room—"you take your bath in this bathroom in here. That way I'm in bed waiting for you when you come in, in your robe and pajamas."

"I don't have any pajamas."

"Well," she said, "then we'll have to forget the whole thing. Scrub the whole marriage. It just isn't going to work if you walk through that door in your jockey shorts. That is obviously not what the architect had in mind."

"Your feet must be soaking wet. Why don't you take your shoes off?"

"Okay." But when Gus had her shoes and panty-hose off, Norman put his hand on her cool calf, and ran his fingers up the inside of her leg, inching them under the elastic leg band of her bikini underpants.

"Take your dress off," Norman commanded.

They were standing by the window in the sitting room but the drapes were closed. . .heavy, figured drapes that made the room seem timeless—as if the room were airtight, sealed against the world and the corruption of change. A languid gold light, overrich as syrup, lay in thick, inert pools on the deep-pile carpet.

Gus reached both arms around her back to unzip her dress, and the action twisted her at an angle so exquisite in relation to Norman that she nearly fainted. Norman had to take his hand away to pull the dress over her head, and he brought her underpants down when he did. Then she shut her eyes as he drew the dress over her face and took her into his arms, dispensing with the bra, and when she opened them again, looking over his navy-suited shoulder in the direction of the door, she saw the bellhop.

She screamed.

The bellboy jumped. He would have put Nureyev to shame. He jumped so high, kicking his legs to turn around at the same time, that he could almost be said to be dancing. But he wasn't dancing. He was running, out of an instinct as old as the Lascaux Caves, an instinct for self-preservation that said it was not safe to look at another man's naked wife. It was evidently an instinct with as much urgency behind it in the twentieth century as in the Pleistocene period, and if Norman was anything to go by, it had retained its validity, because Norman turned around, saw the bellhop, and wanted to kill.

The bellhop had fled, a single, useless, courteous phrase left lingering behind him in the room, the result of a kind of time-lag as if he were traveling faster than the speed of sound. It was, "Compliments of the management, sir," and it had been delivered with a magnum of champagne in an ice pail which the boy dropped clattering on the coffee table as he turned tail and ran. Norman took off after him.

The first leg of the race was a straight stretch of hotel carpeting from the room to the elevator; then there was a hallway-crossing, and the bellhop made a sharp swerve to the left. Norman caught hold of him in front of an open linen closet.

"You fucking popeyed bastard," he said (strictly metaphorically, as the boy, unlike Norman, had not even been thinking of fucking, and, unlike Dinky, was not at all exophthalmic, *and*, as Norman was to learn later, was definitely not illegitimate).

"*You fucking popeyed bastard*," Norman said again, with emphasis, unable to think of anything else—and kayoed him with a left uppercut to the jaw and a right to the stomach (Norman was left-handed).

The boy fell backward into the closet, bringing down shelves of sheets, pillowcases, towels, washcloths, toilet paper, detergent, and a broom. Maids materialized from nowhere, blossoming in the doorways of rooms all along the hall, like primroses springing up after an April shower.

They were standing there, the primrose maids, dumbstruck, and the bell-boy was lying there, among the linen, and Norman slowly began to realize what he had done. Without saying a word to anyone, carefully, like a silent film re-winding, he edged back in the direction he had come. When he was around the corner, he tore back to the room. Gus had locked the door.

"For God's sake, Gus," he shouted in a stage whisper, "let me in!"

Gus opened the door and he whisked into the room but she latched the door again afterward. She was dressed in jeans and one of his shirts but her face was as white as dough and as ready to crumble as a matzo cracker. "What happened?" she said.

"I hit him."

"You what?"

"What do you think I did? Asked him back to play gin rummy?"

"It's not funny."

"I'm not laughing."

Gus was. Hysterically. "Oh God," she said. "I'm sorry, Norman, but you should have seen the look on your face when you turned around and saw him."

Norman didn't at all like being laughed at, and, disgruntled, answered, "I was looking at the look on *his* face when he saw *you*."

This sobered her up. "The whole hotel will know," she said. "You were still dressed."

"What has that got to do with it?" he asked, puzzled.

"Well," she said, "well. . . I don't know how to explain it, but it has a lot to do with it. It's so. . . unequal, somehow."

"You're not in North Carolina," he said. "Nobody's going to be shocked. We were only doing what you're expected to do in hotels. You can guess what goes on in the other rooms."

"But they aren't bridal suites."

Norman was beginning to feel beleaguered, and he did not quite understand why this should be so, particularly on his wedding day. Holding himself in with the last of his patience, he took one more stab at getting through to Gus. She was *supposed* to be a fairly rational person; she was *supposed* to be straightforward, as girls went. How could the simple process of becoming a bride scramble a woman's brains beyond recognition?

"Gus," he said, "that is all the more reason they won't be shocked to hear that you took your clothes off in this room."

"It's not the same thing," Gus said, wistfully. "For you to be dressed and me not is almost decadent. You can tell that by the layout of the bathrooms. We weren't *supposed* to start making love the minute we walked through the door."

Norman flung himself on the settee and tried to think. It seemed to him that lately he was thinking more and enjoying it less.

There, on the coffee table in front of him, was the champagne.

"I guess we could have a glass of champagne," he said. "If I can get the cork off." He was half afraid to try.

But the cork came off beautifully, and Norman managed to pour the champagne into the chilled glasses successfully, and that made him begin to feel better, and after a while he called room service and ordered Chateaubriand. Unfortunately, the radiator went on the blink, and the hotel had to send up a man to fix it because the room was growing cold, and he, the man, came up with the food. He talked all during dinner. He directed all of his observations, which were chiefly about the weather, the plumbing, hippies, and, for some reason, Howard Hughes, to Norman, man to man, dumping Gus conversationally, so that she felt like a dangling participle. She kept looking at him while he was talking—he seemed to think it was all right for a woman to look at him—trying to determine whether he had heard about their contretemps, but she couldn't decide yes or no. After he left, the radiator resumed its comfortable hissing, and the room grew warm again, as if someone had spread an invisible blanket over the settee and coffee table and chairs and carpet. She watched a late movie while Norman read the newspaper which the maintenance man had left behind, and when the screen said THE END, she went to the window and drew the heavy draperies wide open. It was snowing. The flakes were as large and soft as cotton balls. Illumined by the street light, snow edging the sill looked like lace; falling against the traffic lights, it looked like colored sugar—spun sugar, because it was spun in the sky by the winter wind and spiraled downward in a vast and lovely confusion.

"I packed a nightgown for you," Norman said, behind her.

"I saw."

"It's getting late." He was proceeding cautiously, testing gently, wishing he could read her mood in the way she stood. Her hair was so close to his mouth that it seemed it might leap to his tongue, like nylon to a metal comb. It was as if her whole body was breathing, and he wanted to inhale every inch of it. "Do you want me to meet you in bed, as planned by the architect?"

She nodded, not yet quite ready to shatter her mood of snow, but when they were both in the big bed in the other room, she whispered, in the dark, "Norman, I'm scared."

He didn't answer at first, not knowing what she expected of him. "I think," he said, "it's natural. At least, I hope it is, because I am scared shitless. But I'm not sure you should tell me that's how you feel if that's how you feel."

"Why on earth not, if that's how I feel?"

"Look at it, Gus," He lit a cigarette. "You're telling me you're not sure I'm right for you. It may be a natural fear but hearing you state it is not exactly reassuring to me. If you ask me," he said, "it's a classic demonstration of displaced hostility."

"Nobody asked you. Would you mind putting out that cigarette? The smoke isn't good for my lungs."

"You never told me that before, Gus."

"You never asked. I've worked very hard to develop my diaphragm muscles."

Norman stubbed the cigarette out in the ashtray on his side of the bed. He had to use the butt as a flashlight to locate the ashtray on the table, before he could stub it out.

"Anyway," Gus said, "you already got your own back by telling me you're just as scared as I am. I don't know why we shouldn't be a little nervous. It's not every day that people vow to spend the rest of their lives together."

Norman felt as if his heart was a rose planted in the garden of his soul, and somebody was digging it up for transplant, every root torn from its rightful place. "Do you think you may have made a mistake?" he asked her, barely able to squeeze the question past his throat.

"That's not it!" What was it? A sense of missed possibility. She would have liked to marry the world; instead, she was cutting herself off from most of it.

And she did mean "marry," not "sleep with." Or maybe "sleep with" *was* what she meant. How could she know, if she'd never found out? "Norman," she pleaded, thinking of the wide world to be seen, "let's go to Africa."

"Sure. First thing in the morning," he said.

"I'm serious. To see the hippopotami."

"And the rhinoceri."

"And the anthropophagi."

"Wildebeests."

"Elephants."

"Giraffes! Zebras! Gazelles!"

"The poisonous horned viper!"

"Come on, what do you know from horned vipers?"

"You see," Gus said, weeping, sitting up, and biting her knee, "you see how little you know about me? My father used to work in a zoo. When he was putting himself through school. He was an assistant."

"Take it easy," Norman said, "you're hysterical."

"I'm not, I'm not." She did know perfectly well what she was doing, but she couldn't stop herself; she wanted him to be just as alarmed as she was. When she caught the note of panic in his voice, she calmed down.

"Hey," he said, soothing her, "relax." He pulled her down beside him and stoked her forehead until she was still. It seemed to him that he held his future in his arms, and that it was going to require infinite attention and tenderness if it was to turn out the way he wanted. Deep exhaustion seized him.

So Gus pretended to fall asleep in Norman's arms, but he fell asleep first. The radiator stopped steaming. The room grew cold again; Augusta's nose on the outside of the blanket felt as cold to her own touch as a puppy's muzzle. She used to have a dog called Caesar. It seemed to her unbearably sad, that she once had a dog called Caesar and no longer did. She listened to Norman's breathing. There was always something urgent about it, his sleep-breath, something super-intense, as if to breathe by night called for as much concentration as thinking by day. It seemed to Gus odd that she could never know her own night breathing as she knew Norman's, this rasp scrabbling through the netherside of day like a mole through mud: it was already imprinted in her brain along with the coded pattern of her own heartbeat. Time, slowed almost to a standstill, might be measurable only by some such corporeal signature. Then Gus thought of something else, and smiled to herself in the dark: Norman was sleeping with the light off.

Esther and Sidney

It may be, in fact it almost surely was although the unconscious is not to be treated too familiarly but with a certain respect, that one reason Sidney had never divorced Esther was that in the back of his mind he knew this moment would come; and while Esther would not have wished for it, she felt as if her natural talents at last had found a mode of expression. They turned to each other almost with an air of elation, though it was muted by Sidney's dark side, the profound pessimism that always underlay his manic temporizing, and by Esther's unsureness, the habit of self-doubt that came from years of living in a social world foreign to her inner temperament, altering her personality to fit the world when it was the garment of world that was too large, cut unsuitably, like her mink coat. Nevertheless, it was if Sidney and Esther discovered in their old age the reason they had married each other forty-two years before, in 1926, on a day when it seemed to Esther the whole line of her forefathers must have been ranged invisibly along the walls, smiling behind their invisible beards, and the sun had been shining and the trashcans gleamed as if they were made of silver and flashed like diamonds and even what the horses left in the streets gleamed like ebony, and in the distance a radio played "All Alone by the Telephone," and later Sidney kept trying to talk to her father about the Scopes trial, which the day was the anniversary of although it was also their wedding day; and this discovery was a cause of jubilation, however modified it might be for the sake of appropriateness and to the eyes of outsiders. In fact, the only visible sign of it was a heightened flush in Esther's age-soft cheeks, a sharpened modesty in her pale green eyes as if she were newly aware of her husband's affection for her; and in Sidney, the yearning in his glance as he pushed himself up from the sofa and the Désirée pillows in Birdie's apartment and clasped Esther's hand in his. For if Birdie was the twin of his soul, what Sidney needed now was someone to minister to the needs of his body, needs that Birdie could not yet fully understand, and, Sidney felt, ought not, because she was only forty-one or -two, and although Birdie was beginning to think that was old, she was, so far as Sidney was concerned, only a baby yet—too young to be told the facts of death. After all, she had not even gone through menopause yet. And Sidney remembered Esther's hot flashes and erratic depressions with an immediate welling of sentiment. He had fought McCarthyism by day, contending with Esther's change of life at night, and while both had left him frazzled in 1953, the absurdity of the relation now endeared Esther to him tremendously, as if it were a wholly new event and not one which he had just relived in retrospect in the space of a few seconds.

FROM *IN THE WINK OF AN EYE*

Rosita's House

At first there were only the *pawiches* on the edges of the plots cleared from the jungle, tree stumps still smoking. Later, there were tin-roofed shacks, the roofs covered with flattened oil drums and the outer walls slammed together from scraps of old lumber. Finally, for Rosita, there was a cabin constructed of bamboo sticks and mats of woven palm leaves (with even some cardboard thrown in), and a calamine roof.

Miguel pounded nails in the walls as pegs for clothes and backpacks. Rosita hung white cotton curtains at the two windows. There were two rooms, a front room and a back room, one window to a room. In the front room, there were a table, four straight-backed chairs with cane seats, and a cooking platform of adobe with a small fire going on top of it. Soon there would be electricity, a hot plate. . . . In the back room, there was only the bedding of their sleeping bags, but Rosita slashed one side of each open and sewed them together to make one double-sized sleeping bag. In hot weather, they slept on top instead of inside.

One day Ramón showed up while Miguel was out. Rosita asked him in, gave him a cup of coffee.

"I brought you something," Ramón said, flushing under his deep olive skin and reaching into the bag he had hung on the peg by the door when he entered.

Mewing? Rosita heard mewing!

He handed her a ball of fur; it was hardly more than that.

It had blue eyes, a white face with black markings over its eyes that made it look terribly, terribly sad. Poor little thing!

"I saved it from the stew," Ramón said.

Rosita held the kitten tenderly in her arms, snuggling it to her breasts.

As Rosita petted and the kitten purred, Ramón imagined himself in the kitten's place.

The Jungle

The sleepy rivers of the jungle were being awakened by new travelers upon them, virginal rivers penetrated by the insolent lanchas bearing equipment. Reedy passageways parted. Trees over a hundred and eighty feet high, some already dead, were felled, an immense task because their apparently endless trunks were trapped in an elaborate network of smaller trees, woody lianas, and creeper vines. Some of the trees had enormous flat plank roots. Miguel's men swung their machetes. The tall, fallen, defeated trees, bleached by moonlight, were like the carcasses of sharks fouled in safety nets. When they dried up, the men burned or bulldozed them. Drilling equipment, dragged for miles through the jungle and relayed across rivers by pulleys, lay under tarpaulin in the same soft, muted moonlight. In the camp, radios played dance music, as faint as if it were an echo of itself. People played poker. Ping-Pong. Rolled dice. And at the camp's edge, behind mammoth trees and thick grass, men and women made love.

Butterflies, folding their forewings over their backs, gathered in sleeping assemblies for the night, hundreds to a branch—the same branch they returned to each migration. A howler monkey screamed. A timamo ruffled her wings, floated an inch off her perch, settled down again, and tucked her head beneath her wing. A snake slid silkily as a live scarf down a wire-thin smooth-barked liana, as if wrapping itself around a woman's neck—quick and deadly embrace. A heavy silence dropped over the jungle, a shroud. Night died into midnight.

Rosita, in her little tin-roofed shack, slept in Miguel's arms, but her dreams were uneasy, unfulfilled. The sad-faced kitten curled between them, its fur as soft as a sigh against Rosita's sleeping wrist.

Miguel

He had a broken view of a paved side street. It was part of the highway that led from Cochabamba to Santa Cruz de la Sierra. Donkey-drawn carts mingled with automobiles and vans. Engineers in Burpee Hybrid Seed caps mingled with Indian women in bowler hats and unmarried Mennonite girls in white organdy *Kapps*. The road was layered with dust, the sky gray with clouds rolling in all the way from the Atlantic. A cartload of clay pots, bound for the open market, the *mercado central*, rattled past. Out of range of the window, to the right, Miguel knew, was the large government-operated oil refinery.

"Surface rights only," the general manager said, signing with a pen that leaked.

With great flair, Miguel unwrapped the red bandana from his neck, leaned over, and blotted the ink. The general manager scowled.

"Surface rights only," Miguel said, nodding, knowing that a little matter like the legality of drilling for oil in a certain location would be seen for the tiny technicality it was, when backed up by pistols, single-shot rifles, clip-fed semiautomatic Garands or M-1s and fully automatic M-16s, a couple of Belgian FAL automatic rifles, a bazooka, tele-explosive mine devices, and a sixteen-caliber sawed-off shotgun mounted on a tripod constructed by its own butt in conjunction with a pair of legs and fitted with a projecting stick for launching Molotov cocktails.

Besides, the government would be grateful if anything could be done with the Green Hell. They'd try to take it over, of course, but by then it would be too late.

The three officers of the Euro-Bolivian Real Estate and Livestock Co., a sweaty-browed trinity, were dabbing at their foreheads with white linen handkerchiefs. The transaction was complete. Papers were shuffled.

The general manager unscrewed himself from his chair and came around to the front of his desk.

Miguel rose from his chair and stretched. He felt sleepy and relaxed, as if he had just made love.

"It was wise of you," Miguel said, "to cut your losses."

"I repeat. We will find you."

"*Sí, sí,*" Miguel said, laughing. "But, *hombre*, what will you do with us when you do?" And he bared his dogteeth again, at the same time extracting a large knife from inside his shirt and running his thumb along the blade.

He reached out his hand and the manager cringed, but instantly the knife was in his other hand, and he was shaking the manager's hand, while the manager blinked in surprise.

"*Hasta la vista,*" Miguel said, pumping the manager's hand up and down.

Ramón's Dream

Although the Green Hell now offered barracks and cots, Ramón, like many of the men, preferred the old way of a hammock under the moon.

He strung up his hammock; but it was a moonless night. He listened to the dark. The jungle's night-noises harmonized with the twenty-four-hour pumping of the great rigs, the thump-thud of the Kelly and the clink-clang of the engines, the vibrating of the standpipes and suction tanks through which drilling fluid flowed. It was an orchestration of the primeval with the technological, and it filled Ramón with a wild anxiety.

He could smell the oil, mud, salt water, the sulphuric and nitrogen oxides from the refinery which were sprayed into the atmosphere around it and enveloped everything in a haze even during the day. . .could smell the sour-water smell of gas, the open refinery sewers and oil separators and catalyst regenerators . . . could see black smoke rising in columns above the turbines. From the circulating water system in the drilling area came a continuous whining hum, loud, as if it were the voice that all men's voices, mingled together, would make: a plaintive pitch like a thin thread woven through the strangely musical fabric of the Bolivian night. Small red lights gleamed like the eyes of a new kind of creature, the Machine.

Ramón felt the refinery was watching him.

He shifted in his hammock, thinking. How beautiful Rosita had looked tonight! with that flower perched in her hair like a butterfly!

In Madison, Wisconsin, the women all wore their hair straight, parted in the center. Or they frizzed it a peculiar way that made their heads look too big. He had never seen a woman in Madison, Wisconsin, wear flowers in her hair. It was common here.

He drifted in and out of sleep.

There were so many flowers here, they practically fell into a woman's hair as she walked under the bushes and trees. Leathery-leaved orchids grew in clumps on the top of tree branches, pink, red, white, purple orchids, larger than hats. The branches overflowed with bromels, ferns, and mosses—and hydrangea, red hibiscus, roses, and more roses. Roses for Rosita.

He had an image of himself walking beside her, a little ahead, strewing her path with rose petals. He had an image of himself binding her breasts with honeysuckle, while hummingbirds whizzed in and out of the trumpet-shaped flowers. He had an image of himself kissing the small of her back, at the very moment in her body's journey where it began its rise toward her buttocks, while she lay on her stomach, the honeysuckle crushed into perfume, the hummingbirds dipping delicately in and out of her ears.

Their Blue Heaven

The ship rolled, collecting heat first on one side and then on the other. The sun shone like the door of a furnace suddenly opening, and then closed, the blackness of black space as black as an afterimage.

Flashes of light appeared from nowhere. Jane said they must be cosmic rays of one kind or another.

She said the crew's heightened clarity of thought must be the effect of the pure oxygen swishing through their suits and helmets. Maybe, she speculated, if oxygen clarified the brain, cosmic rays could actually charge it, like electricity charging a battery. But she was only guessing.

Miguel thought that this time Jane might be wrong. He had glanced back at the earth, when it was still there, and remembered Bolivia, his home, however poor and war-begotten, however bleak and treacherous, and he thought perhaps this new acuity of vision arose from the loss of an old. He felt sad and lonely, as the dream of his youth disappeared into nothingness behind him, swept by solar winds out of sight and out of mind.

Bolivia, Bolivia!

He remembered a dream he'd had of healing the nations. It had been St. John's dream in the Book of Revelation. The nations would be made whole and new. And he remembered Revelation's angel saying, "Hurt not the earth, neither the sea, nor the trees, till we have sealed the servants of our God in their foreheads." He remembered that, so sealed, the servants of God would endure the disintegration of earth itself. These mysteries had been taught him by the old priest who had cared for him briefly after he ran away from the man who wanted to cut off his leg. That kindly, half-enlightened, half-superstitious priest had rambled on about revolution and revelation, nodding off from time to time as he sat on the hard-backed chair at the cold, wood table. In his fitful doze, his mouth had opened and shut. Flies buzzed around his mud-spattered black cassock as if he were already dead.

The boy Miguel had listened to that low drone and high whine, and the stereophonic sound had put him into a trance, hypnotized him. Soon he saw nothing but the old priest's moving mouth, and it seemed as if every word the man uttered were a fly. Flies poured forth from his mouth in a black cloud, settling on the stale bread, the unwashed wine glasses, the maize in a burlap sack spilling open in a corner of the room. They mated on the window sill, locked in a noisy embrace. The priest woke up, mumbled, slept again. Miguel had imagined an angel like a great fly, rubbing its wings the way flies rub their legs, an angel with the gridded eyes and mosaic view of a fly, able to look in a thousand directions at once, and a mouth that kept opening and shutting, an angel dressed not in white but in mud-spattered black.

Miguel had had a jackknife, a flat handle of bright blue with a blade that flipped open and shut like the priest's mouth. He had carved his name into the cold, wood table.

Only the servants would be sealed. The boy Miguel dug deeper with his knife into the table. He wanted to be a guerrilla. A revolutionary. Could a revolutionary be a servant?

He didn't know. But he knew that he was known. He knew that he had been sealed in his forehead from birth, and that the cosmic brilliance that seemed to focus there now was only what had always been there. The thinker is always thought.

And as the light in Miguel's mind grew, shining ever more brightly, darkness covered Bolivia. Thunder and lightning swept the surface of Lake Titicaca, and rain rolled down the dark blue walls of the sky and fell on the steep streets of La Paz and in the jungle of the Green Hell. The storm moved on to Argentina.

Drops of wetness remained on the purple orchids, on the lianas looped from tree to tree. The sun reappeared; the raindrops sizzled, evaporated; a large, moody silence draped itself over the forest. Giant blue butterflies danced in the sun. Termite ants sped back to their dark holes. A mule brayed. A swarm of sweat bees buzzed through the swamp in a loud black cloud.

The heat glittered. The bullfrogs vanished. The heat hung over the Green Hell like a haze. Everything was green, green with golden sun-spots, green alligators, green sedge islands breaking from the banks and drifting in a silent delirium down the river until they were caught by the next fatal bend.

Green and gold.

Brown.

The blue butterflies.

A tarantula, hairy-legged and leaping, his fat bag body soft as a scrotum above the eight powerful appendages, his eyes, set high above his body, full of bright spite, spun in a mad but cunning love-leap.

And more. The orange trees like trees hung with tiny suns. The plover's scream, the egret's still pose against the thicket of the small deer, the small fox that chases the small deer, the thorns and fever and glades. And the vampire bats asleep in their hollow tree trunks. The lizards asleep. And Bolivia, the world, the world asleep, waiting to be waked into the new day, the day when even the nations would be resurrected.

Rosita and the Soothsayer

Once, when she was still living with the old gentleman in Chile, she had gotten up at dawn to walk barefoot on the cool stones of the patio. There, by the pool, as if poolside-sitting were a perfectly ordinary thing for a soothsayer to do, a woman in a calico turban was drifting her fingers in the green water.

Rosita had gone up to her—timidly, as if it was the woman who lived here, in the rich house, and not herself.

"And good morning to you," the woman said, although Rosita had not yet opened her mouth.

"Good morning," Rosita had answered. "Who are you?"

"It would be much more interesting," the strange woman said, "to ask who you are."

"But I know who I am!"

"And who is that?"

"Rosita. My name is Rosita."

"A girl named Rosita should have a rose in her hair."

And the woman made one appear, by plucking it out of the air, and slipped it behind Rosita's ear. But a thorn pricked the woman's thumb, and a drop of blood fell on Rosita's shoulder.

"A bad sign," the strange woman said.

Rosita shuddered.

"Still," the woman went on, "it is only one drop. Only one lover will you lose."

"The old gentleman?" Rosita asked.

"Do you call him your lover?"

Rosita dropped her eyes. A lizard seeking sunshine slithered across the fine stone.

"No," Rosita said. "I don't *call* him that."

The woman laughed. "Well, then, one lover whom you *call* a lover you will lose, but only one."

"And then?"

"And then, and then," the woman muttered. "Who knows, And then? Did I promise to tell your future?"

Rosita shook her head, her rose-bedecked hair. She felt unfairly chastised, as if she had overstepped some boundary that she still couldn't see.

"All right, then," the woman said. "And don't forget it." And she vanished just as the sun appeared fully over the snowcapped mountains, the calico turban shrinking to a dazzling dot, a spot, a swirl of spots like the dervish, dancing spots you get in front of your eyes when you stare too long at the sun.

FROM *WE CAN STILL BE FRIENDS*

Boyd

He was in his office skimming the trades when the receptionist announced that a friend of his wife's, one Ava Martel, was waiting in the anteroom. Since it was a personal and not a professional call, he told Sally to send the friend in even though she had made no appointment.

She stood in the doorway, with Sally's office behind her like the view into the distance in an Old Master painting, a prospect of ebony furniture and indirect lighting and filing cabinets, and she made him think of art and truth and beauty, of high ideals and the nobility of the human heart, because her silhouette was so pure and sweetly defined, so glowing, like a cool unself-conscious heat, that he instantly recalled his own youthful allegiances and—he could not deny it—his deepest continuing beliefs, underground but ongoing, in the values both of artistic representation and communication among creative minds though history.

He pulled his glance away, glad that Ava Martel could not know how extravagant his response to her had been, feeling foolish that he could overreact like this. When he looked at her again he noticed her long slim legs, the narrow waist, the square-set narrow shoulders, tantalizingly naked—could shoulders be thought of as naked? but hers seemed so, edged cunningly, as they were, by a sleeveless open-necked white shirt. . . .Cunning because so candid. . . .

He rose from his chair.

"It's good of you to see me without an appointment," she said, thrusting out her hand as she entered. He shook it.

"Have a seat."

She was good-looking, with short wavy dark brown hair, thick eyebrows, a kind of feminine precision in all her features and movements, precision in her profile. The kind of easy elegance that comes either though privilege or suffering, though now that he thought about it, he supposed that suffering might just as easily result in sloppiness. Maybe the more a person suffered, the more he backed away from the myriad little decisions each day demanded, the tasks of drawing distinctions and setting standards, knowing how futile it was to fulfill them. Was he thinking of himself, he wondered.

"Sally said you're a friend of my wife's."

"Claire."

"Where do you know each other from?" he asked, hoping to get a handle on why she had looked him up. He began to move things around on his desk: nameplate, scratch pad, pen. He looked at her again, this time in the eye.

"We don't."

She was sitting up very straight, and she had said that without moving a single facial muscle. Remarkable.

"I'm afraid I don't understand," he said, carefully.

The minute hand of the clock on the wall behind her moved soundlessly to the next stopping point. He always liked a clock on the wall facing his desk; it let him control the length of appointments without unsettling visitors.

He was suddenly convinced that there was a trap laid for him somewhere in this conversation. "If you are not a friend of my wife's, why did you say you were? And how do you know her name?"

"I didn't say I knew her. Your receptionist assumed I did because I said that I live in Chicago, as your wife Claire once did. I teach at Midland. Actually, I'm in Memphis until June, though my home base is Chicago. At any rate, I mentioned to your receptionist that your wife used to live in Chicago."

"And how do you happen to know anything at all about my wife?"

"Because she's having an affair with the man I had hoped to marry."

He stepped around to the front of his desk. It was true that her eyes were clear and rational, true that her eyebrows were a Declaration of Independence. It was true that she looked like the Enlightenment, but maybe she was only a French Revolution, a Bastille gone crazy with demands. "Let me guess. Would this man be a surgeon?"

"Yes."

"Then, Ms. Martel, you are not telling me anything I don't already know. Moreover," he said, "I suspect you've been misled by your own feelings into thinking that I would have welcomed this information, had it been new, which it is not, because I would want to act on it. I have no intention of acting on it. My wife is entitled to live her life as she sees fit. Does that surprise you—that I would say that?" He heard his question in stereo: directed toward his visitor, and inside his head. *Did it surprise him that he would say that?* But there had never been anything else he could say, Claire had left him no options—not short of leaving her, anyway, and if that was an option, what was a marriage?

And what was a marriage if someone could walk into your office and within moments you were admitting, at least to yourself, that you were afraid of losing your wife, that you were jealous of a man you knew almost nothing about, you were on the verge of naming grievances, worries, insecurities—none of which were the business of the mysterious visitor who had walked into your office.

For what? What was it she had come for? She wanted something. People wanted things, didn't they. Didn't he.

He kept staring at her, thinking that sooner or later she'd give herself away. He was beginning to admire her self-possession, her Mona Lisa sense of centrality, although a woman who thought she had the right to reveal a wife's secret, or what she thought was a secret, to the wife's husband, was probably a hysteric.

He had told her she was not bringing him any information he didn't already have, but to hear—to have it confirmed—what was wrong with him, anyhow? A sharp pain was working its way up through his chest. It was like being filleted. He took a deep breath and the pain eased.

"Mr. Buchanan—"

"Boyd," he said (almost cavalierly, he noted to himself with satisfaction). "If you're going to call my wife, whom you do not know at all, Claire, you might as well call me Boyd."

"Boyd, I do not give a fuck what your wife does with Tony—"

The pain again, stabbing him. He would have preferred not to know that name.

"—or what you do about it. That's not why I'm here."

"Then I must admit to being confused. Why, if I may ask, are you here?" It seemed to him that his jacket was tight across the shoulders, he should have let it out.

"Tony met your wife, Claire, at a medical convention in San Francisco just before Thanksgiving."

"I know, I was there," Boyd said, dryly.

"Then you know that I wasn't. I was in Chicago. This was before Memphis."

"What does all this geography have to do with anything?"

"At almost exactly the same time Tony was getting involved with your wife, maybe even on the same day, I was having a miscarriage."

Boyd was trying very hard to figure out what he was supposed to say next. Who announced something like that? Bare shoulders—forget bare shoulders. He felt as uncomfortable as if she had shed all her clothes and was waiting for him to give her a gynecological exam. There was nothing sexy about it. No, there was. He lived among people who disguised themselves with personas. Everyone in Hollywood had a persona. For a woman to reveal herself so completely, without prologue or hesitation—it was seductive, after all. As was her mouth, source of all these startling words, kissable lips a natural pink, no added paint, stain, or gloss; none needed. But the lips trembled, turned downward, then pushed outward as she blew a small breath in his direction to get hold of herself, but that puff of air seemed also like a gift she was offering him, a personal, even intimate transfer of biological energy.

He didn't want a hysterical female on his hands, but he still didn't get the connection she was trying to draw. Why was she here?

"When Tony got back from San Francisco, I told him about the miscarriage. He called it a spontaneous abortion, by the way. That's the medical term. He didn't, of course, tell me about your wife. I didn't find out about her until February. He waited until I was in Memphis—so he wouldn't have to tell me in person, I guess—and told me that he was in love with your wife."

"In love."

"Oh yes," Ava said. "She's taught him that real love is intuitive. She's put him in touch with his feelings. It's been a profound experience for him. He's learning so much about himself."

The jacket was definitely too tight, so tight he couldn't breathe. No lobbing back of a breath-ball for him! No anything from him! "I don't want to listen to this. I think you should go."

For a moment, nothing happened, and he thought she was getting ready to leave. And although she had not yet left, he already missed her. He knew he would never again in his life be so surprised. Never again would he be able to look on her fineness, her—elegance was not the right word because it suggested sophistication, and perhaps the delicatest overlay of cynicism as must accompany self-knowledge. Claire was elegant. The woman he had just lost—had actually told to leave—was fresh. Edenic—not innocent but unconcerned with appearance and presentation. Already the day seemed longer, threatening to drag out into a lifetime of loneliness.

"I don't like that kind of talk either," she volunteered then. "I think of it as California hot-tub talk. But I thought you'd be used to it, living out here."

"One thing I'm not used to is having women barge into my office on false pretenses in order to detail my wife's peccadilloes."

"I wanted that baby," she continued. "Do you realize it's even possible that my worry over Tony's not writing or calling when he was in San Francisco may have contributed to the miscarriage? Maybe I was being *intuitive* too. Now I may never have a baby, because the likeliest father is busy discovering himself with your wife."

"I'm sorry. Nobody ever said life was fair."

"Exactly. Which is why we have to do what we can to obtain justice where we can."

"What do you mean by that?"

"I mean I want to have your baby, Mr. Buchanan. You owe me one."

He returned to his side of the desk, removed his jacket and hung it over the back of his chair. Then he detoured to the window. Despite the trimmed woods he could look out toward—planted trees kept free of underbrush—the road that ran behind the building swarmed with traffic of one kind and another: messengers on bicycles, security cops in a car, parking cops in a car, cars traveling to or from the parking lot, one of those little white vehicles that looked more like a robot than a truck (he didn't know what the guy in it did), and a garbage truck that resembled Godzilla. The intense sunlight, falling so equably everywhere, exposed the lack of significance of every object in this scene. The people were carbon, and the people's lives, experienced with such warm emotion, mere arrangements of energy, temporary and ramshackle.

Then he remembered another window, long ago, how it had been open to a spring day and how he had stood there looking out at a yellow warbler in a chinaberry tree. He remembered that the small bird, as pretty as an ornament, flew from branch to branch, and that the leaves shook and shimmied as if doing a fan dance.

Two men climbed down from the garbage truck and fed it the contents of several large trash containers. He could view the scene but he couldn't hear it, because the building had been designed to muffle noise.

He could hear only the clamor in his own head. He couldn't even hear himself think. What did he think, he asked himself, of what this woman had just said to him?

He turned around to face her again, walked back to his desk, sat down.

"How about a walk-on?" Boyd Buchanan said, when he'd finally absorbed what she had said. "That's what most of the crazy ladies out here want—a chance to be in the movies. Would you settle for a walk-on?"

"A baby," she said.

The clock was still marking time. No doubt the garbage collectors had moved to the next building. In his mind, the warbler became a baby—a baby in a chinaberry tree, cradled by boughs. Boughs break, babies tumble and fall.

He could buy a little more time to think by doing dialogue shtick. "I owe you what?" he could ask, and she would say "A baby" and he would say, "I owe you a baby" and she could say "Of course" and they could mix it into a rap beat, but he was not into shtick.

"You can't be serious," he said, wondering why he didn't buzz Sally and ask her to call security.

"I wouldn't be here if I weren't."

He guessed he knew why he didn't buzz Sally and ask her to call security. It wasn't every day a woman walked into your office and said she wanted to have your baby.

"And what," he asked, "would you do with this baby?" Hang it in a tree. Let the wind blow.

"Raise it."

"By yourself?"

"Of course."

"You don't think a child needs two parents?"

"Many children manage with fewer."

He'd had his aunt and uncle.

"Babies become kids," he said. "Kids are a handful. Kids become teenagers, many of whom are monsters. Teenagers become adults. A lot of adults you wouldn't want to have to spend any more time with than necessary." It was the speech he had sometimes given to himself, telling himself that he and Claire were perhaps fortunate not to have had children.

"That's not your problem," she said.

"My problem is you. Why?"

She shrugged. "Luck of the draw, I guess. Claire might have slept with someone else. Tony might have taken me to the convention. He didn't."

"Would you like some coffee? I can buzz Sally."

She shook her head no. Now that she had said why she was here, her face had softened. You let go of a secret and it let go of you, that was one of life's truths though not widely known by people in the business. Her shoulders had relaxed, she looked younger and even sweeter.

"You can't have a baby just because you want one," he said.

She blinked. She blinked a whole series of rapid-fire blinks, to make her point. "I can't? Why else does anyone have a baby, except by accident? Do you mean I can only have an unwanted baby?"

"You know what I mean," he muttered, feeling like a dope.

"You mean I'm not married."

He rolled his pen between his palms and nodded.

"That's why I'm here," she said, slowly, as if explaining that it would not be a good idea to play in the middle of the highway, it would not be a good idea to eat your chemistry set, it would not be a good idea to practice swinging your baseball bat in the living room. "If I were married, I wouldn't have had to come here."

"Maybe, maybe not."

She looked at him sharply. "You and Claire don't have children?"

He said nothing.

"Then," she said, "maybe you need me as much as I need you."

"Oh"—he dropped his pen; it rolled briefly and stopped—"no, I don't think so." But this was a tactic, he knew, and not one of life's truths.

"That's a tactic," she said. "You're saying that as a way of preserving your high ground, but I don't believe you."

"Believe what you want."

She crossed her legs. The red skirt seemed to brighten, as if it were a fire flaring up. He didn't want her to believe what she wanted—he wanted her to believe in him, that he was wise, powerful, gracious, compassionate, and uncompromising. Could one be both compassionate and uncompromising?

"I could take off my clothes," she said. "That might persuade you. I know by West Coast standards I'm a little on the flat-chested side, but then again, what I do have is all natural. No silicone, no saline. Plus I have great legs." It was as if she were playing a scene he had previewed—and now he felt guilty as hell, as if she had said those lines only because he had wanted her to.

"Jesus. You really are beyond the pale, aren't you," he said.

"It's never been put quite that way before."

"What if I call your bluff and say yes, I want you to strip?"

"Do you?"

"God, no. Please, no."

"I was kind of sure you wouldn't call me on it." She lowered her eyes and plucked at her skirt, and he was astonished by how quickly she looked demure as a nun. "It just seemed like something that would be in a movie."

"And were you joking about the baby, too?"

"What do you think?"

"I think you must be a couple of croutons short of a salad."

"I would never joke about having a baby."

"What made you think I wouldn't call your bluff?"

"You seem nice."

Claire had once told him that when a woman tells a man that he seems nice what she means is *You aren't what I expected.* "What did you expect?" he asked.

"I don't know. Slicker. Smarmy. Brutal."

"Brutal?"

"I don't mean physically brutal."

He was quiet, thinking what in her life might have brought her to that word, that phrase.

He set the pen down and flicked it, and it spun briefly.

"You really like to manhandle that pen, don't you?"

He looked at the stopped pen lying on its side on the desk.

"Someday I'm going to buy myself a nice pen," she said. "As it is, I mostly use ballpoints with red ink. To mark up papers— We have to pay the department for them. Can you believe that?"

Claire used a fountain pen. And carried her papers in that wonderful old beat-up briefcase. . . ."Look," he said, "I don't know how to break this news to you, but I don't cheat on my wife. It's just me. I don't like the idea."

"That seems generous of you," she said, "considering."

"I don't use sex as a way to even the score with anyone, for Christ's sake. Neither does my wife."

"Are you sure that's not what she's doing?"

"Aren't you an educator? A liberated woman? Don't you believe in equal rights and opportunities for women? Don't you think a woman should be able to make her own choices?"

"Midland U. would knock those ideas right out of you." She didn't know he'd been a student there; she didn't know everything about him. "You can't teach at Midland U. and go on believing women will ever be treated equally. Not by the administration, anyway."

"Really," he said, amused in spite of himself, "you and Claire have a lot in common. You should hear her on that subject."

"Now we'll have even more in common."

"You're crazy, aren't you," Boyd Buchanan said. "Really crazy."

"It depends on what you mean by that. If you mean *out of touch with reality*, the answer is no, I'm not crazy. Inventive, that's all."

He laughed.

Ava

Another reason for staying awake at night was that if you didn't keep an eye on it the third dimension could go missing, it could just disappear, leaving everything around you flat as flatware. This made it hard to walk, if you decided to get up. You had to hold onto things. And then the third dimension might suddenly decide to come back and pop up in front of you and cause you to stumble. For this reason, it was sometimes necessary to curl up on the floor, since you could not fall off a floor. But then very likely someone would come into the room and tell you to get up, and even if you wanted to, it would be hard to answer because everyone would be talking to you from a great height, as if they were all superior. It was difficult to know how to answer such superior beings. There you were, the lowest thing on earth, the proof of that being that you were lying on the floor, and how could you explain any of this to people who towered over you like skyscrapers, a city of faraway, high-up people?

III

I WAS A TEENAGE BEATNIK

I was eighteen and attending the University of Tennessee at Knoxville. *Attending* may be too strong a word. I was more often absent from than present in my classes, which included Nuclear Physics and Symbolic Logic, both of which I was flunking. In Nuclear Physics students perched high on bleachers and stared down at the Oak Ridge scientist on the stage, whose accent was untranslatable to my ears. The Symbolic Logic professor had a floating eye and bounced on sponge-soled shoes in front of the room. In my literature class, and I believe I must have been flunking that class, too, we were reading *Don Quixote* and James Joyce's *Ulysses*, both of which were over my Junior-Year head, although I kept trying to get through *Don Quixote*, because it was one of my father's two favorite books. (The other was *Tom Jones*.) The Modern Library edition lay on the table in the single back room I rented in a boarding house, and each day I read some of it. But everything was over my head that semester. It wasn't only literature and logic and physics I couldn't grasp; I didn't know who I was or why everything I did turned out such a mess and made my parents angry. I didn't know why the school nurse had sent me to the school psychiatrist or why the psychiatrist said my answers to his Rorschach test meant I had "a male mind in a female body." I was completely mystified about my female body, which at least one graduate student, an Alpha Male from Memphis named Curly Matthews, hijacked to a mountain cabin, there, with the tacit encouragement of friends, to seduce me, except that I sat up all night with my back against the headboard, chewing my nails to the quick and supplying arguments drawn from Symbolic Logic as to why I should not lose my virginity to him.

What the hell was stately, plump Buck Mulligan yakking about, anyhow? If he was going to shave, why didn't he just shut up and shave? What was so amusing about young men behaving pretentiously, showing off their recently acquired knowledge and wanting everyone to admire their wit? The towertop, Babel-onian dialogue between Mulligan and Stephen Dedalus was so arch and so cluttered with signposts directed toward the reader (Don't miss any of these neat allusions to Christian theology and classical mythology! They're here to tip you off! Think Greek!) that I immediately felt wary, hostile, defensive. The author had no intention of leading the reader on a journey into the unknown; like his characters, he just wanted to show off.

At the same time, Joyce's dancing words dizzied me with their dazzle.

When I endeavored to imagine the view from the tower, I felt as if I were falling right over the stone railing. Try as I might, I couldn't see it, "the scrotumtightening sea." I just didn't know what that was. Literature is supposed to expand the imagination, beyond gender as well as other barriers, but I seemed to have trouble conjuring an imaginary world, at any rate while the real one at hand was so unaccountable and strange.

A classmate came to my rented room to talk about writing. We exchanged manuscripts and were offering each other a critique when the landlady's brother burst into the room without knocking and kicked the boy out. The man then turned to me and told me, not so nicely as this, that I would have to move. I moved to an apartment so endowed with cockroaches I did not dare sleep or undress in it. Cockroaches could crawl all over me, my female body. My male mind cringed at this thought, perhaps effeminately. The formerly-a-closet shower, with a sheet hung from tacks on the side where the door used to be, was in the living room and served as a kind of nest or meeting room for the cockroaches. I showered in the gym at the university instead. No wonder, then, that when I went to my classes, I slept through them. I was taking three other classes, and I don't even remember what they were. And those were the ones in which I got A's.

I met people. We congregated in the student union. Someone gave me a copy of *The Well of Loneliness* to read. (My sexuality seemed to be on a lot of people's minds, but I would have been happy just to get through a book, any book.) Another acquaintance spoke vaguely of how a guy named Cruiser had gone to Mexico and brought back "stuff." Well, I did say "those days." This was so long ago, longer than anyone then could have predicted it would be now. The previous summer I had ridden the bus from Richmond to Knoxville, stayed at the YWCA, and searched for a room to rent and in my high heels and pink-and-white polkadot sundress I had felt summery and excited, but already, during registration, I was bewildered, confused, afraid, and now I had lost the ability to read even books that had the advantage of not being class assignments. *The Well of Loneliness* was more eccentric, to me, than *Ulysses*, less sequential than *Don Quixote*, and I didn't have a clue. What I took away from *The Well of Loneliness* was a determination that whatever I wrote was not going to be murky.

I revealed to my new crowd my intention of being a writer, and the leader asked to see some of my poems. He was tall, dark, commanding, with an air of desperation about him; his wife had long blond hair and looked like Mary (the Mary then) of Peter, Paul, and Mary. I thought they were glamorously anti-bourgeois and I admired them fiercely, and looking back, I think they must have been kind people, because they encouraged me in my belief that I was meant to be a writer.

Another member of the group was a fellow I had met back in the summer on my scouting trip, who had written me letters when I returned to Richmond. "I gather from your poetry," he wrote in one of them, "that you are no stranger to the sheets." Wanting not to be murky, I had been imaginatively explicit where, I now realized, murk might have been preferable. I was ashamed to tell him the truth so I let him think he was right, but when I showed a poem to my mother, over Christmas break, in which I used the word "nipple," she had what the doctor explained to us was a "mock heart-attack" and went to bed in her attic room and said she never wanted to see me again. My father was disgusted with me; he thought I had killed her, or more or less killed her, or at any rate sort of mock-killed her.

Whatever guys may have thought about their chances with me, they took to dropping by the apartment, in spite of the cockroaches. They'd come over and we'd sit around talking about books and art and ideas. Answering a knock on my door one night I threw open the door to find myself facing two cops. "There have been complaints," they said, "that you are entertaining men here at all hours. Men have been seen entering and leaving this apartment at all hours."

I was shocked. Could they really be thinking what they seemed to be implying? "I'm not a prostitute," I said, feelingly. "I'm a poet!"

They told me I would have to move.

Luckily, I had met a girl from Shady Valley, Tennessee, who was studying painting. She was the first in her family to go to college and seemed to know what she was doing in a way that I did not. We moved into an apartment together. It was clean and had no cockroaches. Every night people would come to our apartment to read poetry aloud while candles, burning in wine bottles, dripped wax down the glass sides, stratifying over the labels until it looked like a relief map—or the paint on a Van Gogh canvas, the way it threatens the viewer, seems to want to reach out and embrace the viewer (to death maybe), pull the viewer into the painting. We read Ginsberg and Ferlinghetti. I read *A Coney Island of the Mind* and managed to understand it. Maybe I wasn't a hopeless case. I read Celine's *Journey to the End of the Night* and *The Journal of Albion Moonlight* by Kenneth Patchen and Jean Toomer's *Cane* and understood them. Maybe I could even become a hopeful case. We drank the wine before we turned the bottles into makeshift candlesticks, but no one had any "stuff." One of the women kept having to fly to Cuba for, she said, abortions; the way I remember it, she had about three in the space of two weeks. Her boyfriend was Cuban. I say "one of the women," but most of our guests, like mine of the previous month, were guys, and if anyone else besides the Cuban was having sex I didn't know about it. Mainly, we let our brains and tongues grow a little fuzzy with rotgut-red, aspired to the world-weariness of Jelly Roll Morton or Jean Genet or Christopher Isherwood, stayed up too late, and, more and more, skipped classes. Except Maline; coming from Shady Valley, she knew better than to skip class.

In Virginia, my parents were building a house; they were often at the site, where there was as yet no telephone. The dean called me in to his office to inform me that he had spoken with my father at the school where he taught. "He said you used to play the piano," the dean said, as if pleasantly chatting.

"Yes," I said. "I quit because I decided to be a writer instead."

"Your father said you quit because you had no talent."

I left his office reeling with his punches but unable to get in touch with my father. I didn't know how to call my father at work and didn't think he would have liked for me to.

The next time the dean called me in, he said, "There have been reports that you have been seen riding on the back of a motorcycle."

"I've never been on a motorcycle," I said, truthfully.

"That's not what the reports say."

What reports? Whose reports? Why would anyone give a damn whether I was on the back of a motorcycle?

Did I mention that I was finding this world unaccountable and strange?

The dean summoned Maline, too, but she simply let him say whatever he wanted to say and then went on doing what she was doing (and she was still attending her classes).

I fell a little bit in love with a boy who had dropped out or already finished or never had been in college; I didn't seem to know exactly what his status was, but he was an artist, a painter, and kept late hours, appearing and disappearing as if, unlike the rest of us, he had things to do besides just sit around in diners listening to country music on the juke box and holding forth on art and literature. I was intrigued. I tried to get him to notice me, but he told me I was too young, unformed, "a bitty thing needing to be unhooked and thrown back into the sea." Rejected, I consoled myself with daily sundaes at the drugstore, putting on poundage, though since I weighed about ninety-two to begin with I was not in danger of becoming overweight, but I knew the drugstore clerk was concerned about my state of mind (he didn't know it was a male mind) and I avoided meeting his eyes when I ordered another sundae.

The dean kept badgering me. The phone would ring and it would be his secretary telling me that the dean would expect me in his office at such and such an hour, and I would know that when I went there he would tell me how disappointed in me my father was, how my father was so fed up he wasn't sure he even wanted to claim me as his daughter anymore. The dean said my father was going to stop sending me money for rent and food, and sure enough, no more money arrived. Maline and I shoplifted peanut butter and jelly and a loaf of bread from the local market, the kind of corner shop that still had a wooden floor and penny-slot vending containers, shaped like space helmets, for jawbreakers and gum. When someone played rhythm-and-blues on the phonograph I felt I knew rhythm, I felt I knew blues.

"Tell me about your friends," the dean said, "and maybe I can talk your father into sending you some money." He wanted to know about the guy from Cuba: what were his politics? why did his girlfriend fly to Cuba so frequently?

Now, how was I supposed to know the answer to that when I couldn't even read the Great Novels on the reading list for my lit course?

"I don't know," I said.

And, "I don't know," I said again.

I knew better than to mention the word abortion.

"Your father," the dean said, "is very unhappy to hear about your motorcycle riding."

The usual crowd was in Maline's and my apartment the night I received a telegram from my father. "COME HOME NOW STOP," it said. "WILL NOT PAY TUITION FOR NEXT SEMESTER STOP."

I showed the telegram to my current boyfriend—or friend; he was not quite a boyfriend, but he was gentle and caring and I liked him. This was not the moody, mysterious painter but a student who planned to go to law school. Stilton James read the telegram and then held it in the flame from the candle until it caught fire and crumpled into ash.

The next day I went to the registrar's office and officially dropped out. Then, in his office, the dean handed me a bus ticket to Richmond that my father had sent care of him.

The morning I was to leave, Stilts and I were in the apartment alone; he had come over to help me finish packing. Once, I happened to glance out a window, and there were two patrolmen—or state troopers, or campus guards, but definitely a pair, as before—and they were checking around the back of the building. They seemed to be looking for me. The bus wasn't due to leave for six or eight hours but the empty apartment was creepy, and the cops were creepy. Stilts and I were ready to go anyway, so while the cops were still out back we walked down the front steps, got in Stilts's car, and drove to the bus station, where we sat quietly at a little table behind a paperback rack, drank coffee, and occasionally murmured some small comment. A half hour before the bus pulled in, Stilts flipped through the paperback rack and picked out a book. He paid for the book and then handed it to me. "You'll need something to read on the bus," he said. It was *The Dharma Bums* by Jack Kerouac.

I said thank you, and then the bus came, and Stilts gave my suitcase to the driver to stow in the storage compartment, and I got on the bus and found a window seat and waved good-bye to my friend.

It was a long ride—fourteen or fifteen hours. I was too shy to strike up a conversation with anyone. I watched the scenery until the bus began to fill up with shadows, as if all the empty seats were being taken by ghosts, the shades of a Blue Ridge Elysium. Gears shifted as we climbed, we drove through a brief rainstorm, passengers sighed or mumbled or fished in their pockets or handbags for peanut butter-and-jelly sandwiches (as did I), but the bus seemed haunted by silence and darkness. When it was full night, I switched on the overhead light and read Kerouac.

Every so often I'd put the book down on the empty seat beside me. When, at twelve, I renounced the piano—it had been a renunciation, a public declaration of my dedication to writing—I was working on a Beethoven sonata. The only person who had complained about my lack of talent then was me. I didn't think I could be a *great* pianist. (Maline says now—after all these years, we wound up living a couple of blocks apart and, though no longer in Tennessee, still painting and still writing—"You didn't just tell us you wanted to be a writer. You said you were going to be a great writer." "I did?" I ask, disbelieving, wondering how I could have been so bold, so self-revealing, so, above all for a Southerner, impolite.)

My parents met me at the bus station in Richmond but, I learned, they had gone there not expecting me and only because they didn't know what else to do. It seems the Tennessee dean had telephoned my father to say that I had disappeared. "An all-points bulletin has been issued," he informed my father. "We're sure we'll find her." While I was catching the bus, riding the bus, getting off the bus, police were combing the city, scouring the state. The dean told my parents he thought I might be hiding out in the hills, perhaps with a graduate student. Or, he said, I might have run off to San Francisco. It was quite likely, he said, that I had gotten knocked up and had run away to New York City and been chopped into small pieces by a back-alley surgeon who regularly botched his unholy manipulations. Some instinct brought my parents to the station anyway.

As relieved as my parents were to see me step off the bus, my mother was staring hard at my stomach, which was, because of all those hot fudge sundaes, rounder than before. Hardly a word was said on the way home, home being the old house I was used to. The next morning, my big brother came in to wake me; he'd been delegated the task of finding out what was going on with me. (He was often delegated this task.) He picked up *The Dharma Bums* from the chair where I had tossed it. "Aha," he said, "I thought so." I knew from that that everyone had already decided what was going on with me, so I said nothing. For weeks I said nothing, or nothing much. What did I have to say to a father who thought I was talentless? To a mother who cast a shrewd eye on my stomach whenever

I wore anything not black and outsized? To a brother who nodded knowingly whenever I did wear something black and outsized?

My kid sister said she was ashamed of me.

My mother said, "Putting on a little weight around the middle, are we?"

I was not about to explain to her that she had nothing to worry about. *Let her worry,* I thought. *It serves her right.*

I thought if she had a problem because she thought I was pregnant, it was a problem she had created for herself.

After a while, of course, it became clear that I was not pregnant. I lost weight and became again my usual skinny self, although still wearing black turtleneck sweaters and white lipstick. Eventually we began to talk about what had happened. We discovered that the dean had been lying to both my parents and me. Why? Rumors that reached me suggested an involvement within the state of Tennessee with planning for operations in the Bay of Pigs (hence, the thinking went, the trips to Cuba). For my part, I supposed that the university wanted to break up a group of what they considered troublemakers—POETS! PAINTERS!: THEY MIGHT AS WELL BE PROSTITUTES!—and realized I was the easiest student to go after first. Years later Maline told me she thought the university had not liked the fact that our group was integrated, and I now think that is the most plausible explanation. I was officially expelled. My parents moved into the new house, and I, unable to find a school willing to have me, moved with them. In my new room I began to write a novella. The pages piled up. It wasn't Joyce or Cervantes, but neither of them had been himself at my age either. At least I understood what I was reading now. I was making things clear for myself.

What does a novelist or even a budding novella-writer seek to clarify? A question. (A great novelist confronts a great question.) The answer to the question is the unknown upon which the novelist, with the reader, advances (but does not necessarily arrive at or define). The novelist who already has the answer before beginning to write risks no transformation of self and offers the reader no opportunity for a transformation of self. It is the clarity of the question that counts, not the answer. It is the question, not the answer, that moves and involves and educates the reader. Obviously, this is not to suggest that a great question is *all* that is needed to make a great novelist.

I finished my novella, put it in a desk drawer, and began composing letters to colleges. Even now, it would not be easy to find one that would take me.

Meanwhile, the dean had kept after Maline, but she wasn't to be budged. She finished college and was accepted for graduate work in art at the University of Iowa. *After* she was at Iowa, she received a letter from the dean at the University of Tennessee in Knoxville saying she *would not be allowed to return there!*

As Maline says, *What a wuss.*

A few months later my parents, frantic with worry, had to call the Chester-field County Volunteer Rescue Squad for help finding my sister and her long-time steady boyfriend, who were out past curfew. The Rescue Squad shone a flashlight on them in a room over a garage at the boyfriend's house. Reminded of her own walk on the wild side, my sister wrings the dishcloth dry, drapes it over the kitchen faucet, and laughs.

I did find a college to take me. The dean there had a daughter who had been kicked out of Swarthmore, so he felt a certain sympathy for my plight and went to bat for me. The year after I was a beatnik I completed a major in philosophy, wore shirtwaist dresses, kneesocks, and loafers, and got the modern dance instructor to promise me a B in return for sitting quietly in the bleachers, reading, and not wrecking class morale with my total inability to execute a single dance movement.

More time passed. I went to graduate school in philosophy. The Bay of Pigs was a fiasco, Dallas a disaster. Stilton James took a job in District Attorney Jim Garrison's office in New Orleans. Several of our group were drafted, including the intriguingly aloof artist. A second Kennedy was murdered. Martin Luther King, Jr., died by an assassin's bullet in Memphis. Cities burned. I read *Krapp's Last Tape* by Samuel Beckett, was in utter awe of it, bought a recording of it, and listened to it over and over. People gave parties for the Black Panthers. "Ah, Dedalus, the Greeks," Buck Mulligan had mused. "I must teach you. You must read them in the original." Now I took the words to heart and studied *The Iliad*, memorizing some of it. I married, divorced, lived in New York and England. I returned to *Ulysses*, got through it and was stunned by the beauty of Joyce's descriptions of the ordinary world. Mythology aside, linguistic games aside, a "mockturtle vapour and steam of newbaked jampuffs" pulled the reader into "Harrison's," outside which "[a] barefoot arab stood over the grating, breath-ing in the fumes. Deaden the gnaw of hunger that way. Pleasure or pain is it?" Father Conmee's ankles were "thinsocked" and "tickled by the stubble of Clongowes field." Molly recalled "the firtree cove a wild place I suppose it must be the highest rock in existence the galleries and casemates and those frightful rocks and Saint Michaels cave with the icicles or whatever they call them hang-ing down and ladders all the mud plotching my boots." In the "Ithaca" episode, Leopold Bloom carefully observed on the top of the stove "a blue enamelled saucepan" and "a black iron kettle." Joyce's odyssey through Dublin was navi-gated detail by detail. Perhaps the psychiatrist at the University of Tennessee in Knoxville would have said that Joyce had a female mind in a male body.

The Beats were followed by metafictioneers, ethnonovelists, minimalists, and the new maximalists. In 1983 Joyce Johnson published a finely tuned book titled *Minor Characters* in which she described her youthful love affair with Jack Kerouac. When she told Jack she was writing a novel, he asked her to name her favorite novelist. "I said Henry James, and he made a face, and said he figured I had all the wrong models, but maybe I could be a great writer anyway. He asked me if I rewrote a lot, and said you should never revise, never change anything, not even a word. . . .He was going to look at my work and show me that what you wrote first was always best. I said okay, feeling guilty for all that I'd rewritten, but I still loved Henry James."

I love Joyce Johnson.

Terrorists took to bombing and poisoning. Ireland's turmoil—like Yugoslavia's, Africa's, India's, the Mideast's—seemed eternal, but elsewhere the invasion of Grenada, the Persian Gulf War, the devastating fires in Indonesia came and went. Governments came and went—the Soviet Union went!—celebrities came and went. The world changed; it always does, of course, but when you are eighteen, you do not always believe it will. I changed, too. It was a short while a long time ago that I was a teenage beatnik, and I am sure that there is much about that time that I've forgotten, but I remember being kidnaped by Curly, shown the door of the boarding house, evicted by cops who thought I was a working girl, expelled by a devious, ditzy dean, abandoned by books, and dispraised by my parents.

I had thought such picaresque memories would compose a comic memoir. It's not as if I've never earned a laugh or two now and then, spinning them as conversational anecdotes. I have come to understand why my father treasured Cervantes and Fielding, and I would have liked to write a good-humored memoir of innocence-at-large. Or if not that, I thought, then something lyrical and lovely, something just a little bit Samuel Barberish, *Knoxville: Semester of 1959.* Where did all the sadness come from?

It is so interesting how something will appear on a page out of nowhere, or as if it's been hiding in a shadowy corner waiting for someone to walk into the room and turn on the light. I never knew this sadness was there.

But so what. I still spin my anecdotes in conversation, and they still get laughs. "I was a teenage beatnik," I say. "I was eighteen, a junior at the University of Tennessee."

AN UNDERGROUND HOTEL IN LENINGRAD

I was standing at the window of my room in the Sovietskaya, gazing into the courtyard below. All at once a *window* whizzed past my line of sight—a pane of glass exactly like the one I was looking through. It touched down with a tremendous ringing noise and splintered into silence. In the afterhush I glanced up and saw in their various rooms four or five hotel guests, all with baffled and blank expressions. Then the man whose window had fallen out smiled guiltily and shrugged, and the man with him slapped him on the back. The first man began explaining loudly that he hadn't done anything; he hadn't even been near the window. Across the courtyard, another man leaned out of his open window, calling condolences. A fourth man laughed and turned back into his room. Nobody ever came to sweep up the glass. That might have been laziness, or it might have been prudence: you wouldn't want to be under it when the next window came crashing down.

Imant was waiting for me. He had met me at the airport, with Emil, Ilze—who seemed to be Emil's girlfriend—and Rudolf, and then followed the bus to the hotel. Imant didn't know Leningrad well. We were all tired, and Imant's face was drawn. He had a friend in Leningrad and he'd been hoping we could stay there, but it developed that the friend was out of town. Naïvely, I suggested to Imant that we could go to another hotel, surrendering the Sovietskaya to my tour group. That was when he explained the regulations to me: no visitors in your room after 9 P.M. I still didn't understand why we couldn't register as Mr. and Mrs. Ivan Ivanovich Ivanov. Imant's eyes lightened as he saw what the problem was. "Oh," he said, "you thought we could simply sign our names! Is not the way here. One must present one's passport." He meant the internal passport Soviet citizens are required to carry. Once Imant had asked me if it was true that in America anyone was free to travel anywhere.

"Of course," I said.

He didn't say anything for a long time. Then he said, so softly I could barely hear him: "*Free. . . .*Sweet, sweet word."

After further discussion we realized we had no choice: it was too cold to sleep in the car. (We left summer in Riga, and went to Leningrad to catch winter whipping around the corner.) We had to find a hotel: we'd fret about rules and regulations later.

It was still light when we started searching, but the light drained away quickly, as if somebody had pulled out a plug. (Or, seeing that this was a Russian sky, threw the plug away, since all Russians *know* plugs are unhygienic.) Reflected in the black canals, neon signs seemed to swim like brightly colored fish. The streets of Leningrad are broad and beautiful; I opened my window a crack, and air poured in like water. Ilze and I didn't care what it did to our hair.

Imant and I waited while the others went in to see about a room, but there was no room in this inn. We set off to try another hotel, but I felt subdued. And the next hotel had no vacancy either. Nor did the one after that. We had been driving around Leningrad for two or three hours, and in the end Imant took us back to the Sovietskaya. The trio went in to ask again for rooms, it was our last chance, and this time they struck gold, Russian gold. There were still no vacancies—but the clerk at the desk gave them the phone number of an *underground hotel.*

Now that we had a place to go, the others stayed in the car while Imant and I went into the Sovietskaya so I could collect, from the room I was supposed to share with Vera, the overnight things I would want.

"Did Indra bring you something to the bus?" he said, looking around the room. The package was on a shelf. "But you have not opened!" he said, taking it down.

"I waited for you."

"Open now," he said. "I want you to see—"

They were cups. Not the hefty red coffee mugs I had thought I was talking about; these were delicate teacups with matching saucers, two of each, hand-painted against a light brown background.

"Teodor made," he said. "They were very fine, no?"

"They are beautiful." And they were. "I don't want to take them with me. They belong in the farmhouse."

For our farmhouse we now had a painting, a photograph, and two teacups. On winter afternoons when the sun was sparkling on the snow, we would sit in our kitchen and sip tea from works of art.

Imant had said everything in our house would have to be "very fine." He was going to try to get a Dutch sideboard from someone he knew who had one for sale; the furniture in Soviet stories is all knockabout stuff, jerry-built, but you can get good things privately. Still, neither of us had owned fine furniture before, and I asked Imant why he was concerned about it now. He was laughing, though, as always, more with his eyes than out loud. "Someday this house will be famous," he said. "People will come from all over the world to see it, and so, it must be very fine house." That wasn't all. It also had to have alligators in the pond. "You're putting me on," I complained, but he said, "Yes, yes! Russian alligators," indicating a body length of about ten inches. He had already decided we'd have several cats, and a Borzoi puppy for me. And, of course, our allotted cow.

I tied the teacups up again in their newsprint and tucked them back on the shelf.

It was time to ask him about something that had been bothering me.

"You must have been in love when you got married before," I said. "How do I know there isn't going to be a Wife Number Five? I'm willing to live in the Soviet Union as your wife, but actually, I can't think of any place in the world I'd less like to be a divorcée in."

"You are only wife I want."

"Yes, but," I said, unable to stop, "is the way you feel about me"—I didn't know how to put this—"is it any different from the way you felt *before*?"

"You are asking me," he said, "what I cannot answer. I do not know how—" My face felt numb, as if the world had just blown up in it. He said again: "You ask me what I do not know how to answer."

I put together my gear for the night and gave it to Imant to carry. Walking back down the long hallway, weighed down by my flight kit and string bag, he said in a low but distinct voice: "I would give my life for you." I looked up, jolted. "I cannot live without you," he said. "I cannot." I smiled at the key lady at the end of the hall as if Imant weren't saying these things to me under his breath, but words which might be only romantic in other circumstances take on a startling significance when you know they could be overheard by the KGB.

"That's what I needed to know," I said.

We needed a gas station, and it had to be the kind of gas station for which Imant had coupons.

The beauty of Leningrad, simply speaking, stuns. The whole city is a measured spread of pastel set against a pewter sky carefully engraved with clouds; it's like a formal garden in which the ornately trimmed shrubs are made of stone. At night, the city's breath seemed cool and moistened, and the dark streets glistened. We spent another hour looking for the gas station, which we eventually came upon behind another building. I can't exaggerate the difficulty of these ordinary tasks.

And after we found the filling station, we still had to find the hotel. Now: like all underground activities, this "hotel" was certainly known to the authorities. The room shortage being what it is, private citizens, or comrades, rent out spare rooms for a few untaxed rubles. Some of these rentals are quite well organized: word is passed from guest to guest, or through official hotel employees who presumably receive a kickback, and if a "hotel" is booked up, it refers its overflow to another "hotel." Upstairs, it may be, or next door. Again, the room shortage being what it is, the authorities look the other way.

It took us another couple of hours to find our hotel; it was in a monolithic apartment complex in the suburbs. I thought we'd never find it. I asked Imant if the KGB were following us; he said it was possible. I had an idea. "Why don't we let them go in front," I said, "and then *we* could follow *them* to the hotel?" It was getting late, and every back alley and dead end we went down made it later. When we found the right complex, we couldn't figure out how to get into it. At last in utter disgust Imant jumped the curb, drove across three backyards and brought us to a halt in front of a building in a row of buildings. The only thing distinguishing it from the others was its number. We gave three cheers, discreetly.

Emil, Ilze, and Rudolf went on up. Imant clasped my wrist. "Kelly," he said, "do not speak to these people, okay? You will be my Latvian wife, okay? They may be frightened if they know you are American."

I nodded and followed Imant upstairs. Our friends were on the landing, talking (Russian) with the two old women who had answered their knock. They seemed agitated, and I immediately imagined some misunderstanding and dire consequence, but the only problem was that the room had only one bed. Neighbors upstairs had another room, one with two cots. At the time I didn't know what they were discussing; Imant introduced me to the ladies, I smiled, our friends raced upstairs, and I tried to cover up the name tag on my flight bag with my right hand while keeping my ringless left in my pocket and then remembered that in this country it should be the other way around, and kept saying "*Paldies*," the Latvian word for "thank you," whenever anyone spoke to me. Our room was just inside the door to the flat, and as soon as we succeeded in getting inside and shutting our door, I sank onto the bed in relief. The room was small—and wonderful. A window looked out into the lives of other people in lighted rooms across the way. The wide bed had been pushed against a tapestried wall. The mirror was on top of a piece of furniture of indeterminable function. I got out my contact lens equipment—aseptor, cleaning solution, and so forth—and set it on the table and took out my lenses.

There was a knock on our door. Before we could stop her, the larger of the two ladies was in our room, urging cups of tea on us and talking a mile a minute. She was thrilled to be entertaining foreigners—Latvians—and she headed straight for the things I'd put on the table, picking them up and looking them over and seeing, of course, the American labels. Imant launched into an explanation; I could make out that he was telling her that he had to import these things for his wife. I couldn't say anything; I couldn't, for that matter, even see anything. When the woman left, I sighed my second sigh of relief. Then she came in again, with great hunks of bread in her hands. "*Paldies,*" I said. She made motions that plainly meant, even to my myopic eyes, that Imant ought to fatten me up. "Da," Imant said. She seemed satisfied at this and left, and this time she didn't return. It saddened me to think she might not be so friendly if she knew I was American.

After she left, the apartment grew quiet; you could almost see the silence settling, like a cloth over a table. I stood at the window. In the building across the way, lights were going off. Soviet citizens go to sleep at night just as American citizens do: so much the better if they can sleep together, making love instead of war. I put on my long lavender gown with the low neckline. Wind was clawing at the trees, but in our small room we were safe. I could have holed up there a year, at least. Imant felt at home too; while I was looking out the window and musing, he drank both cups of tea and ate all the bread, and I gave him an apple from my string bag and he ate that too, and then he leaned against the tapestry on the wall and began to be happier.

Was everyone else asleep? I opened the door, stealthily. The rest of the apartment was dark, but to get to the bathroom, which was only a few feet from our room, I had to pass an open area from which a prodigious snoring issued. I crossed and recrossed on tiptoe, and then, having accomplished that much without waking anyone, Imant and I discovered that our bed creaked. Someone has told me that at one time the peasants used to overlay their hearths with broad platforms which became their beds at night, so that, in effect, they slept on their stoves. At least stoves don't creak.

We were making so much noise anyway that I asked Imant to teach me some Latvian. After all, I was passing as Latvian. And though the Latvian language, unlike Russian and English, isn't "rich" in vulgarities, it does have some words that were pertinent to the occasion. But Imant refused to teach them to me. When I asked why, he stammered and said that his *māmiņa* had brought him up to be "modest." On the other hand, she had not brought him up to be modest in a foreign language, and he wasn't at all averse to learning a little basic *English*.

Later, with the light out, as I was drifting into sleep, Imant began to speak Latvian. He was speaking his mother tongue, but as far as I was concerned it might as well have been tongues. My face was buried against his chest, and the mysterious words fell softly on my head, as if I were being anointed. I stirred, but he continued; it was almost a chant, alien and ritualistic, and I became alarmed. I thought he might be talking in a kind of half-sleep, that he might have forgotten I was only pretending to be Latvian, even that he had confused me with Frederika. I tried to interrupt, but he covered my face with his hands. His words were swift and sometimes so muted I could hardly catch the hard and palatalized *k*'s that lend the Latvian language its characteristic sound. In Imant's gentle and hypnotic voice the words seemed almost less sound than shadow, and gradually I grew used to them, like beginning to see in a dim room after coming in from a brightly lit hallway. Secure in his arms, I gave myself over to this grave music and closed my eyes. As naturally as day becomes night, the words became silence. The transformation was scarcely noticeable until it was complete, and silence filled the room. Then Imant spoke in a normal tone, in English: "All these things I have had in my heart to say you, but my English is too poor. So I have told them to you in Latvian."

Sunday morning, Emil rapped lightly on our door, took the car keys from Imant, left two boiled eggs on our table, and ducked out again. We were late getting down, and just as we thought we were ready to leave, I realized I'd better pack all my stuff and lug it along with me. I didn't think our landladies were light-fingered but they'd be bound to come in and take a look, and any of a dozen articles could have made them suspicious of my nationality. "Yes, yes," Imant said, smiling, "they are very curious. They are very typical, these old women, for they are simple but they are good." They brought us more tea, more bread, but I was kept busy biting my tongue. Imagine how hard it is not to let slip an "okay" or an "all right" or a "hi" or "thank you"! I was restricted to my *paldies*, which I used indiscriminately, looking helplessly at Imant whenever any longer speech was called for. I'm sure they thought he had married an idiot.

Emil, Ilze, and Rudolf were waiting in the back seat of the car. It was a brilliant day, not too cold. The first leaves of autumn lay on the ground but the trees were mostly still dark green, and the wide streets brought a bright blue sky clear down to eye level. Leningrad's palette is more variegated than Moscow's or Riga's, but its hues remain subtle; only the sky, the trees, the myriad canals will sometimes leap to the front of the stage like the *corps de ballet*, and dazzle. There's also, as elsewhere, the red of the banners overhanging the streets or draped across the cornices of factory plants and warehouses.

I've heard that many of these oratorical oriflammes were hung up to commemorate a given Party congress, and then after the congress no one had the nerve to take them down; and so they accumulate, congress to congress. They all say things like: Communism is the party of peace, or We are making the world safe for all peoples. My favorite slogan was, To live, to work, to study—like Lenin! It struck my funny bone.

*

We parked, and walked to a café—to several cafés, in fact, before we found one that was "open." Along the way, Imant practiced basic English, at the top of his lungs. I tried to hush him up, but he argued, "Is okay! No one will understand," and the more I blushed, the louder his voice grew. He was testing his new vocabulary in sentences. "Is right way to use, yes?" he would ask, and Rudolf, coming up behind us, would say, "What does it mean?" Finally I capitulated: "Imant is learning the English that textbooks leave out," I said. Rudolf begged, politely but urgently, "Please, will you be so kind as to teach me too?"

So I rummaged around in the back of my brain for some expression or idiom that was slangy without being obscene, and so help me, what I came up with was this: "Wow, look at that pair of knockers!"

"Woo, look at that pair of knoak-erz," Rudolf repeated, his face contorted excruciatingly.

"Knockers," I said.

"Please, what are knoak-erz?" he asked.

I tried to explain, "Well, you know," I said, "a woman's chest. That is, her bust." There was complete incomprehension on both their faces, and in desperation I shouted, "Breasts!" I didn't know I was going to announce it so forcefully, and put my hand over my mouth, too late. Imant laughed. "I think you knew all along," I said, accusingly.

He wanted to know "if all American breasts are knockers."

"Only big ones," I said. "You're supposed to stand on a street corner, see, and then when a big-breasted woman walks by, you nudge your sidekick with your elbow, like this"—I nudged Rudolf with my elbow—"and you say, *Wow, look at that pair of knockers.* I promise you, this will make you extremely American."

"Knoak-erz," Rudolf said, with enormous seriousness.

"Knockers," Imant corrected him. "The *s* is between an *s* and a *z*. Woo, look at that—"

"Not woo," I said, correcting Imant. "Wow."

"Is impossible. How can there be such a sound as this: *ow?*" He made a face. "Americans," he declared, "are a peculiar people."

By this time we had reached the café; Emil and Ilze had caught up with us, and we were all standing around waiting for a free table. One of the patrons in the process of leaving was about five feet tall and five feet wide, with a grand smile displaying her gold tooth; as she walked toward us, she rolled from side to side like a sailor. A Russian grandmother, surely. She was reclaiming her coat from the attendant when I happened to catch Imant and Rudolf staring down at her ample bosom. Imant nudged Rudolf with his elbow, "Woo," Rudolf said, "look at that pair of knoak-erz!"

"Oh no," I said.

"Knockers," Imant said. "Yes?"

"Yes. . . .I mean, no!"

"But what is wrong?"

"Those are not knockers," I said (in a low voice, out of the side of my mouth, to Imant).

Imant looked perplexed. "But they are breasts?" And when I assured him they were indeed breasts, he was visibly relieved. "Big breasts," he said. "And so, knockers."

"Right," I agreed, once and for all. Besides, I didn't really want him to become overly American on this score.

The café didn't have the fish we ordered, so we opted for eggs, although we'd already had eggs once that morning. But the waitress tipped us off to the eggs' not being fresh. We wound up with the third—and last—item on the breakfast menu, beefsteak. I asked Imant if orange juice was ever available, and he set off in a search of some. I don't remember what he came back with but it wasn't orange and he'd had to go to two other stores to find it. He didn't mind. Rudolf said to me, while Imant was away from the table, "Imant is cheerful today." Rudolf looked as earnest as ever. "Yes," I said, "thanks!"

We wanted to visit Petrodvorets, eighteen miles outside of Leningrad, an incredibly profligate spill of pleasure palaces and parks centered around the Grand Palace for which Peter himself is said to have done the first sketches, but we didn't know the way. I wasn't even sure it was within the permissible limits except by Intourist bus, but of course it is. I was jumpier than I needed to be. And yet, how do you know what's *appropriately* jumpy? We were heading out of the city, in clear weather, light breaking on the Neva in waves like water. A cop flagged Imant down, and he pulled over to the curb, got out his papers, and walked around to the back of the car to meet the cop. I had no way of knowing what this was all about. I tried to quiz Rudolf but he turned my questions aside. Emil shook his head, but whether he was shaking his head at me or over me, I couldn't tell. I did my best to look natural—also as if I weren't an American staying in an underground hotel—but I couldn't help casting furtive glances over my shoulder. When Imant returned to the car, he didn't say anything. After several minutes of studied nonchalance, I blurted out, "Why did he stop us?"

Imant seemed surprised by my question. "Why?"

"Did we do anything wrong? Did you break a Russian traffic law?"

"No," he said, as if that fact had been obvious to everybody, including the cop.

"Was he looking for someone?"

"For whom would he be looking?"

"I don't know," I said. "Smugglers maybe. Counterrevolutionaries. Enemies of the State."

"He was not looking for anyone."

"Do you mean," I said, slowly, "that he stopped you for no reason at all? Just to check your papers?"

"Yes, of course."

"Of course?"

We spotted a palatial-looking residence and hiked down one hill and up another to get to it. Stone lions guarded the gates. The palace was decayed and deserted, a windswept outpost, as if the czars had dug in at the last affluent fort. There weren't any czars here, however; only two or three contemplative picnickers eating their lunches singly in the "backyard," which looked more like the north forty. We paced the patio, looking down on the solitary lunching people. The formal layout of the former lawn was traceable under the overgrown grasses, and wind rippled the long grasses like green water.

I wanted to take pictures but my companions wouldn't let me; this wasn't our destination, and they wanted me to wait for the real thing. This was just your average spare palace, left lying around like a calling card from an earlier age. SORRY, SIR, says the card, BUT YOU WERE OUT WHEN I HAPPENED.

The real thing was a good deal farther up the road, and a herd of Intourist buses penned in the parking lot made it unmissable. The whole affair is nearly as elaborate and decadent as the Tivoli Gardens, though higher-minded. From Peter's summer palace, steps pitch steeply down an escarpment to a string of parks on either side of a shimmering ribbon of tame water that unfurls into the Gulf of Finland. Viewed from the palace, the figured symmetry of hedgerows and footpaths is breathtaking, but at the bottom of the steps you join the throng of tourists meandering through planned walks past ingeniously contrived fountains and mechanical amusements. You blink before so much gilt—the very air seems like beaten gold. It's all enough to give a good Bolshevik nightmares, or at least dreams of capital gain. Children hop back and forth between a cupola and the sidewalk, giggling and shrieking as they aim to anticipate the next "waterfall" from the rim of the cupola. Toy ducks quack in a pool; you'd have to feed them toy crumbs. The event that took my fancy was a mechanical garden: there were big, painted, metal flowers that spouted like whales, and a tree with spraying branches. Coney Island, Disneyland. . .what won't people do, to entertain themselves and stave off death? We bought ice cream.

As we rounded a bend in the path, the Gulf of Finland came into view. Just before you reach the water's edge, there's a cottage now used as a museum; many of the visitors were headed there. Our friends joined the queue for the current exhibit, while Imant and I went shoreside to talk.

A mere eighteen miles away is Finland. It seemed I could reach out and touch it with my fingertips. We leaned against the railing. There was a bench, but it was totally occupied by two old Russian women, reading. "You could ask them to move over," I said, but Imant whispered back, "I do not dare." The pair held their books up to their noses. Imant ambled "casually" around to the back of the bench and peeked spylike over their broad shoulders. "They are *very* serious," he said, reporting back to me. "I think they must be retired Communists." We tried hard not to let them see us laughing.

"Did you ever think," I said, catching my breath, "of leaving?" Imant followed my gaze to the horizon.

Almost automatically, our voices dropped. "Everyone thinks I want, but this is where I belong. If I had been some years older when the war came, then, to be sure, I would have sailed to Sweden on one of the boats. There were such boats." Imant was five weeks old when the Nazis occupied Riga. Why had his father stayed? "I asked him," Imant said, "of course. He did not think, that it would be like this. Now, is my home, my people, and I belong here. A man must live in his country."

There was never any question of persuading Imant to leave; aside from considerations of law, morality (he thought defecting was wrong), and homesickness, for Imant to leave the Soviet Union would be even riskier for his work than moving to the Soviet Union was for mine; I knew this even better than he did. A young composer who writes on a large scale—symphonies and oratorios—can, in the Soviet Union, be performed and recorded; money is rarely available for that kind of thing—that large-scale kind of thing—in the United States, and although Imant would be able to write his "Magdalen" in the United States, he'd probably have to scrap most of his other compositions. Finding me a typewriter in Latvia, however tricky, still wouldn't be as difficult as finding him an orchestra in America.

"Sooner or later," I said, "after I'm living here, in your country, I'll have to write about it. If only incidentally."

"Yes, yes, is true, I understand."

"Will they make trouble?"

"There will be interference—of this I am sure. They do not know how *not* to interfere. But I think it may not be so bad. They will let you publish in America, I think. They will see that it is good for everyone that you live here and write."

"Will they let me send my manuscripts to America?" Again, it was a question that, according to the Helsinki Accords, shouldn't even have to be asked. My manuscripts would be my personal property, the property of a U.S. citizen, and I should be able to mail them to my agent, who would sell the first rights in North America.

"But why not? I think so," he said.

We looked out over the water—the jumble of rocks first, then the sun-spangled waves, then the jeweled horizon—toward Finland. Our hands, on the stone railing, touched. "Almost it seems," he said, "as if you can reach out and touch—"

I thought he was going to say Finland.

"—freedom."

The day's light had begun to go underground, like all radical activity. Our friends came out of the cottage, and we walked—a little faster, now—through the park, over one of the bridges to the other side of the blue ribbon, and back to the steps. I must say they seemed steep to me. I stopped to rest two-thirds of the way up. "I hope I get to marry you before we get old," I said. "You'll probably be bald by the time they let us get married."

"The men in my family do not go bald," he said, reassuring me. "Only a little."

"That means time is on our side," I said. But I was lying, and we both knew it. The crowd of tourists had thinned, and the weather was growing chill. Imant turned his collar up. We had a long ride back, and it was dusk by the time we got there.

It began to rain, a clear, steady, autumnal rain, the kind of rain that puts things in perspective. We were in the café at the Sovietskaya. One wall of the café was glass, so from where we sat we could watch the rain spattering against it, and across the driveway, the grassy circle changing colors from green to black. I had brought the teacups, Imant's present to me, down from my (official) room—Imant would take them to the farmhouse—and he unwrapped them for everyone to see. Even the waitress oohed and aahed. Just one table was oblivious. While Imant was putting the cups away, Rudolf leaned over to me and said, "KGB." I thought he was pulling my leg, as Imant did fairly often. The only people at that table were kids. "You're teasing me," I said.

"No," Rudolf said.

I looked at Imant. He was tying the string around the teacups.

"Rudolf's joking, isn't he?" I asked.

"No," he said.

I looked again at the table of kids. "How can you tell?"

Rudolf answered, "One knows, that is all."

"They do not talk with one another," Imant said. "They try to hear what others are saying."

"But they're only kids—"

"Very often, a young person does something wrong—he takes something from a store, perhaps, or he tries to buy and sell on the black market. Then when he is caught, he is given a choice: to go to prison or work for the KGB."

We finished eating as fast as possible, got our gear together, and vamoosed. I don't know whether we were followed or whether, if we were, it was by the kids from the café.

It was early evening by the time we found a wine shop where we picked up the night's supply, and dark by the time we found a candy store. Emil and Ilze disappeared into the candy store for twenty minutes. The shop window glowed brightly through the rain, and my red umbrella finally got some use when Rudolf borrowed it to dash in after Emil and Ilze.

I had taught Imant another word: *privacy*. To Emil and Ilze and Rudolf, he had said, "I wish to have some privacy with Kelly tonight." (That was only for show, because he had to say it in Latvian before they could understand.) But Rudolf, in his halting English, said they hoped we would come to their room for a little while first. We would have a kind of party—a very quiet kind of party, in our underground hotel.

At our underground hotel, Emil, Ilze and Rudolf decided to buy cigarettes across the way, so Imant and I went inside and waited for them by the window on the first landing. Light from the streetlamp, made misty by the evening rain—now slowed to a drizzle—shed a nebulous glow on the wet pavement. Three forward-pitching backs made a lunge for the store door, like football linemen. Emil and Rudolf were on the two ends; Ilze was in the center. I didn't know Ilze. She had sharp features, eyebrows carefully etched on a small face, and she spoke only Russian and Polish. I resented her for taking Olga's place, which was irrational of me. I surmised that Ilze herself felt like an interloper and tried simultaneously to defend and play down her position, but maybe I just imagined all this. Maybe not knowing Latvian limited her too. Today she had begun to unbend, be friendlier.

I thought of the other two, Rudolf and Emil: the one, Rudolf, with a young man's acute sensibility lending him outward elegance and a piercing inward sense of betrayal; the other, Emil, so much the man Rudolf would become, the inevitable older version, edges worn, the style grown scruffy with time and circumstance, the passion more accommodating, less ambitious, more forgiving, enthusiasm reserved for the attainable and not dissipated in dreams.

Dreams. Suddenly I wanted something to signify that my life here was real. I asked Imant if he knew what an engagement ring was. "Yes!" he said, excitedly. "I like this custom very much!" He said he would have a ring made for me. "I know a place," he said, "where they are making very fine jewelry." But he didn't think he would be permitted to send the ring out of Russia. "I will send letters," he said. "Each night I write to you and tell you what has happened in the day, and in morning I send." This way I could wake up each day knowing there'd be a letter from him.

We had somehow managed to shrug off the consciousness of time: it seemed as though we could wait forever by that window, speaking softly in a bare, echoing hallway, and never run out of time. I asked Imant if there was any chance we could be married in a church. He was greatly excited by this notion also and exclaimed, "Yes, yes! I have not been married in a church before." Considering the number of his civil marriages, I had to laugh. But Imant was serious.

He is Lutheran, though about Catholicism, he had said, "I like this confession very much." (He'd have had trouble with the Catholic ruling on divorce!) Before the war, the majority of Latvians were Lutherans, about one quarter were Roman Catholic, and nine percent were Greek Orthodox. There were smaller but significant numbers of Russian Old Believers and Jews. In answer to Imant's question, I had explained that I was brought up more or less a Presbyterian. He looked perplexed. "We have no Presbyterians here," he said. However, when I mentioned Calvin, he'd immediately produced a book on Luther and Calvin. The pictures of the two dour theologians were unmistakable in any language.

Now Imant said, "Sometimes it is allowed to marry in a church if it is discreet." (Sometimes the churches are so discreet you can't even find them. We knew there was one church in Leningrad where concerts are held on Sunday morning, but we couldn't discover which one.)

And then I recalled a scene from ten years ago. Night, in the old town of Riga: Imant opens an inconspicuous door, and I find myself in a cathedral. There is incense. People are kneeling, praying, rising. There aren't many of them, and some are so old that it seems a miracle that they can get up from their knees.

There is one young girl, with a kerchief pulled so far in front of her face that I can see her face only when she turns and looks straight at me. Imant guides me out, his hand on my elbow, and neither of us ever refers to any of this.

I had wondered at the time why Imant was showing me this. To show, without stating it, that the Soviets discouraged religion; to show that people worshiped despite that. But did he also mean to convey a sense of his own spiritual longings, to suggest that here, in a church, was where I might find a side of him that not many people knew?

I began to think how much time had passed since we'd come in from the car. "Where could they be?" I asked. And for the first time we looked around us and realized we were in the wrong building. Imant slapped his forehead and laughed. "Well," he said, "they are all the same, these hallways, no?"

We sat on the cots in a room smaller than many closets. There were no chairs, for the simple reason that there was no space for any. Overhead, an unshaded bulb dangled at the end of a string, glaring like an open eye. We had to keep our voices to a whisper. It wasn't the merriest of atmospheres, but we were merry. You're pretty much forced to be, on red wine and marzipan.

Imant asked everyone to estimate my ring size, and, by comparing the circumference of my ring finger with Ilze's, decided what size he'd order. If he couldn't send it to me, it would be waiting for me.

Meanwhile, Rudolf also arrived at a decision: he would learn to speak English well enough to conduct a real conversation in it when I returned. I grew sentimental about the English language, as a language that makes its own music, and then about Russian, which is also beautiful and rich in insight as well. Latvian isn't so beautiful, but it has other virtues, and the most beautiful of all is Estonian. By way of experiment I asked Rudolf to say something—the same something—in Russian, Polish, Latvian, and French. Emil threw in German, and Imant contributed Estonian. Then it was back to Rudolf for the English translation, but he was suddenly overcome by embarrassment. I had to look to Imant to persuade Rudolf to let me in on the little set speech. Rudolf had to struggle through the sentence, putting a period after each word. "We wish to thank you, dear lady, for your company and kindness in being with us." I knew if I started crying I wouldn't stop all night, so I smiled just as if none of us understood that we might never see one another again.

You could of course forge for yourself an iron heart to set in the place of this old mortal heart. This old mortal heart ticks like a time bomb, but the new heart lies in your chest like a dead weight. You try to walk and it drags you to the ground, you try to swim and are drowned. That heaviness keeps you in your place—your only place. This is a type of imprisonment. You would rather explode.

*

We set my travel alarm for six and woke to its clatter. Oddly, we weren't depressed; the thin light outside our window, the sense of secrecy and importance that attends any leave-taking done while most people are still sound asleep, buoyed our spirits. We packed efficiently—we were getting to be old hands at that—and when we were ready, Imant went to pay the landladies. The larger one came to see us out. She was in her robe, her hair looked as if she'd been fighting it during the night, and sleep still creased her cheeks, but she would have liked a chat. She stood with her hand on the doorknob, and she didn't want to let us go. I was afraid I'd muff the whole affair at the last minute, and as soon as we could slip out the door, I began to back down the stairs, saying, "*Paldies, paldies,*" but she wanted a final word with Imant. On the way to the car I asked him what it was. "She told"—he said—"my wife is pretty, I must take care of her." He grinned. I made a mental note that when I wrote my Michelin guide to underground hotels, this one rated four stars.

We waited in the car for Emil, Ilze, and Rudolf. The weather on this last day made it clear that we really were in a new season now: a brisk and freshening wind, sky so blue it seemed as if the last traces of summer had been swept from it only that morning, and a fallen leaf stuck against our windshield like a deciduous parking ticket. The canals glint, glitter, wink, shine, blind, flash, and glow—how can anyone be sad, in Leningrad? But anxiety nips at the heart like a dog at a rear wheel, and by the time we reached the Sovietskaya, I felt emotionally out of breath.

Imant didn't see me onto the bus, because his scheme was to follow the bus to the airport. I couldn't see out back from my seat; I could only hope he was there. Then when we were out on the road that led to the airport, a little yellow Fiat overtook us, horn blaring, and all its passengers waved like crazy at ours.

But at the airport, I couldn't find them. We were driven in one way; they had to come another. We learned that we had a half hour yet, the news I was praying for—but what good was a half hour without Imant? Finally, we collided on the main floor.

"I am as excited as on the first day," he said, "but I know it will be okay. You will be back soon. I am sure of it."

"Before Christmas?"

"Is possible. . . .Yes, yes, I think so! I must make the house warm for winter."

We had gone off by ourselves and were sitting in the waiting room.

"You should keep your name when we marry," he said. "Here, is done very often when the wife has work of her own."

"Don't forget to take the things to the farmhouse—"

"They are calling your plane," Imant said, and suddenly everything became terribly bright and hectic and unreal. I said good-bye to Emil, Ilze, and Rudolf. The room all around us seemed to be in flux, but for that moment we were as isolated as an island. Ilze and I shook hands; Emil kissed my hand, and Rudolf was about to, but he looked so wildly forlorn that I pecked his cheek instead. Then there was nothing more we could say to each other, and we raced to the boarding station, the three of them following Imant and me. Imant, handing me over to the check-out officials, kissed me loudly and proclaimed for all to hear, "I love you." A short while later I was miles *above* ground.

ON THE ISLE OF BARDS

It was not working out. We were two lonely people, and I suppose we were angry with each other for not being the partner for whom we both hoped. He was Welsh and distinguished, a man of numerous and various successes, and a single parent in search of companionship and a mother for his daughter. I was in search of a way to escape the repetitive duties of teaching and the hypocrisy and careerism of academia. We thought we should have been able to make it work and in addition to being angry with each other we were angry with ourselves for not being able to make it work.

With his ten-year-old daughter and her best friend, we had driven north to catch the ferry to Bardsey Island. We parked the car off the highway and carried our baggage and gear down a steep side road to the shore. For a long time, women and children stood around and waited while the men transferred cargo from the ferry to rowboats for the shallower distance to shore. He cut a striking figure, silhouetted against the sky in his raincoat, waders, and seafarer's hat, leaning on his walking stick. The sun glittered on the sea behind him. The tension between us had a kind of glitter too, flashing out and going dark by turns. We avoided looking each other in the eye.

I was dressed all wrong. My shoes were soaked. My arms were cold. When I climbed from the rowboat onto the ferry, I had to hike my skirt up ridiculously high. I blamed him for not satisfactorily answering my question about what to wear.

The two girls had made this trip before. They knew what they were doing.

My sister had suggested that I beg off. *No,* I said, *I'm so bored with my life in Wisconsin. I have to see where this takes me.*

We were going to spend a week on the island, a National Nature Reserve. There would be no electricity, no cars, no hot water. We would have a chemical outhouse out back.

Our cottage was one of a handful of whitewashed stone cottages scattered like rice over the seven-tenths-of-a-square-mile island. My room was on the ground floor. He and the children were upstairs. He handed me sheets and a blanket and exited to make his own bed upstairs.

While they were all still upstairs, I discovered a bulletin board with notices. THERE IS SHEEPFLUKE ON THIS ISLAND, said one. WASH ALL VEGETABLES.

Just before leaving Wisconsin I had seen an episode of *The X-Files* in which Fox Mulder and Dana Scully, FBI agents investigating reports of unexplained phenomena, track down the Fluke Man, a mutant who has been living in the sewer system and eating sanitation workers. The Fluke Man looked like a giant fluke and probably wasn't ill-intentioned, but he was a fluke.

I returned to my room and finished unpacking.

Bardsey Island (in Welsh, *Ynys Enlli*) sits on the northern tip of Cardigan Bay in north Wales. A two-mile-wide channel famous for its furious current separates it from the Lleyn Peninsula. A place of pilgrimage, Bardsey is also known as "the island of twenty thousand saints." And it's said it's their voices, saints' voices, one hears when the shearwaters begin their strange shrieking. The Manx shearwater, one of whose habitats this is, sounds on moonless nights like a slightly crazed, howling dog. This oceanic bird builds a nesting burrow. The male and female produce one egg, caring for it for two months. Isolated as the island is, it is nevertheless a kind of suburbia for shearwaters, who are thought to be quite social, their weird wild cries a kind of gossip.

I couldn't figure out how to put the sheets on my bed (I felt defeated and frustrated and joked with myself that they must be Welsh sheets). But I didn't want to come across as the world's biggest wimp so instead of asking for help I tucked the sheets in like blankets, leaving the bare mattress to sleep on.

He brought me a candle in a saucer; it was only for undressing by, not for reading by.

A window in the small front room (which my room adjoined) looked out across fields to the sea. Sheep grazed freely over the whole island, and would spring up suddenly to land on the "fences"—mounds—that gridded the fields. On a grass-covered stone fence—it seemed the fence needing mowing—a ewe lay sunning herself. In the distance, three horses ran loose along the strand, sleek creatures with the late afternoon sun glancing off their backs.

The girls had lost no time. There were in the front yard, acting out television commercials, forecasting the weather. They took turns being the viewer.

We had brought only minimal provisions, partly because we would have to bring back to the mainland all bottles and tins, and partly because the budget was tight. After a brief supper of undressed lettuce, cheese, and cold cuts, we sat on the couch while the girls played Crazy Eights on the living room floor. He went back to the kitchen and returned with a tray bearing four jelly glasses and a bottle of wine ("recommended by my vintner," he assured me). The now-early-evening light was still pink, swimming across the sky ahead of the blue-black that seemed about to swallow it. He poured the wine. The girls pretended to be winos, staggering drunkenly around the room and passing out cold on the floor, and then raced outside, where they instantly became nuns from the Whoopi Goldberg movie *Sister Act*.

I settled back into the couch. I was thinking that everything might turn out all right after all: the real problem, I thought, was one of communication, and we ought to be able to solve that. "I don't believe the problem is communication," he said when I told him this. "After all, we are both professional communicators."

I felt he was telling me to shut up.

Looking back, I think I was too defensive. At the time I retreated into silence.

We sipped our wine, which was, he reminded me, "very, very expensive."

All at once, a fly landed in my glass. It was as if it had jumped into a pool. "Sheepfly," he said.

It was large and thrashing, drowning before my eyes. I could see its legs paddling the liquid.

I waited for him to get me another glass of wine.

Or—as he did not seem to be getting up from the couch—he could offer to exchange glasses; that would even be romantic, chivalrous. And it would not mean throwing out any of the very, very expensive wine.

"Shall I get that out for you?" he said, and plunged his hand into my glass, fishing out the dead sheepfly.

I thought about sheepfluke and Fluke Man. Fluke Man had been white and wormy, with a mouth like an open wound. Even Scully, who had a medical degree, had been squeamish when confronted with Fluke Man.

There was a knock on the door and the local friar entered and introduced himself. We chatted pleasantly enough, but the friar kept jotting notes in a small tablet. A few days later we learned he was suffering from premature senile dementia. The notes were his way of trying to remember the island's visitors. He also danced by himself in the moonlight and performed private rituals at break of day in the ruins of the thirteenth-century Augustinian abbey, which was not far from our cottage.

It was dark by the time the friar left. I said, "You had been going to say something."

He said, "Let's take the pressure off. You needn't worry about romantic advances. I promise not to throw any passes."

It made me feel sad, his giving up like that. If only we could find a meeting place in our conversation, a space where the gloves could come off and we could talk without lashing out at each other. The pressure was off, but only because we had both moved to our respective corners in the ring.

He called the girls in and they all disappeared upstairs. In bed in my downstairs room, I cried for a long time before I fell asleep. I had had this dream, the dream of meeting someone with whom to share a life and raise a child, forever.

***

I was thrilled and enraptured by the landscape into which I might have moved with my books and manuscripts and blue jeans and work shirts, the stunning high hills of the Wye Valley, the prospects that seemed to be newly created with every hairpin curve one negotiated. Here on Bardsey was beauty of another kind: sunlight on water, bees as fat as tourists in Florida, the butterflies in the back, dizzy with scent. Pink and blue mallow bloomed; sheep fluff waved wildly from wherever it had got itself snagged, on the fences or tree trunks or thickets. Heather, thrift, marsh marigold, nettle-leaved bellflowers, meadow cranesbill, purple saxifrage, and dog rose were everywhere, and so plentiful they seemed to come in flocks, like the birds and sheep.

The girls raced through the field, shouting, "Lambchops and mint sauce!" to scare the sheep.

"Listen," writes Brenda Chamberlain in her book *Tide-race* about life on Bardsey: "I have found the home of my heart. I could not eat: I could not think straight any more; so I came to this solitary place and lay in the sun."

We went fishing with hand lines, using sinker and bait. We perched on the cliffs and cast our lines into the dark water that pooled in inlets and eddied around the rude thrusts of rock. No one caught anything. We ate honey sandwiches the girls had made. "Like Winnie," his daughter said. "The Pooh," her friend explained. Swifts and seagulls and oyster-catchers shot across the blue sky like missiles or dived off the cliffs.

***

I admired his daughter. She was tall for her age, slender, bright and active. She was going to be a model when she grew up. Michael Jackson, she informed me, was washed up. "I might be an artist," she said; "I like to draw." She drew me a picture of a horse.

I had wanted children and missed their presence in my life. It was equally the case that he wanted to marry quickly, the sooner the better, while his daughter was young enough to "bond."

I had already bonded.

The friend was a year older, her beautiful face framed by masses of curls. (They braided each other's hair in the evening right after washing it in rainwater; in the morning, ringlets tumbled loose and wayward, like yellow roses on a climbing vine.) She told me, one afternoon when we were alone together, that he used to date her mother.

I snapped pictures of both girls, separately, together.

After lunch, they became "two posh matrons, Madame Flo and Madame Bettite." Walking back to our stone cottage, we munched apples and listened to the matrons' excited (though also elegantly bored) expectations for the tea-dance.

"When is this tea-dance to be held?" I asked.

"In a fortnight," said the daughter.

"So much to do!' exclaimed the friend.

Each day I wrote poems in a spiral notebook in my room. When the girls found this out, they decided to write poems too. We had contests to see which of us could write a poem the fastest. Sometimes, seizing paper and pencil, they would amble off thoughtfully in different directions. When they returned they had poems to show me. "This is wonderful," I said. "Wow!" They wrote more and more poems. We were becoming a household of poets.

***

The girls and I walked to the Bird and Field Observatory. The chough, I read in the observatory, is another oceanic bird that chooses Bardsey Island as one of its rare habitats. (In *King Lear* Edgar, son of the Earl of Gloucester, persuades his blind father that the spot they stand on is a precipitous cliff. "How fearful / And dizzy 'tis to cast one's eyes so low! / The crows and choughs that wing the midway air / Show scarce so gross as beetles." Gloucester throws himself to the ground, thinking he has leaped off the "cliff." As his son tells him, "Thy life's a miracle."

Edgar's "chough" looked no bigger than a beetle because it was a beetle. The chough in fact is a large, crowlike bird, famed for its acrobatic maneuvers, whose bill curves downward. If the Manx shearwater sounds like a dog baying, the chough sounds like a smaller dog yipping.

We passed a slew of ducks rolling from side to side like sailors with sealegs, their webbed feet large and startling on the dirt path.

Farther along, we came to three Connemara mares standing stolidly as a phalanx in the middle of the path. "Oh," the daughter cried, reaching up to touch the mane of one, "her mane is like Tina Turner's hair!" She was enchanted, and started petting the horse and saying "Tina, Tina, Tina." If we kept walking in the same direction after we visited the observatory we could see seals in the bay, sea-lions basking in the sun on a small rock islet offshore, the lighthouse keeping up its endless silent dialogue with the sea.

***

If poems are a way of talking to their readers, what do our poems say? Do they speak for the author, or do they say more or differently? Is the lyric less dialogue than monologue, the poem itself mere byproduct?

Or is the poem mute, a thing that talks only to itself? The reader, perhaps, is mere byproduct, the author not even that, the author something that is lost in the process, chewed up, spat out, discharge of energy, driftwood, debris, amounting not even to salvage.

There are so many theories of authorship and literary meaning, and most of them are beside the point. Critical method gives us the meaning of critical method. (As intelligence tests measure the ability to perform on intelligence tests.) The poem remains on the page, opaque and mysterious and moving, like the universe itself, that beautiful and so far ultimately incomprehensible ode to existence.

Maybe—just maybe—it's not only we who keep searching for meaning, as we do, in language. Maybe language keeps trying to make *us* mean something. Maybe it wants to take hold of us, push and pull us into some meaningful shape. Are we the materials out of which language composes poetry?

The word, in the beginning, an anthology of infinite variety, incarnation of meaning. . .

***

And still we were afraid to say the simplest thing.

Having but timidly tasted the wine with the sheepfly in it, I had, apparently, established myself as someone who required no more than barely enough wine to cover the bottom of my wine glass at dinner. The daughter's friend looked at me kindly and said, "I bet you'd like some water, wouldn't you? Americans do." I thanked her and she left the table to get the bottle of water I'd packed, and poured it into my wine. This was not what I had expected, but it's not uncommon in Europe to dilute one's wine with water. Our host said nothing, but the next night, wine bottle in hand, he announced that the wine was much too expensive to be wasted on anyone who would ruin it by adding water. The friend and I exchanged smiles across the table. He poured some wine for himself, then hovered over my glass, his eyebrows raised. I shook my head no, thinking that if I drank it without water, the friend would feel she had done something wrong.

We met again at breakfast. Breakfast meant porridge, salted and sugared. He sat at the head of the table, I on one side and the two girls opposite.

"Please pass the porridge, Mamá," said the daughter to the friend.

"Yes, Papá."

"Thank you."

"Papá, there is a dragon in the garden."

"Oh no! Not again! Is it eating all the roses?"

"Papá, Caitlin has put her cold mittens to my leg."

"Well, tell her to take them away, Mamá."

"Easier said than done."

"More tea, please."

"Yes, Papá. Saffron and chamomile and orange pekoe and—"

"Rosehips and lemon and Earl Gray—"

"Black tea and toast," said Mamá.

"Black tea and toast," said Papá. "Indeed, indeed."

"Papá drinks seventeen cups of tea per day," said Mamá, to me. "I think that's enough, don't you?"

***

They might almost have been speaking in Welsh, their impromptu playlets were so lovely and obscure. Welsh poet R. S. Thomas mentions "the possible fascination of the opposite, the different, the alien" (*Words and the Poet*). About the English language, he asks himself, "What is my true feeling for these words? Am I fascinated, repelled, resentful?" A nationalist who studied Welsh at thirty, he continued to write his poetry in English, feeling that the language of one's childhood is always the language of poetry.

I heard the language of the girls' childhood. In my room, in my spiral notebook, I wrote a poem I titled "Welsh Table Talk."

***

Rarely, I would make a very few suggestions to the girls about their poems. Most of the time I thought the usefulest comment I could offer was "Wow."

We say that art "communicates" but what does that mean? I've never thought of writing a poem as primarily an act of communication, and I am annoyed when others assume that it is. It's art, I want to say; it's not a coded message, not therapy, not, in another formulation, a "project" advanced by poet and reader in cooperation. The reader who thinks he knows me should think again; what he knows is the work of art. Yet poems, good ones, do communicate, often directly. Though it is an accepted praxis to speak of the poetic "I" as a construct, as a device or strategy for locating the poem, the irony is that we adopt this way of speaking because exactly the opposite is true: the poetic "I" is usually too close to the poet to be comfortably discussed without this fiction, this little lie we tell ourselves.

The poet has something to say to the reader, something she feels it is important to say. She has waited her whole life to say it. The thing is, it is not something that can be put into words.

It is an expression of emotion, but the emotion can't be summed up. It is an idea, but the idea can't be analyzed. It is a sense of beauty, but beauty always escapes the limitations of definition, because we can never know that our perceptions are the same as someone else's; we can point to what we find beautiful, and someone else may agree that it is beautiful, but we can never really know if we are talking about the same thing. What the poet wishes to convey is a vision, a way of looking at the world—oh yes: a worldview—but the vision, encompassing all, cannot be paraphrased or explained, for the simple reason that the lesser cannot contain the larger.

Besides, what the poet has to say is not so much emotion or idea or sense of beauty or understanding of the world as it is all of these, an awareness of emotion and idea and beauty and knowledge. It is life; it is existence.

C. M. Bowra wrote, "The most powerful and most authentic poetry is a richer source of life than any other form of words." He says that "at their best" words "communicate something so powerful that it makes us live more abundantly. This is much more than a matter of richness of content or intensity of emotion or even clarity of vision. All these may contribute to it, and all these we may recognise in it, but the central, final, and inescapable fact is that inspired words create life in us because they are themselves alive. Just because they are fixed and settled, their vitality is enhanced and enables us to find in them stores of abounding strength secured from the destructive hand of time."

***

I don't know how she knew, but the daughter, too, realized that things were not going well between her father and me. She understood that I was not in love with her father, was not going to be her stepmother, and while remaining unfailingly polite to me, she understandably became protective of her father, edging a little closer to him whenever we walked somewhere, bringing him cups of tea, sitting next to him on the couch.

***

It was not only the emotional weather that had changed; the real weather had changed. It was cold and rainy. The wind pushed against the cottage's thick windows at night. We turned on the propane heater. By gaslight we read, each of us deep into a book that was a still-unopened door to the others. I read *No, I'm Not Afraid* by Irina Ratushinskaya and *The Memory of War* and *Children in Exile* by James Fenton. These were books that had been left by previous holiday tenants. Against the window panes, the rain clicked sharply, like knitting needles.

It was still raining the next day, not hard but steadily. The girls had spread sheets over the front fence to create a bivouac for the soldiers they had become, soldiers on a messy, fatiguing slog through mud and marsh. He and I were in the front room. I was suffocating. "I'm going for a walk," I said. I would show him that I was not a spoiled American woman. "Women," he had told me before we got to Bardsey, "care about money more than anything. Choosing between a man she loves and a man with money, a woman always chooses money." The note of hurt behind this angry statement was so muffled by layers of rationalization that I felt it would be almost unseemly, too bold, too presumptuous, to uncover it. Or I was too big a coward to respond to it. Instead of inviting him to talk about his hurt, as I should have done, I addressed only his spoken statement. I argued. He argued back.

I thought of that now, as I laced up my shoes and snapped a transparent plastic raincoat shut. I would go for a walk by myself. I liked nature; I didn't have to have a man to mediate it for me.

The upward path led me past patches of thrift and purple vetch and mustard seed. At the top of the mountain was a fling of ling, defined in my American dictionary as heather, though the word *ling* was used here on the mountaintop, while *heather* was the word applied in the field. Boulders, draped in lichens as if picnickers had spread green tablecloths over them, jutted into the sky. I was on the island's cliffside, the drop to the sea swift and sudden and probably fatal.

The perspective here was amazing: I could see the entire island. The scale of things was upset: a rooster looked as large as a house. A huge silence took hold of the island and shook it, as if soundlessness could reverberate. There was our cottage, and there was the church where the pigeon sheltered in the loft. Over there was the lighthouse and, over there, the observatory. I could see the fishermen checking their lobster pots.

I was so captivated by the scene and view that I failed to notice it was raining harder. My transparent raincoat had a hood and I raised it over my head. The long grasses bowed under the weight of the rain, the influence of the wind. The fishermen had vanished. I had been able to see everything, and now I could see nothing. I tried to find the path I had followed to the top but the path had vanished too.

Well, I thought, *all I have to do is get down off the mountain.* I took a couple of steps down and then my shoes, which were not hiking shoes, slipped on the mud and down I skidded until I grabbed a branch. The branch was armed with thorns and now my hand was bleeding. I tried to climb back up but my shoes wouldn't let me; I could only go down and sideways. But this course of action brought me to another obstacle: nettle bushes. By the time I realized how far they extended I was in the middle of them. I was mud-bespattered and my arms and hands were scratched all over. What if I was stuck here all night? Could I sleep out here on a bed of nettles, a bramble pillow, the shearwaters—which some people say are the ghosts of the saints—crying their strange, witchy cries in the unfathomable dark?

I had been stupid to walk up the mountain alone. I was stupid to be wearing these dumb shoes. I was disastrously American.

There was no other way: I pushed straight through to the other side of the nettles, ignoring ripped jeans and stinging whiplashes, and slid down a large part of the rest of the mountainside. Near the bottom, I found the path.

I arrived at the cottage door with my hair wind-snarled and rain-gelled (the hood had fallen down), my hands both muddy and bloody, my jeans with torn knees, and what I imagine was a wild look in my eyes.

***

"How was your walk," he asked.

I stared at him. Eventually, as he said nothing else, I said, "Fine."

After a while I added, "I got caught in the rain."

"The rain is ending now," he said to his daughter. "Shall we go out for a walk?"

They put on Wellingtons and windbreakers, she handed him his staff, and they left.

I went to my room, changed into dry clothes, and returned to the front room. The kettle whistled and the friend jumped up and went into the kitchen and came back with a cup of tea. "For you," she said, smiling.

"Thank you," I said.

As she settled herself on the floor by the propane heater, her radiant hair swung forward a bit and caught the rose-colored light from the gas lamp. "He means well," she said, "but my mother just wasn't interested in him. The man she lives with now is a lot younger than him."

"Do you like the man your mother lives with?" I asked.

"Very much," she said. "I like *him*, too, but he has a lot of rules. My mother's boyfriend doesn't have so many rules."

We talked some more about boyfriends and life with stepparents and poetry and horses. I enjoyed the conversation immensely. She told me about her feelings and hopes and likes and dislikes. I told her that sometimes, no matter how much they wanted to, two people just couldn't communicate with each other. "I know," she said, "but you'll find someone. My mother did." I felt a kind of calm enter my heart and spread through its chambers, not because of what she said but because she said it in such a sweet, clear voice, one that spoke to me.

***

It seemed the sick bay was full up, so the last girl to come down with the virus had to be nursed by her roommate in the dormitory. "Your temperature is terribly high," said the friend.

"Am I dying?" the daughter asked.

"No, not yet," the friend said.

"I need black tea and toast before I can get well."

"Coming right up. You don't mind your toast burnt, do you?"

"I mind terribly."

"In that case," the friend said, "I shall give it to the snails."

"I'm quite fond of snails," the daughter said, "provided they've been well cooked in real butter."

***

The morning was bright, the ground still swampy but shining with rain-drops left over from the day before. I came around the side of the house from the backyard, headed for the front. I put my left foot down on the ground and it sank into mud up to my ankle. I had gotten used to mud. Then I realized I was standing in liquefied cow flop.

***

At noon, he came in by the back door to the kitchen. He was holding a Baggie, inside which was a pair of socks. "What were these doing in the trash bin?" he asked.

"I'm throwing them away," I said.

"You can wash them in the machine when we get back to my house," he said.

"But I'm never going to wear them again."

"What a wasteful society you live in," he said.

I shrugged.

***

The day before we were to leave, we had treasure hunts: First, he sent the girls on their hunt, tracking down rhyming clues. I was impressed when one of the clues put "rhyming it" together with "nickel-and-diming it." Then the girls sent him on a treasure hunt; they had secreted clues in places they all knew about from several years of summer weeks on the island. He was wonderful with the girls, easy and doing things that made them laugh at him, and pretending not to be able to figure out the clues.

***

There was a rainbow in the sky. Truly.

***

Someone—I think it was him—suggested that, since it was our last night, we should have a poetry reading after supper. When the last light had fled the sky, we gathered in the front room, each of us to read a single poem to the others.

"If we examine a poem in order to determine what it is that makes us feel it to be a poem," reasoned Benedetto Croce, "we at once find two constant and necessary elements: a complex of *images*, and a *feeling* that animates them.... Moreover, these two elements may appear as two in a first abstract analysis, but they cannot be regarded as two distinct threads, however intertwined; for, in effect, the feeling is altogether converted into images, into this complex of images, and is thus a feeling that is contemplated and therefore resolved and transcended." Croce distinguishes between *expression* and *communication*, insisting that when the poet reads or publishes his poem "he has entered upon a new stage, not aesthetic but practical." (Thus, when he says "works of art exist only in the mind that create or recreate them" he places the artwork in the poet's mind or the reader or listener's, making recreation dependent on communication and leaving open the question of how greatness is to be distinguished from popularity—as it must surely be, even when the great is popular or the popular great—tossing us back onto intuition: "The reader who understands poetry goes straight to this poetic heart and feels its beat upon his own.")

We were entering upon our new stage.

He read first—a poem he'd written this week on the island. "Bury me on Bardsey Island," the poem pleaded. The island was a place of natural purity, sublimely indifferent to mortal man, a refuge from the pettiness of civilization. The alliterative refrain possessed a peculiar buoyancy, perhaps willed rather than found, as if the poem itself were an island afloat on the page, or in our minds.

After him, his daughter read, and then the friend. In the room's profound hush we heard, over and under the poems, a rising wind banging against the windows, the hissing of the gas lamp and the occasional pop of the propane heater, the sea, invisible, battering the beach in some eternal contest that was still a draw. We heard our own sighs and gastric rumbles and shifts in posture, a click of the tongue, a gasp, a hand closing around a hand (his around his daughter's). The drainpipe clanged against the outside wall, iron on stone. A gust of wind knocked against the door.

I read my poem, a short poem that played with sound, a sort of song. It was not a poem that referred to emotion. There was no "I" in the poem. Objects were described objectively. Writing the poem, I had been excited by the patterning of repetitions and rhyme, by the precision of language.

When I finished, I waited for somebody to say something.

Do we come into the world, even Wales, with, perhaps, "innate" and "organizing principles" that interpret form, rhythm, tone, and color as emotion? If Noam Chomsky's notion that we are all natives of the country of language is optimistic, assuming a neurological infrastructure no one has mapped, could it be that he needed only to go deeper into an outback where movement through time and space is made meaningful by emotion? *Music is a language*, my father always said, as many musicians do. *People understand it, even if they don't always understand it right away.* Poetry, too, lets us know what it means.

In my poem were a kestrel, a rooster, a pigeon, a gas lamp, a drainpipe, a window pane, darkness, and a child who brushed her hair.

It was the friend who said something. "Oh!" she said, and again, "Oh!" I looked at her, trying to read her face, but she had cast her head down and her Rapunzelesque locks fell in front of her like a barely parted curtain. I could see that her face was flushed. She had gone straight to the poetic heart and felt its beat upon her own. "Oh," she said once more. "I've never heard a poem as sad as that."

THE PLACE WHERE THERE IS WRITING

The name of the place is Dzibilchaltún, or, translated from the Mayan, "the place where there is writing." Sometimes the translation is extended to "the place where there is writing on flat rocks." The rocks, or stelae, are gone. Perhaps they are in a museum, with the other Mayan hieroglyphics, or buried still in this vast archaeological zone that remains mostly unexplored. I didn't look for them the way a historian might have; I am not a historian. What I cared about was the eeriness of the place, and its implicative name, as layered with meaning as Troy with time.

I had been in Mérida, the capital of Yucatán and thirteen miles south of Dzibilchaltún, only a day and a half. I'd suffered a head wound just before leaving the States, and although the wound was slight, the bandage plastered to the back of my head was impressive. Because I keeled over every time I tried to stand up, and because the bandage so loudly said why, the flight attendants had bundled me in blankets—in August—and wheelchaired me through the Atlanta and Mérida airports.

But now I felt better, and I'd taken the bandage off, found the foreign exchange bank, and hopped a second-class bus to Dzibilchaltún. Dzibilchaltún is not a site most tourists visit; it tends to be overwhelmed by the more fully excavated and therefore more immediately exotic ruins at, for example, Uxmal, Kabáh, Chichén Itzá, Cobá, and Tulum. It was my good luck, as it turned out, to have undergone my mild physical shock. I was obliged to begin by staying close to home base. And so I went to a place many miss—the place where there is writing.

Home base was a *posada*, an inn, in Mérida. It was near the busy *zócalo*, or town square, a pretty square with stone love seats for courting couples, and box yews surrounding benches where old men and women, their courtship days behind them, sat and talked while their grandchildren played. The bus station was on the other side of the *zócalo*.

As the bus pulled out of the city, past double-parked cars, the marketplace, furniture stores, and computer centers, we moved back in time. It happened with a startling swiftness. Mayan cottages, one-room mortared stone dwellings with flat, thatched roofs, lined the highway. Men worked on the highway, cutting back the jungle that would overtake it in three months if they didn't—if they simply, one day, fed up and worn out, called it quits, stuck their machetes and picks back in their trucks, and went home to lie down in their hammocks. They don't go home; they hack away at that jungle every day. The kids mill around houses, at the edge of the highway, and shout, *"Un peso, un peso"*; they'll pose for a picture. They learn early to squeeze what spare change they can out of sentimental tourists.

I was the only tourist on this particular bus, though. There were few other passengers of any stripe. We were not traveling anybody's usual route at the usual time of day, although at other times there are Mexicans and Indians coming into Mérida or going home from work. It was noon. Some grownups lolled around the roadside houses with the kids. To the unwitting tourist, they might look as if they were too lazy to work, but they'd been up working in the fields since 4 or 5 a.m. They'd already put in a full day of backbreaking labor. They would take their siesta, these who'd found a few free moments in a seemingly endless workday, and then put in more hours, crafting gewgaws for the tourist market, weaving hammocks—anything to earn a living, to get by.

There are often nine to fifteen children in these Indian families. They speak Mayan among themselves, but we have forgotten how to write it. The kids play in the dirt, surrounded by the chickens that run loose in the yards. An occasional horse stands stolidly nearby, flicking its tail at flies. Underwear drips from clotheslines, or dries flat, spread out on low bushes.

The breeze the bus's motion made blew in through the open window, welcome on my face. We passed pepper trees, banana trees, hibiscus, a gap-toothed stone fence filled in with a tire and some string, fences made of piled stone, unmortared, with vines growing in and out of the spaces between the stones, and a chapel with a faded mint-green front, three open arches at the top through which blue sky was framed, with a small cross atop each of two of the arches and the third cross missing. I wondered what had happened to the third cross.

The fields along this route, as in much of Yucatán, were planted in henequen—what we call sisal. The henequen plant has wide, tough, rigid leaves; its fibers are strong. I have a sisal rug in my living room in Wisconsin; I bought it because it was cheaper than a "real" rug. Now, when I walk across that rug, I know who paid for it.

Platoons of field workers passed us, going the opposite way, toward Mérida; they leant against the sides of the open backs of their trucks; they were going home, to the look-alike subdivisions on the city's outskirts. The sun was hot; it was, as I say, August. "The wrong time of year to visit Yucatán." I went when I could.

The driver let me off in what appeared to be the middle of nowhere, pointing at a dirt road. I followed his finger; the bus left. I was alone. The absence of anyone made me feel as though someone must be there somewhere, lurking behind the squat trees. But if I turned back, I'd have to wait five hours for the bus to make its return journey. The heat stung; mosquitoes were biting. I tilted my straw hat to keep my face in shade, rubbed suntan oil over my bare arms. After a while, people appeared in the road ahead of me. A Mexican family. A Latino couple, lovers. They had come in cars.

There's an admission stand with a ticket to buy, the omnipresent and necessary soft drinks in a lift-top cooler, and, as you might guess, more children eager to have their pictures taken—for *un peso*. A small girl volunteered to serve as a guide to the one-room museum. Since I knew no Spanish, and she knew no English, and the museum's careful explanations of the exhibition bore no subtitles, I hadn't, for the most part, any idea what I was viewing. But my guide chattered away as if none of this mattered. Maybe it didn't; I knew from my travel book that the seven figurines at which I stared had been taken from the temple I was going to see, and that they were singular in type. None like them has ever been found elsewhere in that part of the world. Each of these figurines is hideously deformed. Historians conjecture that they were used in medical rites, to cure like conditions. They gave me the willies. And, as I say, I'm no historian, so I posed my little guide in another part of the museum, snapped her picture, and reached into my pocket for change. She didn't know that what I was really buying was her smile, a wonderful, shy smile that had to sit on itself not to become a grin. She danced around me, my very own Munchkin, as I set off down the road once more.

Now there were plenty of people, natives, but they were headed for the swimming pool. The pool, of course, is a cenote, a well, thought to be the deepest in Yucatán. There are bones at the bottom, some of them elongated, pointed skulls that were shaped by boards pressed in a certain configuration on the malleable heads of newborn, upper-class infants. This is one of the wells that the Mayans used for human sacrifice. Yucatán officialdom likes to blame the practice of human sacrifice on the Toltecs, a much-later, conquering civilization; the Mayans, they emphasize, were a cultured people, advanced in astronomy and agriculture, living by a complex calendar, rich in art, honoring mind and body, sport and scholarship. This is true, as the most casual tourist can see. The vaguest acquaintance with the mathematics of the Mayan calendar and its adhibitions in politics, art and science, and religion will bowl anyone over. Nevertheless, not all ancient Mayans shared in the benefits of their culture; the societal structure plainly was stratified and elitist. As for human sacrifice, the offering of live bodies, said to have been drugged beforehand, to the rain god Chac, there is evidence enough that the Mayans practiced it long before the Toltec invasion. Evidence is here, in the cenote at Dzibilchaltún. The site at

Dzibilchaltún goes back at least to 600 B.C., when it may have been an outpost or advance settlement of the Mayans then primarily located on the other side of Mexico, along the Pacific, and by still-conservative estimate, it has been dated to 1000 B.C.; many researchers date its beginning hundreds of years earlier. At any rate, it is believed to be the oldest continuously occupied Mayan city-state. It may have flourished before Homer lived; it may be that Troy had nothing on Dzibilchaltún.

Still, these facts—if, given our incomplete state of knowledge, they can be called facts—can be easily looked up or pieced together by anyone who is interested in them; I've nothing new to bring to them, and so, though I am someone who is interested, I set them aside to continue my walk.

From the pool came sounds of splashing—and, yes, transistor radios and portable television sets. I crawled around the Spanish chapel, built in 1590 to "Christianize" the heathen spirit that may have lingered in the surrounding area, hiding behind rocks, swimming far below the surface of the cenote.

There were rocks everywhere, strewn haphazardly as if they'd been a manuscript some author, in a fit of pique, had torn lengthwise and crosswise and tossed to the wind. I followed the turn in the path that led to the Mayan arch. The arch marks the start of the *sacbe*, the ceremonial way to another city-state. I was headed for the one standing Mayan structure here, among an untellable number that once existed; it has been partially reconstructed. It is the Temple of the Seven Dolls.

The Latino lovers walked in front of me; I could see people at the temple, but they were walking away from it, back toward the direction I had come from. A storm was kicking up. Only the lovers and I were walking toward the temple. The path we walked is sometimes called the Road of the Gods. The blue sky had darkened; rain clouds were gathering in the distance, like tribes coming together. Nearer to hand, a great loneliness seemed to sweep over the fallen stones.

Octavio Paz, in an essay titled "The Seed" in *Alternating Current*, tries to describe "[a] time before the idea of antiquity: the real original time." Finding he can reach for it only metaphorically, he calls it "the original metaphor," and writes that

> it is the imminence of the unknown—not as a presence but as an expectation and a threat, as an emptiness. It is the breaking through of the *now* into the *here*, the present in all its instantaneous actuality and all its dizzying, hostile potentiality. What is this moment concealing?

I sensed that presence. I knew the moment was concealing something—but what?

Paz, trapped into describing "the original metaphor" metaphorically, tries again: He calls it "the seed," the future contained—or concealed—in the present. He says that

> the calendar clears a path through the dense thickets of time, makes its immense expanse navigable. . . *[N]ow* falls into *before* and *after*. This fissure in time announces the advent of the kingdom of man.

I have long held that the Fall was a fall into Time, and that there is no time without language. The Fall was a fall into Language. In the beginning was the Word, but we learned to say "I," and that prideful self-assertion was the original sin. It was also the beginning of language. It is not consciousness but self-consciousness, which allows us to see ourselves as subjects, and to see ourselves as objects of our subjective seeing, and so on as in an endless series of mirrors, that separates us from God. That separates us, period. The ability to refer to ourselves grants us history and hope, the foreknowledge of our death and legacy, the knowledge, to put it in other words, of good and evil. For with the reflexive recognition of ourselves as subjects that are their own objects comes the inescapable awareness of cause and consequence. Without language there would be no morality, only perfection; with language comes knowledge. It is a small matter, at this point, whether that knowledge is perceived, construed, imagined, provable or unprovable. It is a very large matter that our capacity to know that we know is a function of language. The original sin was the original metaphor. The original metaphor was the original sin. It goes without saying that this is a guilt of which no writer, especially, would wish to be absolved. The writer prays, Save me, O Lord, but not yet; I have books to write first.

I may not be a historian, but I am, I confess, a writer, and I'll go anywhere where there is writing. I climbed the steps to the top of the temple. It was open on all four sides; the lovers sat on the steps on the opposite side.

The sky had become completely overcast. Rain clouds had dropped closer to the ground. The wind that had come up as I walked was now gusting; it wore an expression of ferocity; it tunneled through the doorways and windows of the temple as if through a wind tunnel; it blew my hair in my face and made a sound like someone blowing through a hollow reed, a mournful sound with an undernote of the kind of despair that leads to a desire for revenge. The lovers had brought their lunch to make a picnic; I opened the plastic bag of trail mix

I'd been given by a new acquaintance at the *posada.*

The sky was black now. I could see rain in the distance, across miles of scrub brush. Thunder pitched toward the temple as if it were being thrown at me. The wind was so strong I had to put the trail mix away before it got blown away. The lovers had packed up their picnic, raised an umbrella, and run off down the dirt road. I was alone in the Mayan ruin.

There was a famous, but unfortunately forgetful, archaeologist who was killed by lightning when he took shelter at the top of another Mayan structure during another storm. He should have known better. I had no reason to know any better. I didn't know these heights draw lightning or that I might well be killed. I stood fascinated in the ruins, letting the wind snarl my hair, watching the lightning tear at the sky, and watching the rain fall first here, then there. I was alone in the Mayan ruin with the rain god Chac.

Rain spattered the rocks; the rocks turned dark with the wet. It was as if Chac were writing on them. We were alone there, Chac and I, and I felt that if I only knew how to read Mayan, I could read rain on rock. What is this moment *revealing?*

I sighed, knowing that I did not know.

Suddenly the rain ceased. The wind fled the temple. I scanned the site. The clouds had crossed overhead and disappeared into the horizon. The sun reclaimed its territory, and the green leaves sizzled, the land hardened, the sun erased the rocks. There were no tablets or glyphs now—only disconnected stones, each as blank as a blank page.

I collected my gear and set off the way I'd come. The Road of the Gods seemed long, empty and long. By the time I reached the little museum, I had to stop to apply more suntan lotion. My guide had gone. By the time I reached the bus stop, I was ready to guzzle about two dozen soft drinks.

I was early. I found a boulder to sit on until the bus came. The ruins were not visible from here. I saw a rooster strutting alongside a rusted fence, as if he were doing guard duty; a pair of male and female turkeys were saying something in turkey language to each other, which, could they possess self-consciousness, possibly had been "I love you" or "Scram"; a hen with five tiny chicks in assorted colors pecked at the ground near a road sign.

Several bikers rode by; they carried firewood tied in bunches on the backs of their bicycles, and hunting rifles over their shoulders. A group of men hanging out beside a beat-up truck smiled in my direction; when they drove off, they waved, and honked the horn.

A few Indians stood on the opposite side of the highway, near the dirt road that led to the ruins. They never looked at me, nor smiled nor waved. They seem to have a trick of turning off the mind in such situations to make time vanish.

189 Kelly Cherry Reader

It looks like mindlessness, but it is not. They turn off the conceptualizing part of the brain, but they remain perceptually awake—they have to, in a land and a country full of threat. It may be a knack for being sensorially aware without having to talk to themselves about what it is they are aware of that accounts for the Indians' frequent long silences; if you do not talk to yourself, you have less need to tell anyone else what you feel or think; you feel and think without naming yourself as feeler and thinker. It follows, then, that they may be closer to God, any god, but I can't say. If they aren't, they haven't told me. If they are, can they say?

Or maybe I was merely suffering from cultural shock, as real but transitory as the physical shock that had started my journey.

But suppose silence does bring us closer to God? I mean the inner silence of a language that does not refer to the self, that does not divorce the "I" from the "Thou" or even the "me." Would that be union, or would it signify the loss of the possibility of love? Is love predicated on divorce?

These are fundamental questions, and we are doomed to ask them. Yet it may be that the very asking of the questions precludes an answer. We cannot ask them without creating ourselves in our own image; we must use a reflexive language. Will our words make right turn after right turn forever, as if we were following correctly a map that can lead us nowhere? Is this an epistemological cul-de-sac?

We cannot know. It may be that it cannot pay off—it may be that the exercise is a futile one—but what we do know is that our disgraced and human condition means that from here on out we have no choice but the making of many books, books without end. This conclusion, though surprising, is logically unavoidable. If there are answers to be learned, they can be learned only in places where there is writing.

LETTER FROM THE PHILIPPINES:
CROSSING A STREET IN MANILA

The creative writing students in the small seminar room at Ateneo University in Metro Manila were answering my question about the relation of language to politics in the Philippines. With that youthful energy that is each generation's greatest natural resource they talked about the "feudal system" Filipinos have lived under, about the centrality of village life, about the Filipino's innately "romantic" soul and love of theater. The electric power had gone off—brownouts were lasting up to seven hours a day—and, in late May, the room's temperature quickly soared. Just as suddenly, a rainstorm rushed across the sky, as if in a hurry to get somewhere else; afterwards, flame trees and acacias seemed to lean in the direction it had gone, like lovers left behind at a train station.

I was explaining to the class that anything might be the subject of a short-short. "A door," I said, pointing at the door through which we had entered. "Or a table." I touched the table around which we were grouped. "This morning," I admitted, "it occurred to me that one might write a short-short about crossing a street in Manila."

The students laughed. "That's not a short-short," one said; "that's a novel! A saga! An *epic*, at least!"

Because of the brownouts, traffic lights often did not work. Sometimes there were police to direct the flow of traffic, and sometimes there were not. That morning I had been making my way with a group of faculty women from St. Scholastica's College to a fast-food Chinese restaurant. I have traveled a lot and have never met a warmer, friendlier, more welcoming people than Filipinos. A good thing, too, I thought, as I imagined, marooned there on the traffic island, that I might have to give up all hope of returning home. I would marry, become a citizen and cast my defiant but losing vote for Miriam Santiago, and grow old on my own little "island" among the more than seven thousand that make up the archipelago that is the Philippines. All around me were trucks, cars, taxicabs, jeepneys, tricycles, and pedicabs. Pedicabs are bicycles with sidecars; tricycles are motorcycles with sidecars; jeepneys, ostensibly another method of public transportation, are a mobile art form. This really is *re-cycling*. Jeeps left over from World War II are painted in elaborate, colorful detail, outfitted with model horses, dressed in flags and pennants, draped with purple curtains, and named. *Banana Magnet*, said one. *Desert*, said another, as if it were the punch line to a running, or rolling, joke. *Last Waltz* was the mournful title of a third. Then there was the jeepney that demanded, apocalyptically, *Saint or Sinner.* I felt put on the spot.

At St. Scholastica's I had read a paper on the short fiction of women in the United States today. Everywhere I went, I met Filipino writers and scholars who were not only acquainted with the work of American writers—they were frequently acquainted with the writers themselves. A number had been to the International Writing Workshop in Iowa City. Ed and Edith Tiempo recalled being in Paul Engle's class alongside the now late Flannery O'Connor. Mimeographing was expensive back then, Edith Tiempo said, so the students read their stories aloud in class. But they had to ask Engle to read O'Connor's stories for her, because no one could understand that Georgia accent. "She had an annoying habit of twisting a lock of hair at her forehead," Edith said, laughing softly, adding that when Engle found unconvincing a sex scene O'Connor had written the author responded, "Come out to my car and I'll show you how it's done."

I loved these stories and scribbled them down in my spiral notebook at night in my wonderful room in The Manila Hotel, where the MacArthur Suite can be booked for $1,400 a day and often is—by the Japanese, who, presumably, think $1,400 a day is not too much to pay for the right to report to their friends that they have slept in the MacArthur Suite! From my more modest room I could look out at Manila Bay with its twinkling cargo ships, the world coming and going and always bigger than I'd dreamed. It is stories like this that link us, make us members of a larger literary community. Gossip makes us real to one another.

Another writer, F. Sionil José, prolific and outspoken, whose *Three Filipino Women* was being published in the United States by Random House, explained to me that Melville and Emerson are the American writers who are "relevant" to him, because they had made an *American* tradition, "throwing off the colonial influence." He likes the contemporary black writers for the same reason.

Weaving—amazingly—among the cars had been adults and children selling single sticks of gum, cigarettes, anything. A boy tapped on a window and opened his palm, begging. No doubt he lived, if he had any address at all, in the poor-beyond-saying Tondo district. I could say how seeing him made me feel, but I can't say how he felt. The Filipino writers will have to tell us that. Every country finds its own words. And out of those words it constructs an idea of itself. Literature, also, makes us real to one another.

At the University of the Philippines, the splendidly lively National Artist Francisco Arcellana ("That means I get to be buried for free") pointed out that deconstructionist theory comes from the French—"an overrefined culture," he said nicely.

To be in search of a language with which to define one's sense of oneself, one's entire country—how exciting! And here in the West we are so eager to discard what we know that we turn a deaf ear even to our own words, eliminating the text, the author, the authoritative voice. I began to understand the lure of the East, the temptation to believe in something besides criticism.

Arcellana was inducting students into the UP Writing Club. He made them raise their right hands. "I promise to write, *write*, WRITE," he had them repeat after him. "And never be silenced!"

On my traffic island I had been clutching a light canvas bag a former student had made for me. She had had my name printed on one side, and the cover art from one of my novels on the other, and I used the bag to carry the books I would be giving readings from. I was also carrying my paper on women writers. And I was also carrying a Sportsac bag that held my money and passport and traveling cosmetics and sunglasses and sunscreen. I had been clutching this stuff and standing there, in the middle of a street in Manila, and waiting for traffic to slacken, and these are some of the thoughts I was thinking.

Why did the writer cross the road? It was never simply to get to the other side.

POSTMODERN POETRY IN ANCIENT ROME: ON TRANSLATING THE OCTAVIA OF SENECA

Russians had roped a wire noose around the neck of the statue of Feliks Etmundovich Dzerzhinsky—founder of the Cheka, the secret police, "father of the KGB"—and were hauling the statue, huge in the Stalinist so-called heroic mode, away. It weighed fourteen tons. It apparently had swung wildly in the air and then listed to one side, a hanged man.

The statue had stood in front of the KGB headquarters—the Lubyanka—in Moscow. Now it looked as if it was about to fall, like all the rest of the Soviet Union.

Eventually even government officials got into the act, engineering a way to remove the statue without disrupting the operations of the subway station directly beneath. Cranes carried the statue to a waiting flatbed truck.

The workers had nothing to use but their chains. In Vilnius, a monolithic Lenin, horizontally attached to rigging, seemed to fly through the air on its way to the trash heap.

Thus did the Romans topple the statues of Nero and Poppaea.

"They're so lifelike, these statues," the people cry in *Octavia*. "Let's smash them on the ground." And this they do, as the Messenger dutifully reports: "Every statue of Poppaea that was put up, smooth marble or shining bronze, has fallen, knocked down by the hands of the mob and smashed repeatedly with iron crowbars. After they've pulled the sections down by ropes, they drag them off one by one, stomp on them, and grind them underfoot, deep into the mud. These barbaric deeds are accompanied by words that I hesitate to repeat." The crowd in Moscow painted a certain word around the base of Dzerzhinsky's statue: *executioner.*

Thus do empires collapse literally to dust, the symbols of them smashing to wonderfully unsymbolic smithereens at the people's feet.

Do I make too much of this correspondence? I'm not alone in calling attention to it. The *New York Times* informs us that Edvard Radzinsky has written a play, produced in Moscow, titled *The Theater in the Time of Nero and Seneca,* which is "about intellectuals living under a repressive regime."

That the Soviet Union should have reached its conclusion (we hope it has reached its conclusion) while I was translating a play about the fall of the Roman Empire was, for me, not merely a coincidence but a gratifying and interesting irony. Years before, I had been engaged to marry a citizen of Latvia, one of the Baltic countries occupied by the Soviet Army and forcibly annexed to the Union in 1940, when the choice—an incomprehensible word in this connection, *choice*—was between rule by Hitler and rule by Stalin. As if economics is a centrifuge, the center of the union had spun and spun—but it was spinning its wheels—until these formerly free nations were flung into freedom one more. (But I have to say, here, that accounts in the *New York Times* and elsewhere seemed to assume that Baltic citizens had begun their fight to reclaim their independence less than two years earlier, in March, 1990, when Lithuania asserted the restored sovereignty of its state by unanimous parliamentary vote, whereas in fact there were those in all three states who had worked toward this aim for decades.)

This, then, was how, that week in August, 1991, I translated Seneca: with network television on, the radio turned simultaneously to National Public Radio, the telephone ready to take calls from a friend who had CNN, newspapers on the floor, my Latin books and papers spread around me on the bed, and my heart in my mouth.

What would Seneca have said about the events transpiring in the Soviet Union? It was not difficult to imagine him as a talking head, holding forth on *Nightline* or *The MacNeil/Lehrer NewsHour.*

Would Seneca have confined himself to the sententious remarks of a—say—Princeton prof? Or a free-lancing Kissinger? Yet the Seneca here, in *Octavia,* is capable of, must have been capable of, awareness of others' perceptions of him, and unafraid to state them. Self-protective he is, conservative to a fault, but he could not survive as well or as long as he does without discerning, and calculating for, the young emperor's adolescent contempt for an old man.

Scholars suggest, of course, that Seneca could not have written this play in which he is one of his own characters. There may eventually be incontrovertible proof, documentary or textual. I rather think, though, that for now, anyway, the evidence for this thesis is at least partly biased by a belief that writers of an earlier age are never so ironic or playful as writers of the current age.

In Michael Grant's translation of the *Annals,* Tacitus refers to Seneca's "pleasant talent" for speech-writing and points out that "Nero was the first ruler to need borrowed eloquence." Seneca the speech-writer might have been at home in modern America, a bureaucrat for the party in power or an overpaid professor on more or less permanent leave from teaching. Tacitus says that Agrippina, angered by her son Nero's defection from her tutelage in favor of Seneca's (because Seneca smiled on Nero's affair with Acte, a slave girl), denounced Seneca as "that deportee with the professorial voice."

In *Octavia*, Nero appears, at times, to be merely hormonally inflamed the way teenagers always are, but Tacitus reminds us that "[a] number of contemporary writers assert that for a considerable time previously Nero had "corrupted" Britannicus, the half-brother he arranges to be poisoned. Incest and child abuse. There is in this play a disarming note of intimacy that can seem to reduce Nero's actions to those of a boy being a boy. But what we have, really, is an emperor being an emperor, assassinating his mother, his brother, and anyone else who dares to get in the way of what he perceives as his due.

Perhaps the young Octavia is the main source of this sense of intimacy. Although she's often self-righteous and self-pitying, her circumstances so clearly justify her that the reader, or audience, forgives her. (But we also can't help assenting, even if guiltily, to Nero's longing for love, even if he has confused love with lust, and to his idealization of love as a refuge from the dangers of his position.) Tacitus says of Octavia that "young though she was, [she] had learnt to hide sorrow, affection, every feeling." And how does one love the man who has pretty much wiped out one's family?

Conventionally this play would have been rendered primarily in iambic pentameter, with a shorter line for the choruses. I found iambic pentameter, with its regularity, its singing extension, which I otherwise love, too controlled, maybe too public, to convey this drama's intimate character. Nobly born the central personae may be, but their personalities tumble off the page in a tangled heap of emotions. They are so psychologically defined that every one of them possesses an irrefutable logic, and the result is a kind of Shakespearean sympathy with points of view that are at variance with one another, that Shakespearean genius for seeing a thing from all its angles. Not that Seneca was in that class, but may I propose that what Shakespeare learned from classical drama was more than plot, was what made Shakespeare even more than a great poet. Made him Shakespeare.

I rendered most of the sexual women in verse: Octavia in a loose, four-stress line; Agrippina in the free verse of an anathematic hysteria that turns, finally, as so much in this play does, on itself; the two allusively erotic recitations of the chorus of women in sonnets, as if their voices flowered like roses in the wilderness of text. Octavia's chorus is another loose four-beat line, echoing her in their allegiance. The nurses are guidance counselors, prosy with pedagogy. Poppaea is in prose—I don't know why. Something about her anxiety, the way her desire for contrition arises from fear for her fate. She is a modernist figure, haunted by bad conscience, the dreams of "a mysterious, subconscious intelligence." The men are all prose.

A Menippean sort of solution.

I made these decisions, but I would not want to elevate them into principles. If I adhered to any principle, it was to an idea of metaphor. Wherever I could, I followed metaphors inherent in the author's Latin language, as if tracing an underground river through the text.

Another principle was not to worry about anachronisms. As I have said, part of the interest of this play, this historical drama, lies in its parallels to a later world.

A third principle, for me, was to stay within the bounds of the established text. I admit I would have liked to rewrite the play. I'd have done this and that, except then the play would have been mine, I think, not Seneca's (or the reputed Seneca's). Translation is a constant denial of temptation, this way. Possibly the translator achieves purity of soul by being willing to compromise! What an odd process, a poet thinks. But I have found it an enlightening one.

The poet and translator Willis Barnstone, whose books include *With Borges on an Ordinary Evening in Buenos Aires*, told me a story. He and Borges were in a taxi on their way to the University of Chicago in spring, 1980. The question of where everyone was from came up. Barnstone identified himself as being from Indiana and explained that Borges was from Argentina. "Hey, buddy," said the taxi driver, "*I* was in Europe too."

"When was that?" Barnstone asked.

It had been during the Second World War. Barnstone asked the taxi driver if he had seen any action. And what it was like, the action. The taxi driver didn't want to talk about it. "I don't think about war, about all those things of the past," said the taxi driver, "because memory is hell."

Elated, Borges seized Barnstone's wrist. "Why, those words could have been written by Seneca!" he exclaimed.

I have thought I might have liked to translate the taxi driver.

The Duckworth edition (1942) of Seneca's plays, including the translation of *Octavia* by Frank Justus Miller, announces, "The *Octavia* enjoys a unique distinction, for it is the only *fabula praetexta*, or Roman historical play, which has survived to our day." Detailing the ways in which the play is indeed Senecan, the judgment here is nevertheless that "it seems extremely doubtful if Seneca is the author of the play. . . .It is not impossible that Seneca wrote the play, which could have been published after his death, and, presumably, after the death of Nero. But it seems preferable to assume, as do most scholars, that the *Octavia* was composed soon after Nero's death by a dramatist who had been an eye-witness of the events described, and who, in his portrayal of the pitiful fate of Octavia, imitated the technique and structure of Senecan tragedy."

This argument has a persuasive Ockhamistic elegance but may be set aside briefly to let us see what it misses: the extraordinary bleakness at the devastated heart of a play in which antagonist and protagonist, joined inextricably in a life-

and-death struggle, do not even encounter each other on stage. What an irony! What a deep, deep cynicism underscores the very existence of this play. If, here as elsewhere in Seneca, questions of how to rule—what is the right relation between emperor and people? *Whose* justice shall prevail?—if these questions appear to provide the philosophical substance, something else, also, is going on. For the question of how to rule, in a historical drama, has already been settled by how the emperor *did* rule: any answers are hypothetical, and useless. And the author, whoever he may have been, knows this. And this knowledge changes everything.

The always marvelously perspicuous Moses Hadas described Stoicism as an "evangelical" project devolving into a notion about how to live. To the Senecan Stoic, Hadas suggests, pain cannot be painful (not even the pain of memory), because all things happen for the good of the whole. I think I want to suggest that in this observation may lie the strongest argument to be made for *Octavia's* having being written by a later hand.

For—let us repeat—the author knows how history has happened, or is going to happen, and the play reflects this knowledge in its despair. At the end of the play, we see the future foreclosing on itself. We see the text, which has already claimed its right to comment on itself, dissolve itself, like a parliamentary government. It is as if there is no longer any question of the good of the whole: as we have said, in a historical drama, history has answered many questions. And it is as if Stoicism has unwound itself even further, becoming a notion about how one has lived. How has one lived? Has it not always been exactly like this: *things end, and then they go on, having already ended?* That, I suggest, is the true temper of this author's mind. We live, are living, after the fact. We are, or know we soon will be, post-empire, post-modern, post-everything. Octavia cannot save herself, because she has already been destroyed. She was destroyed from the beginning, from the moment her history began to unfold. This is what *fate* means. Everything that can happen to her has been foretold—*fatum*, an utterance and the foretelling has sealed what can happen to her. *"Do not pray,"* she chastises herself, *"To gods who have no use for you!"*

But the domestic drama of *Octavia*, as *fabula praetexta*, is an emblematic acting-out of the transaction between individual histories and history, between the self and the state. Octavia is the repository of the people's hopes. She represents themselves to themselves. Their future is hers, and if Nero cleaves to her, and if she bears sons, "the world may rejoice / And Rome's glory endure." But the dissolution of her marriage has been yoked by history to the dissolution of the empire, and all fall down.

Once upon a time, I was married—to an American—and my husband and I thought that if we had a daughter we might name her Octavia. As it turned out, we had no child, no daughter named Octavia. I may have come to this play, in part at least, to search for a daughter named Octavia. I thought this even as I worked on it. And watched Latvia becoming free again.

It was an occasion for rejoicing. But it was also an occasion for wondering why the past had had to happen exactly the way that it did. History!

History is a cannibal, cutting off its own arms and legs to devour them. It is Chronos, the god of time, swallowing his own children. In the Introduction to the Loeb edition (1917) of *Octavia*, much is made of Roman drama's debt to Greek tragedy, but not quite enough of the way in which this particular play negates itself.

A parent devouring his own children is deconstruction with a vengeance. To us, in our dilettantish days of theoretical preciosity, this is the harshest truth: a text that, I submit, chooses to obliterate its own tradition. If Seneca is not his own character, the real author—the Loeb nominates Maternus—may be said to have devoured Seneca. If Seneca is his own character, the text has, in a sense, consumed him. The play closes with a brutal image: other peoples offer only strangers as sacrifices to the gods, but Romans—this civilized people, these people who think of themselves as, alone among the peoples of the world, *not being barbarian*—kill their own citizens. *[C]ivis gaudet Roma cruore.* "Rome's delight is in her children's blood," says the Loeb. Our metered Duckworth has it: "But Rome delights to see her children bleed." In the parlance of today we would, surely, say, *Rome eats her own.*

To avoid slang, which tends to trivialize meaning, and at the same time to express the philosophical underpinning of these words, I passed up the vividness of the metaphor of cannibalism for the richness of another metaphor that alludes to Chronos: "Thus Time itself is in exile." With these last words, the play rounds on itself and writes itself *out* of existence. There is no history, then, because history ended when the world ended, and for Romans, that was when Rome declined and fell. Self-negation, the complete dismissal of everything, of oneself and the world. This is a play that consigns its audience to irrelevance, a text that suicides. It *is* a suicide. We feel, at the end, the way we feel at the death of anyone we knew well. Grief, rage, terror, despair—all of these feelings that the play, the play, understands cannot resurrect one life, ever.

WHY I WRITE NOW

I was in New York for the week, staying at a hotel that was formerly a flop house but was now mentioned in see-America-on-a-shoestring travel guides published in Europe, so that French, German, Swedish tourists crowded the lobby. Dialing from a pay phone on the street—to avoid room charges—I telephoned a friend who lived in the city. It was April, and the streets were loud with cars, trucks, messengers on bikes, vendors hawking wares, and pedestrians clomping across intersections, but in tiny square yards about the size of a square yard greenery flourished as if it were growing in a meadow.

My chum was close to fifteen years younger than I, but we were both writers, we were both living the single life, we both wore eye makeup, and we got along well. It was difficult to hear over the phone with so much noise in the background, but she gave me directions and when I arrived at her apartment she said, "I have two tickets to the opera. Would you like to go with me?"

Tickets to the Metropolitan Opera—orchestra seats, no less—were beyond my budget and, I'd have thought, hers. She made it clear that she had planned to ask a male friend to join her but that, seeing me in the doorway to her apartment in the meat-packing district, she impulsively asked me. I was grateful for her generous gesture.

For the opera we both dressed in, of course, Manhattan black. Her skirt was long, my dress short. All around us swirled the beautiful people in designer clothing. We found our seats, and looking at the rich and famous she asked, "Which would you rather be, unknown in your lifetime but famous after death, or famous now and forgotten later?"

It was not that I had never heard this question before. Every teenager who has ever wanted to write, paint, sculpt, or compose has encountered it. It's almost a rite of passage.

The auditorium lights had blinked in warning; now they dimmed and as they went dark my friend added, "Oh, that's ridiculous! One has to hope for fame in one's own time."

The orchestra plunged into the overture. The curtain rose. I heard and saw nothing. My entire life had just been invalidated.

I had been one of those kids who test themselves with that question. Why did it now upset me so?

I guess: because I was no longer a kid. Fame in my lifetime had ceased to seem something that might someday happen.

For my friend, fame in her lifetime was still a possibility—even, it already seemed, a likelihood. The time I had been born into had changed, and young women writers now received a major publishing push, where before they had been relegated to minor or exceptional positions. There had been Eudora Welty and Mary McCarthy, Katherine Anne Porter and Hannah Arendt, but in general, if not always in the specific case, women writers, until the eighties and nineties, were considered lesser life forms. Nor was circumstance the only reason few people knew my work. All on my own, even without the help of sexism, capitalism, and bad timing, I had managed to make every mistake a writer could make in the commission of her career. I'd left New York City just as my first novel was being published. I'd hooked up with a literary agency without (but I didn't realize it then) credence in the publishing world. Instead of immediately publishing a second novel, I brought out two books of poems. Instead of immediately following those up with a third collection I let eleven years lapse before I published *Natural Theology*. And those are only *examples*.

So I had missed the brass ring. I wasn't even on the merry-go-round. Shoot. I wasn't even at the fair.

I was just writing, with the same blind devotion I had always had.

For posterity? Who knows? Books that receive attention in their own time are more likely to be remembered: there are more copies in libraries (many libraries throw out books that nobody has checked out in a year, or five years); critics and scholars are more likely to write about them. Fame in one's own lifetime might not guarantee fame after death, but it increases one's chances.

If there *is* posterity. There might not *be* posterity. An asteroid may wipe out human life, including all the readers. Libraries have been known to burn. Entropy may turn the entire universe, including literature, to soup.

And if entropy seems far-fetched, illiteracy does not. If there is posterity, it could very well be illiterate. Apple icons could supplant the alphabet.

So why not do everything one can to win fame, acclaim, while one can enjoy it?

Sitting there next to my friend, singers projecting their vocalizations, I couldn't formulate any of these thoughts. Not yet. Anxiety had shut down my brain. The one thought I had was, *Something is wrong with what she said.* But what?

I had other places to visit after my week in the city, and wherever I went I was nagged by the thought that something had been wrong with what my literary chum had said, and still I couldn't figure it out.

One night at a writers' conference I lay in bed recalling that evening at the Met. I heard my friend's words again. Then I sat up and turned on the light. The work, I thought, she left out the work!

In her equation there had been only two terms: the artist and the audience. If that were all there was to be considered, of course it was only logical to think in terms of the relation between the two. But there was a third term, and it was at least as important as the other two. The third term was the art.

The artist, the audience, and the art.

Faulkner, in his Nobel speech, said he wrote "not for glory and least of all for profit." He said that "the basest of all things is to be afraid," and he worried that the atomic bomb had caused younger writers to turn away from "the old verities and truths of the heart" to a near-sighted focus on the self.

We live in our own time of terror.

Art is more important than the artist. It is even more important than the audience, no matter how elegantly dressed (and wouldn't it be fine if opera gloves came back into fashion). A writer does her best for the work—not for its own sake (I am not speaking of art for art's sake)—but because only if it is coherent, whole, complex, and stable will it endure.

Endure, perhaps, for no one to read. And what is the good of that?

Faulkner believed that man will prevail "because he has a soul, a spirit capable of compassion and sacrifice and endurance." The writer's voice, he said, can "help him endure and prevail." I may be less sanguine than Faulkner, less sold on the idea that man will prevail, but I believe that the human spirit, whether human beings survive or do not, is magnificent and fathomless, breathtaking in its aptitudes for both good and evil, and capable of the most exalted action. It deserves to be recognized for what it is—a transformative power.

I am speaking of art for the sake of the human spirit.

The human spirit survives and prevails in the written word (the well-written word). Literature is testimony and tribute; it upholds our world. When people have gone from the world, literature will still bear witness to the breadth and depth of humanity, of humanness. No—not *bear witness to*: it will *be* the human spirit, extant, alive. Our books are us; they will be what we were.

And if the books themselves are lost—burned, or buried in an avalanche or on purpose to avoid warehouse storage costs, or overwhelmed by melting polar caps? If they are seized and destroyed as contraband? Annihilated in a worldwide computer crash? But there is, after all, a limit to how much a writer can worry about.

A writer craves a little fame, a few prizes and more readers, but that is not why she writes. Her deepest concern is not for herself, here or hereafter; her concern, her dream, is to make a thing that does not, cannot, die. So what if it goes unread. Her dream is to create an object of beauty and power that gives to the human spirit a home in eternity. Her dream is to discover the shape and substance of the soul. That shape, that substance: that is the work of art.

IV

ANNIVERSARY

A man and a woman lie down
together, and when they get up,
they leave the imprint of their love
in that place, and it is a kind

of fossil, invisible to
all but the trained eye. The trained eye
spots the fossil and reconstructs
the past, as if a symphony

were to be unraveled from a
single note. The trees of the time
reappear, ringed with light, and the
cardinal returns for a bow.

Encore, encore. Even the man
and the woman return, white-haired
now, complaining of aches and pains,
and they wonder if they need new

glasses, as they take in, first, their
surroundings and then realize
each other's presence, the last man
or woman they had expected

ever to find themselves with, here
at the end of so long a time.

from *Death and Transfiguration*

FALLING

The air fills up with ghosts—
mother, father,
even dead movie stars (so far past their prime
they're willing to audition, for the role of a lifetime).
And they are like stars,
if also like shadows at night,
a concentration of space,
crumpling of light,
fiery and not quite invisible
(though invisible)
billiard balls of bright spirit
rolling overhead,
underfoot,
until you are afraid to move,
you might step on them they might
trip you up send you falling
down the stairs you
clumsy thing you,
arms and legs all in a scrawl
like handwriting on a wall.

from *Death and Transfiguration*

PASSING PEOPLE ON THE STREET

To think of where their lives will bring them is
to be without breath of your own, for that
thought will take it from you, leaving you gasping
for air. The young man with his arm around
the girl who looks as him as if he were
a walking god will one day lie in bed
catheterized. And she will see her face
in a plate-glass window, and wonder who she is,
this woman uninhabited by love,
living alone on the past's small pension.
                                      And you

will be an old fool, wanting to rush in
to save them, as the buildings of their bodies
topple into dust—ruins, long forgotten
temples of a city of the dead.

from *God's Loud Hand*

BERLIN: AN EPITHALAMION

In Berlin,
I lived in an attic, crawling
through a space barely big
enough, while
the men below drank
tea and ate hard rolls, arguing
economics. In Warsaw, snow
covered the abandoned tables
like white linen, and my boyfriend's sword on the wall
gleamed like a mounted fish. In Riga,
my boyfriend smoked
French cigarettes and promised
to marry me
and I believed him.
Snow fell in a scattered field
on the dark expanse of his leather jacket
like shrapnel.
I imagined him exploding
inside my body
like a grenade and when I pushed
his head between my legs I felt
I was getting ready to die.
There were people watching us—
there always are,
in cities like those.
Informants, blackmailers—one gets used to them.
In the morning,
he was always gone.
I would watch the sickeningly bright sun banishing the snow from the sill,
the glittery January icicles, no backbone, surrendering,
and turn on my side,
thinking *What will they do to us*
but I already knew the worst
thing they could do
would be nothing. I am
telling you all this
because I want you to

know that even though
love happens over
and over, riddling
our bodies until we are
scarred beyond recognition,
faceless,
and frozen,
I have chosen you
and only you
over all.

from *God's Loud Hand*

READING, DREAMING, HIDING

You asked me what is the good of reading the Gospels in Greek.
—Czeslaw Milosz, "Readings"

You were reading. I was dreaming
The color blue. The wind was hiding
In the trees and rain was streaming
Down the window, full of darkness.

Rain was dreaming in the trees. You
Were full of darkness. The wind was streaming
Down the window, the color blue.
I was reading and hiding.

The wind was full of darkness and rain
Was streaming in the trees and down the window.
The color blue was full of darkness, dreaming
In the wind and trees. I was reading you.

from *God's Loud Hand*

WAITING FOR THE END OF TIME

Behind the window, in that room where rain
and wind were instrumentalists playing
on the windowpane, you were asleep, again,
and never heard the words that I was saying.
I didn't say them for you to hear, I said
them to your heart, that listening, third ear.

What anyone's heart knows is what has been bled
out of it . . . .

          It's February, a different year,
and spring seems something that a season might do
for the sheer delight of being sprung,
a kind of rhythm, a heartbeat, or *parlando*
(the words are spoken even though they're sung),
and everything is different now, except
time itself, which goes right on being kept.

from *God's Loud Hand*

SUNRISE

An egret on the river's edge,
            a sky as blue as if it were
the backdrop for a Renaissance
            view of the Ascension (that slow, sure

stately flight from earthly sorrow
            into Paradise,
where angels patrol
            the hallways of God's highrise,

looking a little like egrets
            themselves, so long and white
and winged), a morning
            risen from the night.

from *Rising Venus*

QUESTIONS AND ANSWERS

In the beginning was the Word . . .
        —John 1:1

And about the ninth hour Jesus cried with a loud voice, saying, Eli, Eli,
lama sabachthani? that is to say, My God, my God, why hast thou forsaken me?
        —Matthew 27:46

In the beginning is the beginning
and all beginnings, points of darkness becoming
points of light, the pulsing dot of yellow
or red or blue shimmering in the space
where a soul is about to create itself
out of the surrounding unnameable
nothingness. After this stage you can expect
a great silence to descend, like a cloth
dropping over the smooth top of a mahogany table, forever.
This silence is the way you felt when you were a child
and counted inwardly for three days, stopping only to eat,
holding your breath as the numbers mounted higher
and higher and seemed as if they would surely topple
like a tower of blocks, trying to reach
infinity. Or when you stared at the electric clock
(the one with Roman numerals on the kitchen wall),
and you fought back the desire to blink, desperate to catch the minute hand
at the moment of its fatal jumping. All this failure
lies in a heap on the floor of your heart,
scooters with one wheel, blind Teddy bears,
Chinese checkers with two colors incomplete in their triangles,
the new puppy dead on German School Road.
There is always that: the hole in the side
of eternity, through which time leaks into the world,
a plasmic spatter, heart's blood on the hillside
running off into the gullies like the rain
which is said to have been as dark as ink.
They used to make a fountain pen that was transparent,

so you could see when you needed to fill it again.
Torn pages: you will go to the library and find
that in every book you take down from the shelf
a page has been removed by someone who has
preceded you in the night, and it was precisely
the page for which you were looking, your hand trembling
as you turned to the table of contents. *I always knew,*
she says, *it was ridiculous to say a thing
like that.* Here we will be sorrowful, bitter,
sardonic, and the light that flashes in the brain
like the blue light on a patrol car will turn and turn,
looking down alleys lined with garbage cans,
while rain soaks into the cop's pants legs and he curses
somebody, the night, the anonymous tip, you.
There are mini-rainbows in the oil-slick puddles, luminous
under the cloud-streaked moon. You have made a mental portrait,
pieced from photographs, of her face, her impassive eyes,
her bleached blonde hair, pale white as the pulp of an apple,
and the question is, How are we to step outside
of all these likenesses and dissimilarities
which surround us like a container with no outside?
Did *he* glance startled back at the one who had suddenly recognized him,
disbelieving that the reflection could be greater than the thing reflected?
Did the anxiety in his heart presage an instant when love
would spin away, screwing itself like a tornado
to a vanishing point, leaving only
the vertigo of despair, the giddy view downward to hell,
or was it merely the consequence, the scar, of discovering he had been
from the beginning one who would come after, always after,
a feeling as when you sat in study hall
and carefully pulled against the closing of your notebook's three rings
at the same time you released the spring, but the snap,
when it came, was too loud anyway, and you made a face
as if to disassociate yourself from the event.
You must answer this question. You do not have
all the time in the world. The shadow of the dove
is flickering on the concrete pillar. A bird
like a brushstroke is swerving idiosyncratically
or along unseen lines, dipping
in and out of sight over the sailboat

and glittering water. Have you thought how it will be
when you are no longer present at this window,
and the autumn leaves turn red and yellow
and loosen and swoop and hang-glide even without
you to watch them? The squirrel collecting acorns,
the hiker rounding a curve—what will not go on? You may become
resigned or angry, thinking about this.
What is inevitable is that you should recall
with a clarity so intense that it seems astonishing
in spite of its inevitability
the expression on the face of one man
whom you have loved for so long that loving him and being you
appear to be the same, that loving him
may even be what called you into existence
in the first place, so that who you are, is
an afterthought, but inescapable.
You heard someone saying your name
in the night, and woke with a start,
blinking at the sound which threaded its way
into your brain and heart like Beethoven's
music, feeling created and new. His hands
covered your face and in the darkness of his palms
you lived a million years, every day
of which was like an emerald and a ruby.
What does this mean? What does it mean? What?
That there are portents if you look for them?
This is not a question, and the only possible answer to it
is ambiguous. For the sake of the poem, it is
September in Wisconsin, becoming October,
and the colors are blue and gold and green, with white
clouds which, if the day were colder, you might imagine
were made by God's breath, the Hidden One revealing his presence
in the divine huff, if you believed in God and were not,
as you are, called upon to perform these actions
in a variety of moods, all unanchored by any confirmation.
You know only that you have been abandoned
among twigs, pebbles, grasses, hubcaps, and bits
of broken bottle glass, and the thing you must accomplish,
after your friends have been picked off one by one
by the sniper in the radio tower and dusk has settled

over the construction site, a few shreds of light snagged
on the barbed-wire fence, like pieces of caught cloth, is
forgiveness. This is the hard part. This is the feeling
you were chasing down corridors, the feeling you were seeking to capture
when you sank the dragnet into your mind's depths
and came up with everything but. Here we are thinking of
rejection slips, the KGB, murder.
A man has been nailed to some sticks of wood
and his insides are sagging into his bowels.
Time is swirling around the sparse weeds, eroding
and seeping into the sandy earth, and the question is,
Who is this man? There are holes in his wrists
through which wind roars like wind in a wind tunnel,
and the sound slices into your skull like shrapnel, a fragment
no surgeon will ever be able to excise. It will stay
with you always, that memory of how it felt,
hanging there, pierced, and tied to the crossbeam by leather
thongs. The bad taste in your mouth had nothing to do
with vinegar—it was knowing you had been last, and only
for this. Not the *cross*; that was to be expected.
What was insupportable—what was wholly beyond reason—
was that you were supposed to feel no dismay about it.
No resentment. *None.* It was too much to ask.
It was like the time you looked into the mirror
and discovered that your future and your past were written there,
in minute detail, and the sole way you could revise
a single line was by slowly and painfully
erasing yourself. Later, though you had tried,
the people were staring, they kept looking at you
and laughing, and you didn't know why, but then, in the middle
of the crowd, you saw one man who looked at you
with such tenderness that it confused you, and you lowered your eyes,
blushing, pleased. The valentine box in fifth grade,
lace-edged, crepe-covered cardboard on which red hearts
were pasted, heretofore charged with residual anxiety,
has now been completely transformed by this reassurance
to an object of deep nostalgic affection! And the memories
drift gently down around you, falling like leaves,
until you are walking through your past, each memory
an ash of burnt air, a poker chip, a thin shaving

of sky colored and curled. There was a turn
here, and it has been very subtly made.
We have arrived where we can examine the situation
in its entirety. This is no elephant tusk or ear.
It is the view from all sides simultaneously,
or, to put it another way, it is
the present status of Observatory Drive
as seen from that remembered instant long ago
when you knew you had rounded a curve
and gone on into a lifetime of longing and joy,
though the two were not—or you, being unfond of tension,
were not ready to accept they were—linked.
The football fans are leaning on their horns
and waving flags from tiny Buicks, and
the final question is in sight. *You will
do this or that:* Is this declarative,
or is it a command? *This* is the question.
You will, say, one day go into your parents' bedroom
and discover that no one has slept there for years.
If you lie on the bed, dust will rise from the spread
and sift back through the still air onto your white silk sleeves.
Was this prediction, or did someone send you there,
someone who is not willing to show himself
yet? This *is* the question, this *is* the question.
Things are not so simple, it seems, as certain ones
who have gone before us have suggested:
there are implications everywhere,
whispering in the tops of trees, urgent,
restless, waiting, darting across the ground
just a second before you turn your head,
so you never quite see them, just their shadows,
the light stabilizing itself after the sudden disturbance.
Today's sun has moved on to California, leaving behind
a rose sky that flattens out over the lake, widening into darkness
and deep blue ripples. And now the far shore is gone,
vanished, the island is bleeding into the margin,
and here on the bank the reeds rustle uneasily
in a rising wind, the shed feathers of forgotten sparrows
are stirred, ruffled, and dropped, a large rat
slips into the water—does he touch your foot?

You are surrounded by unseen eyes in the dark,
and the wind has snuffed out the fire in your tin box.
And there are sounds in the forest, there are coals in the campsite pit
not from your pack, still warm, warm as a baby's breath,
and you know that the others, the ones who were
here first, are now hiding not far, only
outside the rim, in the woods beyond the cleared place,
whispering. *Come,* say the voices, *come with us.*
For you will, you know. And they say:
We will go into the unknown together,
drawing the long sentence of ourselves after us,
until only the tip end of it is visible,
a scant bit of blackness, a point, like a period.

from *Natural Theology*

ALSO BY KELLY CHERRY

POETRY

The Life and Death of Poetry
The Retreats of Thought
Hazard and Prospect: New and Selected Poems
Rising Venus
Death and Transfiguration
God's Loud Hand
Natural Theology
Relativity: A Point of View
Lovers and Agnostics

FICTION

A Kind of Dream
The Woman Who
We Can Still Be Friends
The Society of Friends
My Life and Dr. Joyce Brothers
The Lost Traveller's Dream
In the Wink of an Eye
Augusta Played
Sick and Full of Burning

NONFICTION

Girl in a Library: On Women Writers and the Writing Life
History, Passion, Freedom, Death, and Hope: Prose about Poetry
Writing the World
The Exiled Heart: A Meditative Autobiography

CHAPBOOKS/LIMITED EDITIONS

Vectors: J. Robert Oppenheimer: The Years before the Bomb (poems)
The Globe and the Brain (an essay)
Welsh Table Talk (poems)
An Other Woman (a poem)
The Poem (an essay)
Time out of Mind (poems)
Benjamin John (a poem)
Songs for a Soviet Composer (poems)
Conversion (a story)

TRANSLATION
   "Antigone," in *Sophocles, 2*
   "Octavia," in *Seneca: The Tragedies, Volume II*

DISCS, BROADSIDES, POSTCARDS (EXCLUDES MOST TAPES)
"The Right Words." Limited edition broadside "in honor of Kelly Cherry's term as Poet Laureate of Virginia." Virginia Arts of the Book Center, 2011. Pen and ink drawing by Frank Riccio. Plate design by Kevin McFadden.

"Reading, Dreaming Hiding," "The Lonely Music," "The Raiment We Put On," "At Night Your Mouth," "Song of the Housewife," "Appoggiatura," "Waiting for the End of Time," "Yalta Rain," "I Went to Find You," "Remembering." *Research Review*, The University of Alabama in Huntsville, Fall 2000. Compact disc.

"The Universe Creating Itself." Limited edition broadside. Emory and Henry College, Virginia. 1999. On the occasion of Leidig Lecture in Poetry, delivered by Kelly Cherry.

"A Lyric Cycle." Text for the final movement of the Fourth Symphony by Imant Kalnins. U.S. premiere (and world premiere for text and original orchestration) by the Detroit Symphony Orchestra (Maestro Neeme Järvi), May 29, 30, 31, 1997. Text printed in program. Recorded for broadcast on syndicated national radio (50+ stations). Videotaped for television broadcast in Estonia and Latvia. Videotaped by NBC affiliate.
   Also, premiere European performances of restored original, Liepaja, Nov. 17, and Riga, Nov. 18 and 19, 1997. Translation of text printed in program.
   Also, CD recording, Liepaja Symphony Orchestra, Imants Resnis conducting, 1998. Riga: MicRec, 1999.
   Also, performances by Singapore Philharmonic Orchestra, Lan Shui conducting, Victoria Concert Hall, Singapore, August 27, 28, 29, 1999. Also, CD recording, Singapore Philharmonic Orchestra, Lan Shui conducting. Sweden: BIS, 2000.
   Also, first studio recording (CD, vinyl, tape, Resnis conducting Liepaja Symphony. With text in the original and in translation. 2009.

"Reading, Dreaming, Hiding." Limited edition postcard. Orlando, Florida: Liquid Poetry Series, 1996.

"Gethsemane." Limited edition broadside designed and hand-set by Nina Morlan. University of California at Santa Barbara, 1994. 12 copies.

Natural Theology. A book of the title poem from *Natural Theology.* Designed and hand-set in 14 pt Spectrum by Nina Morlan. Santa Barbara: College of Creative Studies, University of California at Santa Barbara, 1993. 8 pp. (one fold), col. ill; 15 cm. Printed on Somerset paper, with original monotypes. Binding hand-sewn. Cover is Evanescent Moss paper. Limited edition of 14 numbered copies.

"As Between Wisdom and Youth." Hand-printed postcard. Santa Barbara: UCSB, 1993. 20 copies.

"The Getaway." Postcard. Greensboro, North Carolina: March Street Press, 1993.

"Loneliness." Limited edition broadside. Winston-Salem, North Carolina: Palaemon Press, 1980. 100 numbered copies and 26 alphabetized and signed copies.

Also, *The Palaemon Broadside Folio, No. 18,* published with O. B. Hardison, Robert Morgan, James Applewhite, and Robert Watson, 1982.

ABOUT THE AUTHOR

Kelly Cherry has previously published twenty-two books (novels, stories, poetry, autobiography, memoir, criticism, essays, and reviews), nine chapbooks, and two translations of classical drama. The most recent book is *A Kind of Dream: Stories*. Her newest full-length collection of poems, *The Life and Death of Poetry*, was published by L.S.U. Press in 2013 and her newest chapbook, a group of poems titled *Vectors: J. Robert Oppenheimer: The Years before the Bomb*, appeared from Parallel Press in December 2012. She was the first recipient of the Hanes Poetry Prize given by the Fellowship of Southern Writers for a body of work. Other awards include fellowships from the National Endowment for the Arts and the Rockefeller Foundation, the Bradley Major Achievement (Lifetime) Award, a USIS Speaker Award (The Philippines), a Distinguished Alumnus Award, three Wisconsin Arts Board fellowships, two WAB New Work awards, the Dictionary of Literary Biography Yearbook Award for Distinguished Book of Stories in 1999 (2000), and selection as a Wisconsin Notable Author. Her stories have appeared in *Best American Short Stories, The O. Henry Awards: Stories, The Pushcart Prize*, and *New Stories from the South*. In 2010, she was a Director's Visitor at the Institute for Advanced Study in Princeton. In 2012, she received both the Taramuto Prize for a story and the Carole Weinstein Prize for Poetry. In 2013 she received the L. E. Phillabaum Award for Poetry. A former Poet Laureate of Virginia, she is Eudora Welty Professor Emerita of English and Evjue-Bascom Professor Emerita in the Humanities at the University of Wisconsin-Madison. She and her husband live in Virginia. Further details appear on her Wikipedia page.

CPSIA information can be obtained at www.ICGtesting.com
Printed in the USA
BVOW03s1217270215

389530BV00009B/14/P